Diagram of Death

A Detective Harper Stowe Mystery

A Novel
by Andrew Spradling

Diagram of Death A Detective Harper Stowe Mystery is a work of fiction. All names and characters are the product of the author's imagination and completely fictitious except for historical figures or historical references germane to Hilton Head Island. Any resemblance to actual persons, living or dead, events or locales, is entirely coincidental unless acknowledged by the author.

Cover photo by Mylissa C. Spradling

© 2021
All rights reserved
ISBN: 9798514571345

Diagram of Death

A Detective Harper Stowe Mystery

A Novel
by Andrew Spradling

This book is dedicated to all the devoted, hard-working educators of my youth, but especially Ramona Caincross, Ross Culpepper Harrison, and Thomas S. Morgan, all of whom impacted me greatly.

And to my parents, Ruth and Alan Spradling, for all their nurturing, support, and love.

When you understand, things are just as they are. When you don't understand, things are just as they are.
- Old Buddhist saying

The light shines in the darkness, and the darkness has not overcome it.
- John 1:5

CHAPTER 1

My experience has taught me that the most important first strike of the abduction – since a scream in a residential area is so out of order -- is to silence the victim. I don't want to bloody my new partner, nor do I want her groggy or asleep. I want her wide awake. I want her eyes screaming. She owes me that.

And, I have big hands. The Admiral always mentioned it. My "big mitts," he'd say. They're so large, in fact, I can secure two strips of duct tape in my palm with just a quarter inch of overlap, turned under and taped to the heel of my hand and to my fingertips. The second piece affords me a little extra coverage in case I'm slightly off. It's not always easy, depending on my approach. Covering the mouth of an unwilling female isn't like slapping a butt. If I have to peel a little back off her nostrils, it's okay. I want her breathing to the end. Once I have her quiet, she's mine. The physical domination has never been a problem. When they see the gleam of the hunting knife I pull, their eyes begin to beg. That's when the thrashing stops. That's when she realizes the stakes. I can cut away the necessary clothing without so much as a nick to her skin. That part gets me going. I find it so erotic I can hardly breathe.

Choosing my next victim isn't difficult either. Not around here. If they're running the trails or walking the beach alone, chances are their neglectful old man is playing golf, maybe deep-sea fishing, or possibly still back at the ranch busting it to pay for their beach house. Not always. Sometimes you follow one back to find a home full of fellow-travelers, with ten screaming kids in a twelve-foot pool, her walk but a brief reprieve. No matter. This place is a delicatessen. A

Diagram of Death

smorgasbord of delectable treats. I can stand at my kitchen sink and through my windows watch them run, walk, or ride by from dawn till dusk. I can sit on the beach and they'll approach me and ask what book I'm reading. If I'm walking Dexter, my lab, they're putty in my hands. I have that wholesome, trusting look about me. One stopped me at my garage and asked if I could please put air in her bike tires. Twenty-five minutes later, she was gone. I can't remember a feature of her face, but I can still taste the salt on her skin. But that was before, when we still rented our house to tourists through summers.

I'll admit in the beginning I wasn't perfect. Along the way I recognized the need for some tricks. I learned to muddy the water, leave false clues. Part of a shoe string from a work boot – this place is deluged with laborers daily -- a hair sample I'd pick up from my barber's floor, a receipt from some touristy spot I'd find somewhere, from a golf cart or a restaurant barstool. But the true genius of it all was the dumbest luck. I hadn't even considered it. My first here was discovered on a Saturday morning. Saturday around here is getaway day. To police detectives, that meant ten thousand suspects just crossed over the Wilton Graves Memorial Bridge from the William Hilton Parkway, back to mainland, USA. And that, my friend, is a hopeless feeling.

CHAPTER 2

Harper Kathryn Stowe paced the floor in front of her desk, studying the horrific details of case documents in her hands. Her spacious office had become the nerve center of the worst crime spree in Hilton Head Island's history, and she was its lead detective. The eight-foot wide bulletin board, mounted to an interior wall for just such a purpose, was filled. The last two victims' cases were taped to the wall to the board's right: numerous eight by ten color glossies of the victims and the crime scene, with printed fact sheets placed beneath. The total was now four. With that unfathomable number was a riptide of panic among permanent residents, city officials, and the Chamber of Commerce.

The crimes had all taken place in the gated community of Ocean Oaks, which was a mixed bag of four thousand households ranging from ten million dollar beach-front mansions to three-hundred-thousand dollar condos. In between was a good number of relatively affordable ranch-style homes for professionals willing to make the commitment. New owners often rented their homes for much of the season to supplement their second mortgage payment, looking to cash in later or own their retirement home outright. Rentals typically ran from Saturday afternoon to the following Saturday morning - noon being the latest departure. Within the gates of Ocean Oaks was Bay Harbor, which included high-end stores and restaurants, the Lighthouse, the Marina, and annually, the Professional Golf Association's Bay Harbor Golf Classic. On the south side of Ocean Oaks' tip of Hilton Head was the popular Parrot Perch, conceptually the same, though on a smaller, more casual scale. Forming an inland triangle was Ocean Oaks Resort, a two-hundred and fifty-unit hotel. Found

Diagram of Death

there also was the clubhouse for two of Ocean Oaks' four signature golf courses. All three establishments also had dozens of tennis courts available, and numerous tennis tournaments and camps were held there in the spring and summer. Throughout the five-thousand acres of land that was Ocean Oaks were paved trails for residents and renters to run, walk, bike ride, roller blade, or skate. Just off the trails, on each of the yards of the affluent was an oasis of green shrubbery, fanned palmetto palms, and live oaks with dangling Spanish moss meant to provide privacy for pools and hot tubs.

    Despite her youth, thirty-two years of age, there was no one better suited on the island to handle the case than Harper Stowe. The daughter of a Savannah doctor and lawyer she was steeped in southern pedigree, southern tradition... and southern criminal behavior. Her mother, Muriel Lancaster Stowe, was a beauty pageant winner who also had the intelligence for law school, and she pushed Harper in that direction through her childhood. Her father, Carter Stowe, was a sought-after orthopedic surgeon with enough handsome features – and pocket - to snag a beauty queen with brains. Carter was out each day by 5:30 for his first round of daily surgeries, so Harper took her breakfast each morning before school with her mother, an assistant prosecutor with an excruciatingly-painful family history. Harper was reading *The Herald of Savannah* by the second grade. At the age of ten, a newsworthy local kidnapping swayed her attention towards law enforcement. Then in 1996 in her fourteenth year, the JonBenet Ramsey case sealed the deal for Harper. She became consumed with the events around the investigation. Her parents' workload was so heavy at that time that Nanny Sylvia was on daily from two to seven, and as long as Harper was being productive, she was not monitored. The internet provided her every fact she could digest about what she deemed "a tragically-mishandled case" that to this day remains unsolved.

Harper earned academic scholarships to her choice of southern universities, and though her father deemed it overkill to study criminology and forensic science out of state at the University of South Carolina – he longed for her to be closer - that is where she pursued her higher learning. She finished summa cum laude. Her mother's secret agenda was to promote the relationship between law and law enforcement through those four years. But, while her friends applied for law and medical schools and planned their post-graduate lives with nervous apprehension, Harper signed on as a Bluffton police officer – just across the bridge from Hilton Head and sixty miles up the road from her parents' Savannah home - and stayed on in Columbia to attend the South Carolina State Justice Academy. A middle-distance walk-on to the Gamecocks track team, she was both physically and mentally prepared for the academy grind. Her IQ separated her from her class, and ten years of jujitsu training made her a slippery opponent in hand-to-hand battles. She was also a dead-eye shot with a pistol.

A repetitive bang on her office door interrupted her focus.

"Why so formal, Chief? I can't believe you knocked," she said.

"I wouldn't just walk in on you, Harp. I respect a closed door," said Lester Beaumont. He knew she couldn't stand being called Harp. He walked past her to the board, put his hands in his pleated trouser pockets, pleats he couldn't see for his gut, and stared at the photos.

"So what can I do for you?"

"You know I have complete faith in you, Stowe. That goes without saying."

"But."

Diagram of Death

"But, I've just come from Mayor Sneed's office. He expressed *deep* concern about the case. He assumes we've made no progress."

"Does he understand that we're keeping quiet intentionally?"

"Yes, but you have to understand, he's catching heat too. The Chamber of Commerce runs this town and they're petrified. The media's all over him too."

"What do you mean, *The Island Packet*? I still don't understand what's going on at *The Beaufort Tribune*. It seems they couldn't care less."

"I believe your world is officially about to change, my dear. The national media is now on the island. Matter of fact, I saw two vans setting up in the parking lot when I came in. Do you want me to handle them for you?"

Harper Stowe sat the document she'd been studying down on the edge of her desk and looked at the floor. The cold steel of a knife blade flashed in her mind. She didn't fear it. In fact, it made her blood boil. She pictured the last victim, Anita Williams, running the trail behind a line of houses in Old Hilbert Woods, off Hilbert Road. She could hear the rhythm of Williams' Nikes touching down on the blacktop, her stamina perhaps dwindling. Tired and vulnerable. Unsuspecting. Just 5-foot-4, 125 pounds, 34-years-old. What chance did she have? The backyards there dipped to the trail and ditch line, causing a blind spot for anyone looking from their homes. Two of the five houses with visibility to the abduction site – the rape and murder - why sugar-coat it? - sat unrented that week. Did he know that? Could the suspect be a realtor? Add that occupation to the list of island suspects to check. Is the unsub calculating enough to know these houses are empty from his own observation? From his runs? Or rides? Could he be a resident? The few clues they had thus far pointed in the opposite direction... maybe a day laborer. Hilbert Woods was a perfect spot for an ambush, and he knew it. But, the first three had been as well.

There is a like-minded feeling in Ocean Oaks – "we all have this love of beach, this beach house, and the ability to pay for it, in common" - that brings the renter a sense of safety and security. Not that they don't lock their doors, because Ocean Oaks is infiltrated daily by multitudes of pool cleaners, landscapers, carpenters, handymen, trash collectors, as well as a large sales force - food and apparel vendors hitting up restaurants and shops, keeping the roads hopping with traffic even without the regular visitors. But the workers – white, black, Hispanic, Asian - seem to do their jobs properly and keep moving. The companies they work for are bonded, thus a mere complaint would be the end for an employee. Therefore the laborers don't seem threatening or intimidating, they don't slow down to look at the smartphones or Ipads left by teenagers on the poolside tables at the private houses. The safety and well-being of vacationers never seems in question. If they wish, they can take long walks alone to clear their heads, re-charge their batteries. They can run the beach or through the trails without being harassed, or hit on. They trust that they have put in their rearview the crimes they read about in their daily newspapers and see on their local newscasts, that they have left behind the embezzlers, drug dealers, rapists, and murderers and entered a world of the affluent, a world where men dress for dinner in nicely pressed shirt and shorts combinations, and women in colorfully patterned summer dresses that display their newly-tanned cleavage or equally revealing spaghetti-strapped tops with shorts or skirts and matching sandals. They trust that they are safe.

Stowe cautiously weighed her next words. Her silence caused Beaumont to turn and face her. She looked him straight in the eyes.

Diagram of Death

"I've avoided the cameras thus far, Boss. I think it's time I go undercover… pose as a renter or something. Maybe a new home owner," she said, with conviction.

"No. I won't allow you to use yourself as bait," Beaumont said. Her chief was a 58-year-old family man, father of three, grandfather of eight. Despite occasionally needling Stowe, he respected and felt genuine fatherly affection for his lead detective. He'd never worked a case of this magnitude. He was stuck in the side-car with South Carolina and Beaufort County investigators driving during the '08 John and Elizabeth Calvert extravaganza, high-profile, real estate royalty who disappeared, never to be found. The admitted-by-note embezzlement of their accountant Dennis Gerwing, followed by his "suicide" days later, sealed the deal for the state boys. But the case was still on the books – unsolved, bodies unfound, presumed to be dumped in the vast Atlantic Ocean. Beaumont hoped to ride out his career having never worked anything so bizarre again.

"What choice do we have, Lester? All we're doing now is cleaning up the mess, documenting the bloody details. Four blond vacationers, all killed on Fridays, all two weeks apart. I *have* to get in there and try. Maybe I'll get lucky, spot someone suspicious," Stowe said. Her expression turned deadly serious. "And if I'm really lucky, maybe he'll choose me."

Beaumont again turned his back to her, and took a step closer to the case pictures taped to the wall. She could hear him mumbling under his breath.

"What was that?"

"I can't let you do it," he said.

"Lester, it's Monday of the second week – the tenth week. I don't have to tell you that. He's got to be out there looking, making plans."

"If we did it, I would want you watched constantly," Beaumont said.

"You know we don't have the manpower for that. Plus the pattern is established. Friday it'll feel like invasion day, all the help we have lined up."

He sat down in a chair in front of her desk and exhaled in a way that seemed to make him deflate.

"Well," he said finally, "you certainly fit the profile. Except for the hair."

"I've got a plan for that," she said. She opened a drawer, reached in, and set a plastic bag on her desk. She glanced at her closed door, then pulled at her shoulder-length, brown locks until they came off in her hand. Beneath, her actual hair was cropped short in a flattering pixie, the bangs – now released – fell slightly, to just above her eyebrows. It was colored an elegant, sandy blond. Beaumont's mouth dropped open.

"Damn Harper. Do I have to say out loud that you find me predictable? You got the house picked out too?"

Stowe smiled. Then her expression turned back to business.

"I've seen three online. Two go for more than our annual budget. One is small, mostly unfurnished, and 'as is.' "

"And?"

"I made a call. It's an estate deal. The owner passed away and her kids just want to split the sale price. It's close enough to the beach where it'll probably be demolished and rebuilt. We just need to commandeer it."

"Please don't make me regret this, I'm not sure my heart can take it."

"Boss, we can't fail. I believe we'll win."

"Oh, and Stowe, by the way, it looks good," Beaumont said. He gave her a wink and a smile. "Very becoming."

CHAPTER 3

The impromptu press conference ended with all the vagaries and banality expected by the media. Chief Lester Beaumont wouldn't allow his feet to be held to the fire concerning specific details related to his investigation or his plan for surveillance. Of course, without specifics, the media was likely to draw unwarranted conclusions. Beaumont's goal was to make sure the visitors and residents of Ocean Oaks remained on alert. He stressed that at no time should women exercise alone on the trails, but especially as dusk approached and certainly not after sundown.

The national media had learned from the local beat reporter, Randy Simpkins of *The Beaufort Tribune,* that Beaumont was a figurehead administrator. At least that was what *he* had been told. Simpkins was new to the beat and his knowledge of the Hilton Head Police Department was minimal. Relegated to misdemeanor police blotter items thus far, he'd never laid eyes on Harper Stowe. The editorial stance at the *Tribune* seemed to be to downplay the murders. Stowe had openly questioned her colleagues about the paper's lack of interest, but no reason was forthcoming.

Beaumont's one slip while addressing the media came when asked who was heading up the investigation, and at what time that person would be introduced to the media.

"Shh - I - am the lead in this investigation," he said. "But the entire staff is working overtime, and we are adding reinforcements from nearby departments and the state police as well."

Most of the press thought he'd cut off an expletive. Rhett Richardson was closest to Beaumont. He was the only press corps member to hear – or at least imagine - the vowel. He was certain Beaumont said or was about to say "she." Richardson was an independent cameraman freelancing for the British Broadcasting Corporation. He was hungry for a scoop that would give him an opportunity to go to the networks, to go big time. He longed to be, and was brave enough to be, a foreign correspondent. He was twenty-nine, tan, with brown hair and eyes. A three-day beard grew like wild brush over his strong features.

    His legitimate attempts at climbing the ladder, stints at small-time television stations, two years in Roanoke, Virginia, seven months in Knoxville, Tennessee, fifteen months in Salisbury, North Carolina, three weeks in Savannah, Georgia, all ended with dismissals due to his aggressive, erratic, "unprofessionalism." In Savannah, Richardson was filming ankle-deep in blood during an ongoing turf battle between blacks and Mexicans. His mistake was dragging his female talent along with him. She was petrified and filed a grievance with the station against him. Despite the dismissals Richardson continued to take crime journalism to the limit with no apologies. He wanted this story, and he would be tireless in his efforts to get it. His hunch was that Beaumont was hiding a female colleague. Scenarios ran wild in his head as to why, but he knew the aging boss didn't have the stamina for the lead on this case.

    The media corps departed the HHPD parking lot to edit and file stories from their respective hotels. Richardson, traveling by SUV, decided to edit there. He need only a strong internet signal to reach wetransfer.com to file – anywhere in the world. In the not-too-recent-past it would have taken a satellite feed to get his story to London. Besides, he wanted to play out his hunch. He edited in his backseat and waited patiently. It was only forty minutes later that he saw her. A beautiful woman, dirty blond, sunglasses, blue dress pants and

Diagram of Death

a sleeveless, ivory blouse, exit from the department's back door. She was tan and her curves were apparent at eighty yards.

"Damn, hold the phone," he said aloud to nobody. He sat his laptop down and climbed into the driver's seat of his Envoy. The woman passed a row of unmarked police cars and flashed the lights of a pale blue Mercedes coupe, opened the door and slid under the steering wheel. Assuming she was law of some sort, he gave her a wide berth. After tailing her three miles from a distance, he watched from two cars back as she cut out of the traffic circle that took her into Ocean Oaks Visitor's Center. Ten minutes later she left that building and drove through the owner's side of the guard gate. He purchased a day pass from the right, visitor's side from an out-of-shape but friendly white guard, likely a retiree, he thought. The transaction was quick enough for him to reacquire the woman's trail just before she hit the traffic circle that could send her first to Bay Harbor, second to South Beach, or third to Ocean Oaks Resort and Golf Center.

She took the second right to South Beach, remaining on Greenbank Drive, Ocean Oaks' main thoroughfare. After another right then a quick left, she pulled into the driveway of a gray, ranch-style beach house with a vaulted ceiling, typical of so many wooden structures within the gates. Its only distinguishing feature was its canary-yellow double-front doors - more of a war-cry than simply loud. As he drove past the house he could see a middle-aged woman carrying a "For Sale" sign to her car's open trunk. When the second woman saw the first, she smiled and waved. Richardson, driving on, saw dunes ahead, which told him the street was perpendicular to the beach. With so many branches overhead, Spanish moss hanging, and with the twists and turns of the road, it was difficult to keep one's bearing. At the end of Slack Trimmer Road, he backed his vehicle into the driveway of a home he guessed would go for every penny of five million dollars: wide, two stories, nearly as much glass as brick and wood siding, in-ground pool with a built-in hot tub. He knew because his parents owned a similar second home on Fripp Island, just not on the water. He watched from four houses away as the women greeted each other warmly. He sat and watched until he began to feel conspicuous in his spot. He slowly inched his monstrosity of an SUV back into the street. When he reached the house numbered "12," the women were walking in the opened front door.

"This seems unlikely. No way a young cop could afford that home," he thought. "As run down as it is, it would still sell for six-fifty or seven. Maybe I was wrong about her. Hell, she could be the attorney general for all I know. But if I was chief of police, I'd damn sure plant a woman inside the gates. I *have* to keep an eye on her. I've got to rent a place of my own."

Richardson drove directly back to the Welcome Center and found the business office. In charge was a robust but pleasant woman of forty-five.

"I'd like to rent a house as close to Slack Trimmer Road as possible please," he said.

"Ok," she said, maneuvering within her computer with a few mouse clicks. "Looks like I have three. Is this for a family?"

"No. Just me. Make it the smallest one you have."

"I'll be glad to do it, but it seems like a waste of money. The price is eighteen hundred dollars."

"Ouch. That's nothing to sneeze at Miss…"

"Ms. Monroe."

"Oh, like Marilyn," he said. She giggled until she blushed. Richardson's rugged good looks were getting to her.

"Well Ms. Monroe, I'm with the international media. In fact I'm here working for the BBC," he said, pulling his credentials from his pocket to show her. I have a hotel room

Diagram of Death

outside the gates for two hundred per. But I came in on a day pass, and, well, I found I just had to stay here. The place spoke to me as if, I don't know, I was in need of a sanctuary. It's crazy out there at the Marriott. You can imagine, I'm sure. Since the week has started and the unit was going to be sitting empty anyway – and still will be at that rate - wouldn't say, nine hundred be enough? Who makes those decisions?"

"Well, I do, Mr. Richardson," she said. Her finger tips fiddled with a plastic button on the red vest she wore over a white, long-sleeved blouse. "I'm Rita, by the way."

"It's better than nothing, isn't it Rita?"

"Oh, it's much better than nothing," she said, giving a sigh that lacked hope. "Ok. You're in. There's a little paper work to take care. I'm sure you'll have a wonderful stay."

CHAPTER 4

At seven that evening, Harper Stowe decided to step out to get a feel for the lay of the land. She'd driven into Ocean Oaks at least two dozen times for various reasons in the past few years - prior to the murders - but she hadn't overnighted or lounged on the sand there since she was a pre-teen. Visiting Hilton Head from Savannah was a parents' dream: beautiful, secluded beaches without the long drive so many American families had to endure. It was perfect for her parents and their demanding careers. If either had to sneak back to Savannah for a professional emergency, the hour drive was manageable. Savannah had its own retreat, Tybee Island, but to the Stowes, constantly running into neighbors, associates, clients and patients was more of an aggravation than a break.

The paths of Ocean Oaks were less developed back then. She'd never run there in her youth. That was before she'd developed her passion for pain. She knew she could run a marathon if she had to, looking for something or someone out of the ordinary... or very ordinary.

Of course, in the last eight weeks she'd been in and out of Ocean Oaks more times than she could count. With brown hair, and with police credentials. She walked out on to her front porch and began to stretch. As she turned, her reflection in the window made her do a double-take. She'd already forgotten about the hair. It didn't look bad on her, she thought. She smoothed the running shirt she was wearing with her palm. As she did, she wondered who, if anybody, could connect her as that police detective. A guard might think she looked vaguely familiar, but dismiss it due to her hair color. There was just too many people in and out, and to keep the traffic moving the guards' line of sight went directly to the date on the

Diagram of Death

visitor's pass on their dashboard. What did it matter anyway unless a guard was the unsub? Their stories all checked out. And to them, each week brought a new crop of fresh faces.

She turned her back to the window and the loud doors of her dwelling and spread her feet wide. She stretched her hamstrings by first dropping her head straight down, and then from one knee to the other… slowly, with no bounce, pulling, her hands on her Achilles tendons at the tops of her Nikes. She didn't think about it. That was routine. She thought about the first victim, Linda DeShea, who had stayed with her family just a few streets away, on Royal Fern. She'd run the beach, and was attacked as she made her way home, apparently cooling down. She'd been found in an undeveloped lot, not twenty-five feet from the beach access pathway. There were forty-five of those on the South Beach side of Ocean Oaks alone, numbered signs on the beach for the vacationer's convenience, every fifty yards or so. After a long walk or run the beach houses often looked quite similar. Landmarks were needed. Some had wooden stairs that went up and over the dunes to concrete sidewalks, some were wooden walkways that snaked their way straight to the beach and were used by bicyclists to get on and off the sand.

DeShea was a beloved elementary school teacher, her husband a stock broker, from Richmond, Virginia. She'd left her two teenaged children poolside at her rental house while she ran. Same body type: 5-6, petite, blond. He was finishing up a round of golf. They were going out for a late dinner on their last night. She had most all their belongings packed up to leave Saturday morning. She never returned. The images continued to flash in Stowe's mind as she made her final stretches, the opened-eyed, lifeless stare, tape over her mouth, the slit throat, shirt on but cut open, shorts and panties cut off. One fact amazed Stowe: not one shred of D.N.A. evidence from the fingernails of the victims.

She put her feet together and placed her palms flat on to the concrete, then locked her thumbs behind her ankles for leverage, and touched her forehead to her knees.

"He has to be binding them, but there's been no bruising," she thought. She jogged to the end of Slack Trimmer, crossed the two-lane South Beach Drive, turned left on the trail and began running at a modest pace. She reached a juncture at the far edge of a lake where she could turn right to Bay Harbor or go straight, down South Beach to The Parrot Perch area. She could do both with minimal effort, so she turned right for the route to the posher of the two areas first.

"Why is that?" She thought, of the lack of bruising. She tried to imagine the scenario, as she had ten thousand times already. Arms bound how and where. And how is it no one has seen this man afterwards? If he uses a rope, he's never left one behind. Nor has there been even a fiber.

She left the lake behind her to her right and entered an oasis of trees, thick palmettos, and green shrubbery growing wild, the backs of houses on either side, more distant to the left. The homes were often barely visible. Soft, silent pine needles everywhere - right up to the edge of the asphalt. In the first hundred yards she recognized at least a dozen spots that would be adequate for an abduction if it were dusk. That ratio was a huge advantage for evil, if evil was present.

"I can't think in terms of what I would do," she thought, knowing and trusting her lethal instincts. That was one of the pitfalls she fought against. Her mind shuffled through the hot spots to neutralize an attacker – the eyes, the nose, the Adam's Apple, the testicles – a quick punch or poke. Or a sidekick to the knee or shin. Anything to gain an advantage, or at least a second or two to escape. With her hands gripping an arm, Stowe could step in and throw a 250-pound man over her shoulder and on to his back. She'd once punched a resisting-turned-violent "public intox" in the lower

Diagram of Death

abdomen and caused him to urinate in his pants as she squeezed the pressure point in his wrist and twisted his arm up behind his back to subdue him.

"How does this man gain such an advantage?"

As she glanced again at the never-ending privacy thickets it dawned on her.

"I've been studying the trails. He's likely taking his own well-known shortcuts through these forests or thickets. He could be three streets over in twenty seconds. I need to see the map… think of his escapes 'as a crow flies.' "

CHAPTER 5

Ray Finney sat down at a table opposite Ralph Sneed, the honorable mayor of Hilton Head Island, at Rayburn's, a reservation-only, sixty-dollar-an-entrée eatery near the entrance to Wexford, another of the island's gated communities, once home to Michael Jordan, among other celebrities. Finney, proprietor and publisher of *The Beaufort Tribune*, also owned twenty-two rental units in Ocean Oaks, fifteen houses and seven condos, value on paper, some forty-four million dollars. It was his retirement package. He was finally right-side-up on the majority of the properties – closing in on full ownership on some - and he didn't want his equity compromised by canceled rentals due to sensational journalism. The editorial line at the Tribune had been to downplay the murders. Finney was a slight man in his seventies, a Navy veteran of the Korean War. He had scratched and clawed his way to success, attending night school while working his way up from the bottom rung of the newspaper ladder - obituaries.

"Mayor, what can I do for you?" Finney said.

Sneed was a thirty-three-year-old dot-com near-billionaire who bought his way into office after relocating from Washington State. He was looking for something semi-interesting to occupy his time while his fortune grew. After spending nearly a half million dollars on a campaign that called for fifty-thousand, he'd earned little respect from the forty-thousand permanent residents of Hilton Head and absolutely zero from Finney. He'd hired the highly-respected and glamorous owner of a powerhouse public relations firm, LaDonna Reynolds, as his campaign manager. After the election, he kept her on as a consultant – on his own dime. The

Diagram of Death

fact that his sexual orientation was a mystery had become a point of contention on the island. The unmarried Reynolds, if anything, quieted a few rumors.

"Mr. Finney, thank you for meeting me," Sneed said.

Finney waved the back of his hand. "I take it you have a problem?"

"The island has a problem."

Finney watched him, waiting impatiently. "Am I supposed to guess?"

Sneed tilted his head in protest of being forced to state the obvious.

"Mr. Finney, we have a serious problem in Ocean Oaks – a serial killer – a sexual serial killer – and your paper for some unknown reason has given it no more ink than the local Little League results."

"All right. First, cut the Mr. Finney. You know it's Ray. Use it please."

"Yes sir," Sneed said, militarily.

Finney again stared, this time with more disdain. His head turned slightly as he studied what he considered to be a youth. If it had been confirmed to Finney that Mayor Sneed was gay, he'd never have taken the meeting and would go out of his way in the future to make sure Sneed failed in the next election. They'd had conversations before. Finney owned shares in a number of businesses around Hilton Head and in Ocean Oaks, businesses for which issues had occasionally arisen, dropping on to Mayor Sneed's radar. Finney had also been a financial and vocal supporter of the incumbent, longtime Mayor Freddie Silver.

"Do you think that renters from North Carolina or Virginia are in the habit of checking our headlines before booking?"

"No, but, how many papers do you sell on the island daily? You could certainly do a little better job of keeping our year-round residents informed. You live in Ocean Oaks don't you?"

"Yes I do."

"Daughters?"

"We're empty nesters."

"Granddaughters visit?"

"Look Sneed, you're wasting your breath. I'd think you'd want it covered up. You've seen "Jaws" haven't you? In the reruns? Mayor, bad jacket, running around, 'the beaches are staying open, the beaches are staying open.' The Chamber certainly isn't crying about my coverage. Oh wait, you don't *have* any business interests here, do you."

Sneed turned his water glass ninety degrees, as though a water spot discouraged his vantage point, then lifted it to take a sip.

"You know that I don't," he said. "But that's not the issue here. The issue is responsible journalism."

Finney again stared, until a waiter entered his line of sight. He flagged him down.

"Double scotch, neat," Finney said. "What'll you have?"

"Martini. Very dry, please."

"I'll tell you what, Sneed. I'll send our top reporter to your office for an exclusive. How about that? You can share with our readership what is being done to catch this maniac."

"I've spoken with Randy Simpkins."

"Simpkins? That moron. He's not qualified to cover the instate crop report. No, I'll send our political editor over. He came down from New York about a year and a half ago... has a bit more of an edge to him. He does all our tough stories."

"What's his name?"

"Tyler Bishop," Finney said.

"Oh, yes. He grilled me in print a few months back."

"I'm sure it was nothing personal," Finney said, flashing a half smile, his first of the meeting, which wrinkled his face up to his crow's feet. "He's leasing a condo from me in Ocean Oaks, so he has a vested interest."

"What's the vested interest?"

"He has a daughter nearly grown."

"So he's married."

"Well, yes, Mayor. That's usually the way of it. Wife doesn't come around. Not much for get-togethers. That's all irrelevant. This is about our island's problem, correct?"

The waiter returned with the drinks. Finney downed half of his in one gulp, as Sneed took an unimposing sip.

"She's enochlophobic? Fear of crowds?" Sneed asked, completely ignoring Finney's cynicism.

"No, I didn't say that. I think maybe she's just a little shy."

"Kind of a hobby of mine to study phobias – and predators," Mayor Sneed said. "It's wrong to call our killer a maniac, Ray. He might be unbalanced, but he's very calculating."

CHAPTER 6

I haven't always been this way. Maybe it was lurking in me somewhere. The childhood wasn't a Norman Rockwell. My father would rather beat me than hug me, when he was there. My mother was... odd. No excuses. I can say that now because I know I'm not crazy. There's not a voice telling me to do it. Just a pull — like a gravitational force. I find the act intensely gratifying. My wife is a bore. She never grew out of her initial frigidity. Just never diminished, no matter what I tried. Then she faded completely away, like the snow screen of an old television. Give her a glass of wine and she gets a glow on and just sinks into the furniture.

    One day I was walking – cooling down from a run – it was dusk. I was on the trails here, way back when we were still renting the place out most of the time. When I was still working and we lived on bases. I glance at an upstairs window and see this gorgeous young woman getting fixed up for dinner, wearing just a towel, from the waist down. Vacationing, with a group likely... I saw no kids. Her man comes out of the bathroom and starts kissing her. I look around. I'm alone. I hide in the shrubbery just off the path. The bedroom is mostly windows, floor to ceiling. They stay after it, getting worked up. She's willing. Next thing I know she's on top of him on the bed. A light from the bathroom shone on her. Watching her was enthralling. Then she looked towards a window. She saw me. We made eye contact. She looked away and kept at it. Then she closed her eyes. She was so enraptured with her mate she didn't care who saw. I'd never felt that. Suddenly I was so empty inside I cringed with loneliness. I came out of the bushes and walked away. A month later, on the west coast, I started again.

CHAPTER 7

Harper Stowe pushed off of the base of the lighthouse at Bay Harbor with her foot, having stopped to re-stretch her hamstrings. She'd slowed her pace to weave her way through groups of minglers, swarms of rocking chairs – impatient tourists dressed for dinner -- and lines of satisfied others craving ice cream, and felt her legs tightening. The slips in the water to her left were overrun with a variety of vessels, from million-dollar yachts and sailboats to more mainstream gas cruisers. A few blared music for the owners partying on their decks, the sounds colliding with those songs from the nearby Tiki Bar, or the amplified solo guitarists from the restaurants.

She still intended to make the return run to South Beach Drive, then turn right and head to The Parrot Perch. Impulse took her on to the pier, where pairs of lovers, and a few individual stragglers, were wandering, though the businesses that operated from there – boat tours, kayak, parasailing and seadoo rides – were closing for the night. Still, the sun was just beginning its dancing wane and the sky was creative in its expressions, the light reflecting on twisting clouds that were lonely in the blue abyss.

The give and bounce of the wood of the pier under her feet gave her new awareness, and away from the crowds of people she could actually distinguish bits of conversation between the couples she dashed by. The pier made a ninety degree left turn after eighty yards, the remaining twenty acting as shield and protector to the large, double-decked, diesel-powered ship, *The Pirates Of Hilton Head,* used to take vacationers on tours out into Calibogue Sound and around Daufuskie Island. It also provided a wonderful opportunity for crabbing, and one lone teenaged-boy took advantage, leaning over the rail, pulling at his rope, his hopeful eyes gazing down at his rising trap. No one she encountered seemed suspicious.

Stowe was a trained observer. As she left the pier to run the outside perimeter of the area, she continued making quick studies of the male faces she saw. It was easy, of course, to distinguish vacationers from workers. But identifying a rapist was not so cut and dried. The predator could live on his boat, or a nearby fifth-floor condo, or bartend through lunch, or dress as a tourist visiting Ocean Oaks on a day pass, or be a pool cleaner or exterminator. She had to narrow the search. The fact that the victims' bodies had not been moved lent credence to the killer being a runner, someone a woman would be comfortable with on the trails. But no victim seemed to fight back, there had been no near misses, so it also seemed that the women were ambushed. It was just as possible that the stalker could again be almost anybody... and yet someone who walked around without detection or arising suspicion.

As she left the sand and crushed-oyster-shell path she'd been on for a parking lot she was certain of one fact: most men's eyes latched on to her as she ran through. A few saw her as a mere distraction, a couple others smiled respectfully, but many more, she felt, saw her as an object of their lust, even if they gazed quickly then returned their look to their wives.

That was harsh. Am I jaded?

She knew men. She just knew *bad* men well. She knew evil men like the lighthouse at her back knew wind. She knew every inclination of the sadistic man, and she could anticipate the impulse of the criminal. Her record with non-criminals was better, though she'd never found the right man. She'd loved a boy in high school, but he ultimately took the path of least resistance when it came to companionship, so she left him behind. In college it became much more difficult to determine who the serious-minded young men were, and who was just trying to get her out of her jeans. As a freshman, she'd attended

Diagram of Death

a frat party and warded off a potential date-rape situation. As she exited, with her escort crumpled in a corner, she passed three more young men in a hallway. They were so in tune to her abrupt departure, she realized that she may have thwarted a pre-meditated gang rape. That kept her away from wild parties the rest of her time on campus, though she did date a few young men.

But her knowledge of the unchivalrous went even deeper than that. Distinguished by her affluent background and classic beauty – almost haunting light sky-blue eyes behind what seemed to be clear crystal - she was approached by numerous professors, their lines much smoother than those of her classmates. She became mildly interested in one young, untenured prof, even had drinks with him. But he was married, and she refused to merely be someone's something on the side. The occasional office visits that her parents had preached was "a good routine for college" became a nuisance to her, especially since she was acing all her courses. Come-ons became so banal and tiresome that she did her best to register for classes taught only by female instructors.

At the academy, she felt a reversal of affection. The attitude of the young men there was more of aggressive resistance. Any interest shown in her would alienate the trainee from his buddies, and subject him to the same harassment she was enduring. It was only when the training neared its conclusion that she felt any acceptance or respect.

Though her eyes darted from tree to tree as she sped along the wooded paths, this stream of consciousness – images of so many interested males, males that saw her as an object only - stayed with her until she reached the deck of The Parrot Perch, which was also crowded with customers. Unlike the benign bits of conversation she'd overheard at Bay Harbor, the talk here was more of a worried nature, though possibly brought on by her appearance as a twilight solo runner.

She stopped and filled a plastic cup with water from an orange cooler beside the ice cream window. At the first table she passed, two couples in their mid-thirties discussed the murders. The woman who faced her glanced up with a surprised but sympathetic look of "Wow, she's brave to be out alone."

The second table was a mother and her adult daughter, both blond and wearing patterned-sun dresses. They stopped her, the mother gently reached and touched Stowe's arm.

"Sit down here with us a minute," the mother said. "Do you know about the murders, darling? You shouldn't be running at this time of the day."

"Yes, I do, but they've all been on Friday haven't they?" Stowe said. "I've just moved here but that's what I was told."

"Yes, but who can depend on that? If a man has a taste for murder, how can you rely on a routine?"

A woman at the next table, fiftyish, more robust, with dark hair and features – i.e., not fitting the victim profile – joined in. "My bet is he's moved on," her smoker's voice said in a northern accent.

"Why do you say that?" Stowe asked.

"Too much heat. This place will be crawling with cops on Friday. There'll be a presence."

"But there's just so many places he can attack from," the mother said.

"That's right. We've been running in the mornings," the daughter continued. "Together, I might add. I'd be scared to death to run by myself after seven-thirty – on any night."

"He could take the additional protection as a challenge," Stowe said, wary of not getting overly-technical or seem too informed. "It gets to be a badge of honor in them. But that's how they get caught."

Diagram of Death

"We're leaving a day early," said a woman at a fourth table, her husband and two children listening intently. The boy – the older of the two kids, at ten-years-old - couldn't hide his disappointment. "I heard about the school teacher. I just can't let that happen to this family."

A waitress approached with more purpose than drink refills. She was in her early twenties.

"I heard there was a home invasion – an attack in a home – before the first murder," she said, unapologetic for her intrusion. "But the guy ran when he realized there were more people in the house. I think that means he'll try anything... any night."

Stowe had heard a similar story, but it didn't fit the modus operandi, or m.o., of the unsub.

"From what I've read," she said calmly, "sexual predators usually stick to the same pattern. I don't think we'll have to worry in our homes."

"I can't stand it," the waitress said. "I'm never home alone anymore. If my parents leave, I call friends over. I get that creepy feeling after dark, like I'm being watched."

Stowe looked around the deck as the girl spoke. All the tables within earshot had halted their conversations and had begun to listen. At least ten women close by had a look that bordered on panic.

CHAPTER 8

Cold introductions were usually not a problem for Rhett Richardson, on the job or socially. To say he was a bit of a flirt was a gross understatement. Professionally, having a camera perched on his shoulder worked wonders, depending on the scenario. It opened more doors than a police battering ram. High school and college kids always loved being part of a broadcast. He'd worked hundreds of games for ESPN as a regional lens-for-hire, to the point of knowing on a first name basis dozens of cheerleaders from the schools of the Atlantic Coast and Southeastern Conferences.

He realized though that this woman that he'd followed into Ocean Oaks, despite just returning from a run, had a sense of purpose. He had enough professionalism to show discretion as far as her cover was concerned. What he hadn't considered was that he could immediately be considered a suspect. He walked across South Beach Drive from his rental. Having settled in, he approached her wearing shorts, a faded Pearl Jam T-shirt, and flip-flops.

"Hi. Good run?" he asked. He'd met her at the entrance of Peachtree Lane.

"Yes, it was," she said. She stared at the man, on guard for any sudden moves, though they were out in the open. She'd made it back from the enlightening conversation at The Parrot Perch just as the sun began to set.

"I just wanted to say hello. Welcome you to the neighborhood."

"You saw me arrive?"

"Yeah, this afternoon."

He was beside her as she began walking down her street towards her home. Their hands grazed at one point.

Diagram of Death

When they did, she recoiled her left arm and took a step to her right.

"Look, I don't mean to be rude, but keep your distance, please."

"Oh sure. I understand."

"Do you? Do you know what's going on here?"

"I do."

"So you realize that approaching me like you did would put a woman on edge?"

"Uh, yes? Wait, no... I didn't think that - "

"But you did it anyway?"

"Well, yes."

"Well..." she said, almost mocking Richardson. Her sense that he might be a threat was diminishing. "Why would you do that?"

"I... I wanted to meet you. As I said, I happened to see you earlier."

"What're you, casing the neighborhood?"

"Uh, no," he said, exhaling. "Can we start over, please?"

They walked on in unison. Their feet on the pavement, consistent, was the only sound at that moment.

"I suppose so," Stowe said, smiling to herself.

"Look, I'm trying to be discrete. I'm working for the BBC right now... covering the murders," he said. Then he glanced at her, barely turning his head. He almost whispered the next line. "I saw you leaving the police barracks today. I followed you thinking I might get a scoop on the story. Then I kind of put together a theory of why you're here."

"Oh, that's just great. Are you driving a big news van?"

"No. I have my own car. I'm freelancing. I won't blow your cover... if that is what you're doing here."

More silence, broken only by the metronome of their steps. Stowe's eyes busily darted from house to bush to tree though her head remained still. She wondered if they were being watched. The sense of relief she'd felt turned to irritation. She didn't need a journalist on her tail this week.

"May I ask if my theory is right?"

"No. You may not."

Stowe looked at Richardson. She was torn between playing it tough and cutting this handsome young man some slack. She didn't want to hinder an approach by the unsub, and she certainly didn't need to kick off a new romance at this pivotal juncture in her career, during what will likely be the most memorable and possibly historic crime spree she ever works. Yet she found his verbal stumbling just before to be as touching and honest as a child's confession.

"Well, whoever you are and whatever you're doing," he said, "I've rented the house across the way there. Nothing illegal in that is there?"

"Of course not."

"I'm Rhett Richardson."

Stowe turned her head slowly until she locked in on his features, masking her surprise in his name.

Mom would get a kick out of that.

"Can you keep your mouth shut, Rhett? I mean to everybody... editors, bosses, friends, colleagues?"

"Yes, I can." He'd become distracted by the fact that her dress clothes from the afternoon somehow hid a level of fitness he'd rarely seen in any woman, any time, any place.

Again she looked at him as they walked, her eyes narrowed with study and diminishing irritation. They were approaching her house, which she assumed he knew. She was upset that he had that knowledge, but there was no getting around it. She made the decision: better to control him than have him trying to follow her constantly.

"Ok. My name is Harper Stowe. Yes I'm a detective with Hilton Head P.D. I'm posing as Carrie Stowers. So that's

Diagram of Death

the name you use. I need to be alone on my runs and walks… my surveillance. Do you understand that?"

"Yes I do."

"I can't have you underfoot – or beside me – or watching me from the bushes, while I'm trying to draw this man in."

"I got it," Richardson said. "I won't get in the way."

"If you do you'll be wishing that *you* were gone with the wind."

He laughed.

"Does that mean though that you'd be free for a late dinner? Or a sandwich or something?"

"Well, I don't have a morsel in the house… "

"Great. I'll pick you up in what, an hour?"

"Make it forty-five minutes. And just for something quick - got to be out early in the a.m."

"Okay. Oh, I meant to tell you something earlier."

"What would that be?"

"It's a beautiful evening. Isn't it?"

Stowe hid her smile and looked at the colors of the western sky. She turned to walk up the driveway of her commandeered home.

"Forty-five minutes," she said.

CHAPTER 9

I've always dealt with disappointment well. That's what life is all about isn't it? Dealing with gut-wrenching disappointment? I may have lashed out a bit after my first female rejections. It's quite insensitive of a girl to tell a boy no. Who is she anyway? Especially after the preparation. When you're eleven-years-old, you spend hours – weeks – visualizing the encounter: how to approach her, what to say exactly, rehearsing the lines. Will you go with me? Want to see a movie? The opportunity approaches, recess, free time, after school, you're almost paralyzed with fear, your mouth is dry, uttering a sentence is like spitting up gravel, you work up the courage finally, fighting the dizziness you feel in your head, the nausea, the heat, then without so much as a sincere thought, she instantly says "no," or "I don't think so," or worse yet, "no way."

Lashing out later is a given, right? She asked for it. She deserves it. You have to put them in their place. The pulling of the pony tail on the playground, or a slick "accidental" trip or bump in front of her friends. Turning the tables with a verbal assault. "I wouldn't go to the movies with you if you were the last girl on earth. I was just asking out of pity." They were on to me, but what do you do?

The teen years get a little dicey. Girls flaunt their maturing bodies with no regard for their male counterparts, knowing that they're driving us crazy with desire. On fire. Knowing that we want to explore, not hurt, just touch. "I'm not ready," they say. But the teasing goes on. I couldn't tolerate the teasing, the smug little attitude that goes along with it. Who are they to withhold? I began to punish the teasers. The teasers didn't deserve to live. It was good to have a car, a bribe from

Diagram of Death

my parents for my affection. I never hurt a girl I went to school with. Ever. That would be dumb, right? "Don't shit in your own backyard," as they say. Can't say that about a few girls in some neighboring towns though. And of course, our family was always on the move. I didn't mind it so much. I never had any close friends anyway. It was a pretty good life. That's why I decided to follow my father into the Navy. See the world, one port at a time.

CHAPTER 10

"So, why did you leave New York, Mr. Bishop?" Mayor Ralph Sneed asked. He thought some light conversation might soften the edge of the reporter who'd called him a "gunslinger who pulled his checkbook out of its holster with lethal precision" during the election. Sneed guessed that Bishop was in his early forties though he looked younger.

"I can't say it was just one thing. It's a long story, boiling down ultimately to where we wanted to raise our child versus dealing with the boatload of pretentiousness and pseudo intellectualism we faced daily," Tyler Bishop said. "If I ran into one more liberal having an existential crisis I think I would have jabbed my own jugular with a pen. And those were our friends."

"Not a big philosopher?"

"Hey, I just try to string sentences together... not interpret the meaning of life. Everybody wants to go to New York to write, sing, paint, act – be discovered. But the internet killed a lot of good jobs - magazines and smaller papers. No offense."

"Why you bastard!"

Bishop laughed. Sneed felt he'd smoothed any rough edges, like a comedian whose first few jokes were home runs.

"I think there were more out-of-work writers than out-of-work actors," Bishop said. "My wife was a traveling nurse when I met her. It just felt like it was time to hit the road. And, besides, I wasn't born there or anything."

"Oh no?"

"San Diego – father stationed there. What about you? This certainly isn't a west coast hacker gig."

Diagram of Death

"Oh, I just got lucky there... good timing. I was upper-middle management at Microsoft. Everybody got rich. I parlayed that a time or two. But it really wasn't my scene. I'm a searcher."

"Asking would be redundant."

Sneed laughed as he leaned back in his leather chair.

"Oh, I don't know, happiness, fulfillment, a sense of civic purpose. It was so dreary in Seattle. I liked the idea of getting some sun, but I didn't want to go down to Miami. I'm not a big partier. Not that I'm anywhere as stern as your boss. I still like to have fun."

Bishop gave an obliging cough of laughter.

"Yeah, I've got you. Ray's a little, how-should-we-say, gruff. A man's man, no doubt about it. But the paper's budget is surprisingly robust."

"Generous is he?" Sneed asked, presuming Bishop's annual salary didn't equal the monthly increases in his savings account from compounded interest.

"Well he kept the conglomerates at bay. Staying independent makes it easier. The giants are killing the soul of the business. They want to pay everybody like they're right out of school - despite making their millions in profits."

"Well it sounds to me like your wife has the right idea. She's helping people for a good wage."

Bishop shifted in his chair. The thumb and middle finger of his left hand adjusted his glasses from the outside rims, covering his face as he looked at his lap, shielding the downturned corners of his lips. He cleared his throat.

"She's taking some time off, actually."

"Oh. Good for her."

"Yeah."

"Does she enjoy the island?"

"My daughter does. We hardly see her. She's at that age, you know? Seventeen in a couple of weeks, lots of friends, senior year, college looming on the horizon."

"What a lively time."

"So, Mr. Mayor, why am I here?"

"I told Ray Finney I didn't feel the Tribune was giving this crisis adequate coverage."

"I see. And his response was?"

"Well he made me feel like a naughty school boy. But you're here, so I must have said something right."

"What can you tell me about these murders that I don't know?"

"Well how much do you know?"

"Just what I've read in the paper: four victims, every other Friday, raped and throats slit, attractive blonds in their thirties, runners, no evidence to speak of, hands tied with a rope."

Sneed's head turned slightly as he studied Bishop. He started to speak but stopped.

"Anything else?" Bishop asked.

"My goal here, Tyler, is to warn people about the dangers Friday, not necessarily re-hash the past."

"Well, I've got to have my facts straight. What's the textbook age and race for the perp?"

"Oh, thirty to late middle-aged man, fit, strong. Caucasian most likely. There seems to be a lack of apprehension on the part of the victims."

"Quite a gap on age."

"Yes, but he's cunning, patient… very calculating. That probably leans it more towards middle aged. I don't believe he's rashly attacking the first woman he sees. There would be witnesses."

"Have there been any cases in the past of a similar nature?"

Diagram of Death

"From what I understand, some random rapes. Nothing so… pathological."

"Actually, I'll have to go to the police for that answer. Neither one of us have been here long, right?"

"Well, there are safety statistics. I've got a file there with annual reports dating back fifty years. But it's true that they don't always give a complete picture. I've discussed it with Beaumont. He's the link."

"So what's your safety message?"

"Do not run, walk, or bike alone. Certainly don't run alone after 5 p.m. – any day, not just Friday."

"I assume there will be a heightened presence of law enforcement?"

"Of course. There'll be L.E.O.'s from ten counties in here Thursday and Friday, uniformed and plain clothes. But there's still opportunity, even if he remains true to his pattern. If he breaks it, there's certainly more."

"Meaning?"

"Home invasion mainly, or a parking lot abduction. He could change his selectiveness. If he added brunettes to his taste his scope widens by hundreds. If he dropped the age group to sixteen it would increase by a thousand. Thus far he's been very specific… and undeterred."

"Of course, he could be gone," Bishop said. "It might be over."

"I doubt it."

"The threat of getting caught is certainly higher."

"Right. That raises the question of whether it's a worker within the gates or a resident," said Sneed.

"Have there not been any clues in that regard?"

"Nothing concrete. Circumstantial – items that could have been there prior to the attacks."

"Or he's intentionally… My guess is that he'll have moved on."

Andrew Spradling

"I hope you're right. But I don't think so. Maybe that's why I've been fretting over your paper's coverage. I don't have a good feeling."

CHAPTER 11

Harper Stowe continued to study Rhett Richardson from across a small table. Her mind constantly calculated and dissected. Over time, she'd lost the ability for idle chitchat. He was bright enough to recognize her mind was still on the case.

"You know, sometimes the greatest revelations come after you've put it aside for a while," he said.

"That's a good notion, but it's never worked like that for me."

"Well, can I ask you a few questions about the unsub?"

"Sure."

"Are these acts about lust or about a need to murder?"

"I think it's about a desire to dominate."

"Could he have a split personality?"

"It's possible, but not likely. There definitely seems to be some recognizance and planning. That doesn't really lend to the split mind deal. Impulse triggers multiple personalities to act."

A waitress approached their table through the surrounding chaos of the deck at Carley's Grille, an island staple just outside the Ocean Oaks gates. She was carrying two plates: a grilled chicken sandwich for him, a salad with grilled chicken for her.

"I'll bring two more drinks," she said. "See anything else you need?"

"I think we're good. Carrie?"

She grinned slightly at his use of her alias, then she scanned the plate for her side of low-cal balsamic vinaigrette.

"No, looks great," she said, smiling up at the teenager.

They began their meals in silence, but Richardson was eager to learn more about a woman brave enough to take on her current duty. The reminder of her obvious courage made small talk seem superficial, but he pressed on anyway.

"So you're a southern girl. Where'd you grow up?"

"Just down the road... Savannah. You?"

"Charlotte. But we spent a whole lot of time down here in the low country. I think I've been on about every island from Kiawah to Jekyll. The folks spent my whole life looking for the perfect spot for a beach house."

"That's a good childhood. Did they find it?"

"They bought a place on Fripp."

"What do your parents do?"

"They're both bankers. High finance. Part of that Charlotte boom. Mom got out of it. I'm the oldest of four kids, so her hands have been pretty full."

"Wow, four kids," she said. The reoccurring and disappointing twinge of having no siblings struck her. At the same time, Richardson wondered how he'd lost the interrogation floor.

"You know, it's amazing really," Stowe went on. "All the waterways and bays and sounds and rivers on the southeast coast. All the *fingers* you see on the map. There's so many I don't think you could count them. You could spend a lifetime trying to see it all. It's so gorgeous. And I'm sure some people think it's all the same."

"Some people think a true island has to be freestanding, out in the ocean somewhere. By comparison, it's only a trickle of water that made Hilton Head an island."

"Yeah, a 'Sound' that has two lanes of constant boat traffic."

"I can take a kayak down the May River, cross Calibogue Sound to Hilton Head in no time – faster than a car sometimes," Richardson said. "Because of bridge traffic."

"For some people, crossing that bridge is sanctuary - the only thing that gets them through the rest of their year."

Diagram of Death

"Some people don't like sand. Or salt water. Or heat."

"True. Different strokes, though I think you're just taking a position to push my buttons," Stowe said. She wanted to shift gears – or depart, the food and length of the day starting to weigh in. "I'll bet there was some chaos on those family trips of yours."

Richardson laughed. "I could go on for hours about that. Even with three seats there was never enough room in the family vehicle. What about you? Siblings?"

"Nope. I'm the pampered only-child of a surgeon and a lawyer."

"I think I got that air. Abundance of pedigree."

"Oh I reek of it, darling," she said, with an aristocratic tone.

They both laughed. He was glad Harper was lightening up. Her smile made her even more stunning. He couldn't stop his next question. It was as if it were loaded in a gun and the trigger already pulled.

"Is your mother aware of what you've volunteered for? I mean - I assume you volunteered."

Her fork, on its way to her parting lips, stopped. Stowe lowered her hand back to the table. Her attention shifted towards the front door. Without saying a word, she put down the utensil, stood and walked away, returning a minute later with a flier. Richardson watched her with uncertainty.

"I'm sorry I…"

She put her free hand near his lips to stop him.

"It's okay," she said. "I had a thought while I was running earlier."

"And that was?"

"That he would know shortcuts through these wooded areas. Between houses, across fairways, around waterways that butt up close to the houses. We'd been looking at it from the standpoint of trails. And that if he was a resident, he'd likely live nearby on one of them."

She opened the map, found the Ocean Oaks portion of the shoe-shaped island, and folded the rest under. She took a pen from her tiny purse and marked the locations of the victims: Royal Fern Road, Old Hilbert Woods, North Live Oak, Painters Woods Circle. Using the dull-side of a butter knife as a straight-edge, she drew two diagonal lines that crossed just due west of the traffic circle on Greenbank Drive. She drew a circle around the "X."

"I'd done this after the third murder. The center of that triangle had a much smaller number of houses."

"Which was fourth, Painters Woods?"

"Yeah, see. I'd studied what we were bringing in about the owners. Nothing suspicious. Nothing seemed to click."

"There's a lot more houses in this center for sure, but you're still throwing a dart in the dark aren't you? I mean a fifth murder would move that circle again most likely right?"

"Sure. But, in this zone, maybe there's someone who fits the profile."

"How many people do you have crunching data?"

"Half dozen."

"Well, you've got three days."

As he drove her home, chatting about his own work to fill the air, he pointed out the house he was renting.

"In case you need anything," he said. "It's fully stocked. Yours?"

"Looks like the owner's kids took what they wanted to keep and left the junk they didn't," she said. "There's an old chair and a love seat. A breakfast table, a guest bed. It's going right back on the market when this is over."

Not considering what she would or wouldn't allow, he jumped out of the Envoy to open her door. She met him at the hood.

"This was not a date, Richardson."

"I know. Just trying to be a gentleman."

"Well, no need. And I don't want you to contact me again," Harper said, and turned to walk to her incandescent front door.

"Ever?"

She paused, looked over her shoulder, and smiled slightly.

"Just let me do my work… neighbor."

"That sounds better," he said, regaining hope.

As she watched him back out of her drive, she looked across the street at the darkness between two of the houses. The hair on her neck and arms tingled. She felt she was being watched.

CHAPTER 12

Ray Finney was true to his word. The placement of Tyler Bishop's story Tuesday morning in *The Beaufort Tribune*, top of the page, bold headlines, was as dramatic as if the murders had occurred the previous evening: SERIAL KILLER STILL ON LOOSE, with a subhead "Mayor Sneed Issues Safety Warning for Ocean Oaks, Hilton Head."

The story included headshots of the four victims: Linda DeShea, Barbara Robinson, Tammy Pauley, and Anita Williams, with brief bios on each. DeShea, 34, the school teacher and mother of two, from Richmond, Va.; Robinson, 39, an accountant and mother of three from Raleigh, North Carolina; Tammy Pauley, the youngest at 31, one daughter, from Greenville, South Carolina; and Anita Williams, 36, mother of two, from Gaithersburg, Maryland, a Washington D.C. Drug Enforcement Administration office worker.

The pictures, all submitted by the families, weren't typical news print mug shots or blurred surveillance images. They weren't even phone selfies. They were studio portraits. All four victims were attractive, but each was in some way stunning. The crystal blue eyes, the pronounced cheekbones, the cutting jawline and neck, the subtle curls and twists in full hair. They were living examples of God's artistic flair. Individually, each would make a reader stop and ponder the senseless waste of life. Collectively, the impact of those four faces on the general public was like a California wildfire. Even Mayor Sneed, who knew the story was coming, was taken aback by the grouping. The television news stations - local and national - also ran stories, also with headshots and background information. The murders were the topic of conversation all over the island, at every café, restaurant, and bar, at every

Diagram of Death

corporate meeting, real estate office, golf course, and rental kiosk. Residents and renters began looking at unaccompanied men suspiciously, especially men walking or running on the beach or on the trails. They began to formulate hypotheses on motive, plan of attack, even ideal victims.

What reservation clerks learned at the hotels was that for every cancelation, there were three requests to book. No rentals at Ocean Oaks sat empty. Guards at the Ocean Oaks gates tirelessly sold day passes – exceeding output of the Bay Harbor Golf Classic. The toll booth for the island's short bypass that leads guests to Ocean Oaks' gates were continually backed up. Traffic on Ocean Oaks' interior roads was noticeably greater. Pedestrian numbers parking and taking the trolley to Bay Harbor, The Parrot Perch, or the beach, multiplied in the early a.m.

Harper Stowe could feel the additional presence as she leaned into the curve of a paved path on her morning run. She could accelerate to a quarter-mile pace if she chose to, and keep it for a mile. Her legs, core, and heart had that kind of speed and stamina. Which didn't necessarily help her popularity at the department. The men generally loved her. But once a year, the overweight male officers who crammed their mile-run training into the days before the annual fitness requirement by jogging a few laps - topped with a prayer - to finish within the 10 minutes loathed her. Some were good-hearted about it, many were not. She could break a 5:30-mile without bearing down too hard on it.

As Stowe ran on, she could see the shaded paths were crowded with men, and men with their women. Were these individuals there to help? To answer a distress call? Or were they curious onlookers, hoping to witness the aftermath of a crime. Chief Lester Beaumont had called Stowe at 7 a.m., to tell her about the front page of *The Beaufort Tribune*.

"I got a call from the mayor last night – at 11:15," Beaumont said.

"You guys are getting to be great buds."

"Don't get smart, Harp. Sneed said the guy interviewing him mentioned rope being used. That had never come out, right?"

"No. And really, not even sure about that. No trace of it... or bruising. Who is this guy?"

"Tyler Bishop. We're running a deep background check."

"I remember his byline. Seems like a longshot."

"I don't know why. This sicko could come from any walk of life."

"It just seems that in his position, he would be pretty well-adjusted. Not to mention that would be the most coincidental fall-into-our-lap conviction in law enforcement history."

"Well get this. Quick DMV scan – he lives in Ocean Oaks."

"Damn. What's the address?"

"He rents a condo in the South Beach Villas at the end of South Ocean Oaks Drive. Apparently Ralph Finney, the publisher, cuts him a deal on rent. He just pays the mortgage amount. It's unit 206."

"Text me his DMV picture right now."

"How would I do that?"

"Are you kidding me, Dino?"

"Dino?"

"Dinosaur."

"When did you become such a jackass? Yes, I'm just playing. Sneed said he's around forty or so. Records have him at 42. Definitely physical enough to be our man – 6-1, 180. Came here from New York."

"Ok. Call me when you get the rest.

Diagram of Death

"Take care of yourself, kiddo."
"Bye-bye, Lester."
"I mean it, Harper. Be careful."

With one typically-bad DMV-impression to go on in a sea of moving faces, she pressed towards the villas past The Parrot Perch. She jogged on to the parking lot as though in cool-down mode, 88-degree cool-down mode, a low country-living furnace. The assigned parking, some beneath the buildings, where a first floor would be, was clearly marked. As she walked closer to the 206 slot, she got a glimpse of Tyler Bishop throwing what looked to be work items – lap top bag, notebooks hanging out of the pockets - and a sport coat in the backseat of his BMW sedan, which was already running to cool the inside.

Pay dirt, she thought. *What're the chances?*

As he stood and shut the back door, Bishop noticed her walking his way.

"Looks like you got a good one in," he said, politely. Harper was a waterworks, sweating openly from all pores.

"Yeah, it got hot fast this morning."

"Well, have a good day," he said, turning away.

"Do you run?"

He faced her again, this time studying her features and form attentively.

"Uh, not nearly as much as I'd like… grindstone you know," Bishop said, smiling. He was unaccustomed and intrigued to be having a conversation he didn't initiate through the interview process. He could also feel the heat of the asphalt through the leather soles of his shoes. He was on a moral fence. Implications were bouncing in his head. His wife's condition was frustrating him. He'd recently initiated a slow-moving affair. It had been years since a younger woman, a stunning woman, was the least bit engaging. "Are you renting this week?"

Andrew Spradling

"Me, no. Just visiting… family," she said, pointing casually at a structure for effect.

"That's nice. Maybe we'll see you again. Enjoy."

"I'll look for you on the trails," she said, and watched as Bishop sat down in his car, pulled and fastened the seat belt, and shifted into reverse. The attention was a stroke to his ego, his testosterone was stirring. He looked in the rearview and watched her as he drove away.

Stowe walked on as though headed for the elevator of the next building of villas. Once he was gone, she doubled back. There was a dusty, second vehicle parked beneath the building, obviously the wife's. On a small shelf in front of that car were a few items you don't take into a three-quarter million dollar condo: two quarts of motor oil, tire gauge, car wax, a tackle box to match the hanging rod and reel, and, the most common of all American household items, duct tape.

Diagram of Death

CHAPTER 13

I'm not sure I have the actual count on what I've done. As a world traveler on a white horse, these events mount up. Stateside, there's so many crimes for the authorities to solve. And, I read the literature on those who have preceded me. I don't take trophies. I don't "need" to be in charge, though how else would these events take place? Sure I like to dominate, just like all the Admirals and Generals above me. This is greater than their domination. I wouldn't imagine they'd have the nerve and will it takes to violently invade the space of a passerby. Most men couldn't do it for love or money. Then close the deal, with all that pressure. But my hormones aren't out of whack, as others have claimed in their defense. Nor did I think I was narcissistic. They're obviously not lucky to be in my world, and I've never felt above anyone. Maybe the reverse is true. I thought I was done. How foolish do you have to be to perform in your own neighborhood? But, that one woman got me mad. Wouldn't speak to me out there. How can you walk by someone, practically brush arms, and not speak? Especially in this vacation-land. No worries: swim, lounge, run, shower, dress, drink, eat, make love. Rubbed me the wrong way. Enraged me, I guess. I felt a need to make her pay. I wasn't far from home. Ran back for what I needed, met her just where I expected. She wanted to speak before it was over. For her I had no remorse. So that's where I went with it, punishing the unfriendly. You won't find that characteristic in their bios in the newspapers. That would be cold and uncaring, even for the press. And impossible to ascertain, after the fact. So that brings me to a new question: High alert. Slimmer pickings. Raised stakes. As of this moment, I guarantee I will never get caught. So, do I lay low, change the day, the time,

Andrew Spradling

take it inside, lower my standards, my tastes? Do I ignore the supreme challenge? I don't think I will.

CHAPTER 14

Wednesday morning Harper Stowe rose at 5:30 and, travel mug of coffee in hand, stepped into the darkness in route to the beach. She had to clear her head before she began her day. A short walk from Slack Trimmer Road put her on South Beach. She turned left towards the rising sun. It had been so long since she'd seen this blessed event from this familiar sand, something her parents would awaken her for in her youth at least twice every vacation.

"Come watch the birth of a new day," her mother would tell her. "God's painting a new sky. Take it all in and let your dreams run wild."

The world seemed so big then. She would walk with her parents and chatter away, asking question after question. Why, why, why? Medicine and the law. People in need. People suffering. The great-grandfather story. Crimes. Accidents. Sports injuries. The pace of her parents' life was frantic. Never enough time. Long days. Focus. Purity for their professions.

Muriel and Carter Stowe had followed their fathers into their respective fields, and had met at Emory University in Atlanta. They were deeply in love. Harper could see it on those walks, the spontaneous rekindling of romance and play. Their hands would find each other as they walked, and for a while they would overlap their inside footprints by placing one leg and foot in front of the others' until they would become entangled, sometimes tumbling into the sand. They didn't care. He would take her hand to dance wherever they heard music, in the rental kitchen or waiting for a table at a restaurant. It didn't matter. Their southern upbringing meant that they were both proficient with the Shag. He'd spin her, extend their arms, pull her tight to him, then dip her. She would laugh at his antics, so enamored by him, so floored by his love. They would play tennis together, part of their weekend routine in Savannah – mixed doubles with friends. The friendly opposition was part of Carter's clientele: injured shoulders, elbows, hips and knees. His reputation was so widespread he became Atlanta's professional athletes' surgeon of choice despite practicing in Savannah.

The tide was nearly low. The expanse it exposed, one hundred fifty yards of smooth sand from dune to surf, caused a surprise reaction – the beach's reality was huge compared to the memory. The Atlantic tide battled its way up the beach in soothing tones. The squawking sea gulls with their rounded breasts hunted for food, some hovering against the wind, seemingly suspended in mid-air. The brown pelicans in their unbalanced "V" formations also flew high, some breaking off to dive for food.

The eastern horizon was so huge to her, and the distant clouds added color to the canvas as her sandy patch of earth turned into the sun, pinks and reds changing to orange. The water, cut off by the island to the left, went on and on as she turned to her right. The isles of Tybee and neighboring Daufuskie seemed almost touchable. She'd taken off her flip-flops after crossing the wooden overpass and left them in the sand. She looked at her toes as she walked in the surf, dodging the occasional sand crab. The sand was coarse to her feet. The murders began to creep back into her mind and she pushed them out, again thinking of her father and mother. They always tried to make up for lost time on their trips here.

"Work hard, play hard, that's the southern way," her father would always say. "That's our way." She admitted to herself that at 32 she was lonely. The pace of her career to that point had hidden the signs.

Which is why, perhaps, she had allowed Rhett Richardson to again take her out for an evening meal the night

Diagram of Death

before, this time to Hudson's, an island restaurant simple in its construction and interior, yet with a huge deck - bar and many tables – constructed over the waters of Broad Creek, a salt water inroad that nearly cuts Hilton Head in two. As dusk gave way to darkness, the couple drank wine and ate seafood – shrimp and grits for her, a steaming, broiled sampler platter for him - watching a lonely laborer tend to his boat on a nearby dock as a female guitarist played and sang from her barstool. Harper had an undeniable fondness for this man. Constantly around law enforcement-types, she'd forgotten what a man with an appreciation for the arts could offer. In her world there was little room for culture, unless the appreciation and knowledge of it was used to combat a specific crime.

She also listened intently to Richardson's first-hand tales of Savannah's growing violence, her parents still two of her hard-working citizens, and its gates only twenty miles down I-95 from Hardeeville, SC, the exit that begins the half hour trek to Hilton Head for many tourists. She recognized the closing gap from Savannah to here, and wondered if its convergence wasn't inevitable. There was already an element moving in, hidden for the most part. The drug busts were becoming more frequent, the brazenness and carelessness of the sky-high user more evident. There were signs popping up everywhere daily: A user walking into traffic in the middle of the night, struck and killed, just a human vessel with no driver; and increased petty theft for fixes. Sometimes it was a matter of the lack of stock put on a human life. The pushers were using the interstate highway system, and probably bringing more in by boat. Hilton Head didn't seem to be home base for any particular organization or any particular drug, as it had been in its marijuana heyday.

The couple sipped a second bottle of wine and talked into the night about their professions.

"So, what made you decide to go into journalism?" Stowe asked. "Especially with bankers for parents. I'm sure you experienced the same high-browed recruiting influences I grew up with."

"I did, sure. Doing what I felt was – not necessarily the opposite of their profession – but something with a different rewards system. That was part of it," Richardson said. "They made great livings, but what do they have at the end of the day? They helped the rich get richer... Dad still is. I wanted to track down and investigate the big story, tell it to the masses. I read a lot of crime books growing up."

"I did too. That's what got me hooked on law enforcement."

"You ever hear of Dorothy Kilgallen?"

"No, I don't think so."

"Well, she was before our time. She was a syndicated columnist and kind of a celebrity. She was on the game show *What's My Line?* because she was famous. That crossover that was common then. But she twice interviewed Jack Ruby one-on-one *after* he shot Oswald... during his trial. She was going to blow the doors off the 'lone assassin' bullshit I think."

"So what happened?"

"She was writing a book about it..."

"And?"

"She died. Overdosed... suspiciously. Just like Marilyn Monroe. She was found in a bed she never slept in, which a thug wouldn't have known. There are pictures of her and Marilyn together... she knew them all - Kennedy, Sinatra - too close to the mob boys. All her work, her notes with Ruby, disappeared. There're books and websites about her now."

"So, you want to die?" Stowe asked. She looked deeply into his eyes. A hint of a smile betrayed the sternness she usually practiced.

Diagram of Death

"No, of course not. But man, that's cutting edge. Those things were connected. That's how deeply involved I want to be – I'm trying to be. Break a story that changes the way we think, expose something we don't even know is affecting our lives because of greed… corruption."

Still seemingly-relaxed in her listening, she thought intently about Rhett Richardson's drive, his depth. She found herself respecting him more.

"See - we have that in common," he continued. "Wanting to expose and catch people doing wrong. People who think they're above the law."

"Yes, I guess we do," she said. "But you need a partner don't you? Or a pen?"

"Stuck under station guidelines, yes. But getting hired as a freelancer I sometimes step in front of the camera too. I just have to find the right story."

Their evening again ended professionally, Stowe maintaining her "nothing-physical" policy with him. But there was no denying her enjoyment of the situation, an attraction to this man. She thought of her parents. Could she find love out of this scenario? Everlasting love? This guy can't seem to hold down a job - and is looking to roam the world chasing stories.

She was approaching a man standing in the surf, fishing. She considered turning around. She needed to get her running surveillance started soon. But there was something about the man. He was barefoot, had crumpled khaki slacks rolled up to his knees, untucked polo shirt, thick glasses, hair blown everywhere. He was thin, 5-foot-10, looked to be around 60. He cast his line as deeply into the ocean as he could, walked out of the surf, picked up a large Styrofoam cup, and walked back in.

"Morning. Having any luck?" she asked him.

"Not yet, that was my first cast. Last week I caught a 12-foot shark. Drug it up to the house and cut it up. That's been some good eating. Freezer is full."

"Wow. Sounds good. I would've liked to have seen that."

"She was a fighter," he laughed, taking a gulp of what she had presumed was coffee.

"Are you… is that red wine?" she asked. It was 6:10 a.m.

"Yeah. I'm only drinking it 'cause we ran out of beer. You can get wine pretty cheap around here…the big bottles even."

She laughed. He lived in a stretch of multi-million-dollar, beach-front houses and still considered the price of a bottle of wine. She thought of the muddled profile of her unsub, which could essentially be anybody.

"You retired here?"

"No, I'm still at it… own a handful of businesses. Started out with a regional chain of brick oven pizza restaurants – sold that. I kept evolving. I have an H.R. software business I thought might interest my neighbors here. I live in a shack, compared to them," he said, pointing up the beach.

"Oh, yeah, that must be rough."

He laughed.

"Well, one of my neighbors is a foreigner - Russian I think - owns a ball team. I was gonna drop a business card at his house, thought the program might be able to help him. His guards – armed with AK-47s – met me at the porch."

"Oh my gosh. Which house?"

"The flat one there. I really don't think he's ever here. I don't know why they'd need assault rifles."

"Hmmm. Bodyguards," Stowe said, shaking her head. She was considering a dialogue about the case, and this was the

Diagram of Death

perfect opening. "What do you think about this serial rapist running around?

"I saw that story. It's a sad situation," the man said. "I don't know how he does it, performance-wise."

"Meaning?"

"I don't want to be, uh, lewd. I can tell you're a nice lady."

"Please. I've heard it all."

He tilted his head in an "Ok, here goes" moment.

"Well, you get to be my age, conditions have to be next to perfect just to… perform. If I tackled some dame, taped her mouth, pinned her down, pulled a knife, cut off her shorts, kept the blade to her throat, I'd have about as much chance of getting a hard-on as I would catching Moby Dick out here. The guy is deranged. Personally, I think he would have to be on the younger side of that age range I read. Unless he's on the little blue pill."

"Ever see any runners you'd be suspicious of?"

"Sure. About fifty times a day. As you may have guessed, I'm not really in to exercise. Hell, actually, I don't know that any one of these vacationers looks any more or less guilty than another."

"What about a resident? One who runs?"

"You some kind of law, sis?"

"No, just a potential victim."

"Hm. I do see some runners that I recognize as locals."

"Any specifically in the evenings?"

"Uh, yeah, a couple."

Stowe was faced with the same dilemma Rhett Richardson had put her in Monday. This time she wasn't backed into a corner.

"Ok, I didn't quite tell you the truth. My fiancé is working the case," she said, as she stepped closer and leaned in. "So that's my second vested-interest – the first, of course, is staying alive. I'm kind of a busy-body. He appeases me by letting me chip in when I can. So what are these two dusk-runners like?"

"Both white. One is olive, you know, Italian or Greek-looking. Moves pretty well, I think he still works."

Stowe envisioned Tyler Bishop.

"The other is long-limbed, big feet. I remember thinking once I could water ski with his shoes. Anyway, white as they come, kind of dorkish."

"If my man thinks it's worth it, could you describe their faces to a sketch artist?"

"Sure. If he doesn't mind getting his feet wet."

CHAPTER 15

Harper Stowe made it a point to constantly remind herself that not everything was as it seemed. Especially in law enforcement. So simple in theory, so difficult in execution. She knew though, first hand, the lengths and premeditation to which serious criminals would go to pull off their plan. Not every crime was an act of sudden impulse or passion. She knew all too well that after apprehending a subject proof was often fickle, and the hoped-for result – a conviction – was never guaranteed.

Where does this man fall in that scale of planning – does he plan? Or has he just been acting on impulse and been lucky to avoid witnesses? It was Wednesday afternoon – just over 48 hours remained before his next strike, if he stuck to his pattern.

She'd just returned to her commandeered home after her morning surveillance. In 100-degree heat Stowe had spent just over five hours running, walking, sitting on benches, rocking chairs, even those low-growing Live Oak branches that vacationers flock to with their children for pictures. She watched men, hoping that an observation of a suspicious look, a raised eyebrow or turned head, would spark a thought that would lead to a clue, even lead to a lead. Though her grim task in Ocean Oaks – one man's lack of humanity - caused disappointment, the boats in the harbor, lighthouse and open sea for a backdrop, the green ceilings of the trails themselves, made this job better than staking out an office-building or a house while stuck in a car.

After a long shower she felt the need to prop her feet up, which she accomplished by laying on a couch, her calves resting on one cloth-covered arm. Still wrapped in a beach towel, she could feel the blood in her legs moving through her body towards her head. She exhaled and started to relax.

"Thank goodness the air conditioner is top-notch," she said out loud. She smiled. This was when she did some of her best thinking. She was reminded of her last case before being promoted to lead detective.

It involved a rental house in one of the few seedy neighborhoods on Hilton Head. The house was occupied by suspect renters, two males and one female, possibly in the drug trade, possibly peddling sex. There had been a few disturbance calls because the renters were clashing with a homeowner across the street over parking issues, high-visitor traffic, and late-night noise. The complaining homeowner wasn't completely innocent. A hard-nosed, former-convict working as a mechanic at an off-island car dealership, he was trying to keep his own life in order. It seemed he began going out of his way to irritate the renters whenever possible. Temperatures rose between the two households until they seemed to be at the boiling point. An obvious-arsonist fire overtook the rental house one early-morning, burning it nearly to the ground. No one was hurt. The entire police force pointed to the ex-con, Theodore "Teddy" Carson, to be the torch. Especially when his alibi, "sleeping alone," was so flimsy. Stowe saw something in him no one else did. She interviewed him at length, when everyone else wanted only to book him.

"I'm sure what I did was taken the wrong way by you cops," Carson said. "But that's a bum rap. Just harmless stuff – standing my ground - returning trash that had been dropped in my yard, putting notes on their cars when they – or their visitors - blocked my driveway. Banging on their door if I was blocked and had to leave. You can't be timid or back down. Prison taught me that. Dogs sense fear, and so do thieves and dealers. They count on it. I could sense it in the owner of the place back when I moved in."

Diagram of Death

"The owner lived there?" Stowe asked.

"Yeah. It was his residence at the time. He's not a big real estate or landlord dude. He'd inherited some money, found a bigger place. Couldn't sell that house when he bought his next one. He liked *nothing* about me moving in, I can tell you that."

Stowe began investigating the owner, Pat Willingham. Armed with a physical description and the make and color of his car, her investigating – she found commercial surveillance-cameras blocks away - eventually proved he was in the area the morning of the fire. She also found where he'd bought the accelerant he used, weeks before. With no respect for Carson or anybody else that might hold a grudge against the renters, he intentionally made the job look sloppy. The final nail came in the form of an eye-witness down the next block, who saw Willingham cutting between houses on the morning of the fire to get to his car two blocks away. No other cop considered exit strategy, because everyone was hot for Carson.

Willingham was trying to rid himself of all his problems at the same time, pin the fire on Carson, get rid of the headaches caused by problem renters, and pocket the insurance payout for the house, which he never intended to rebuild. Stowe put him away for arson, endangerment, mail fraud, and attempted insurance fraud. Chief Lester Beaumont rewarded her with the lead detective job he had just vacated. Beaumont said in a small ceremony that Stowe was magnificent at continually looking at cases from different perspectives - and through the web of deceit put forth - a must in solving crimes.

Stowe could feel herself drifting off to sleep and did not fight it. She believed the short, afternoon nap was beneficial. She turned her head to the side as her eyes began to close. She gasped. A man was looking at her through a window.

CHAPTER 16

"Stowe's never been late for a meeting that I can remember – in near-ten years," said Chief Lester Beaumont. He looked at his watch, and then at the clock on the wall as if a discrepancy would offer an explanation. It was 5:12 p.m. If his eyes showed any emotion, it was concern.

"She's been spending most of her mornings and evenings on the trails over there," he continued. "And this wasn't a scheduled meeting… had to leave a message on her cell. Not that we don't appreciate your being here. Fresh eyes – especially with your expertise – could certainly help."

Beaumont looked at Mayor Ralph Sneed sitting at the table, flanked by representatives from the Beaufort County Sheriff's office and the South Carolina State Police. The purpose of the meeting being held in Stowe's office: three agents from the Federal Bureau of Investigation had arrived from Quantico, Virginia, to assist in the on-going manhunt for the serial rapist. They had to be brought up to speed.

"Yes, we're thankful the FBI sent you down," said Sneed. The trio had been deployed from the National Center for the Analysis of Violent Crime (NCAVC).

"Why don't you run us through your suspect pool," said Paul Clark, who at 45 was the most tenured and highest-ranking of the three agents. His muscle tone protruded his snug-fitting, gray suit. His tan face was chiseled, his brown hair cropped tight. "We read the overview on the flight."

"I'd rather let Stowe give you those particulars," Beaumont said. "Let's start out with the lay of the land. Ocean Oaks is 5,200 acres, roughly 10 times the size of the Academy. Over thirty-eight-hundred homes and two thousand villas, 600 acers of forest preserve, four golf courses, a hundred tennis

Diagram of Death

courts, five miles of beaches, ten times as many trails and inroads."

"Quite a few attack points," Clark said. "Can the beaches not be ruled out?"

"Only as an abduction site," Beaumont said. "But he could pick his victims there. Plenty of wooded, empty lots and secluded paths coming off the beach – long ones. There's over forty on South Beach alone. That's where he got the first victim – DeShea."

"That's right. She'd been running on the beach," Sneed said.

"Hell, at 8:30 the beaches are so quiet – everybody off to dinner – there're areas he could probably pull it off in the sand," said Beaumont.

"Our studies show over 65 percent of approaches are ruses or cons. Are you sure he hasn't gotten to know these women somehow?" said the agent to Clark's left, Jeff Hudson. Hudson was similar in age to Clark, but of contrasting stature. He was a powerlifter, thick, with black hair combed from one side to the other, a mustache, and thin-wired glasses.

"We haven't ruled out that he's choosing his vics that way," Beaumont said. "We've questioned family members and fellow vacationers extensively – looking for connections. But we've come up empty. And these are surprise attacks."

"In a large hunting area," Clark added. "He obviously knows it well."

The third agent stood and walked toward the bulletin board, covered with photos and printed information about the four victims. At the top of each was the portraits provided to the media. The rapid click-click of the heel then ball of her shoe with each step was the only sound in the room.

"The victimology is always the same. They are available, vulnerable, and desirable," said Arline Thorn. A brunette, her shoulder-length hair was brushed back over her head. Her eyes were a deep brown - walnut. Her pale but pleasant features were covered with base, rouge, and eyeliner. She wore a navy-blue skirt and matching jacket over a pink blouse. She wore no jewelry. "You know, the intimacy of the act usually lends to strangulation."

"Maybe he slits their throats because he's lazy," Hudson said. "He leaves them 'as is.' No attempt to conceal."

"That's about his quick escape," Clark said. "Besides, he has to be just as close – closer even – to use the knife."

"Either way he's still right on top of her," Thorn said. "It's amazing no one has seen this man when he flees. There has to be blood splatter that sprays him."

"It's looked like he's pulled their shirts up to block that," Beaumont said. "That might be why he never removes them. Sometimes he has cut them up the middle."

"That's smart. So in the twilight of evening or early dark he could possibly have been seen running and still not look suspicious," Thorn said.

"That's why we've presumed he's a runner rather than a worker," said Harper Stowe, from the doorway. "He might even be running around in a crimson T-shirt, just in case he has to wipe blood off himself. You know… Roll Tide. A lot of vacationers wear their college or home-state colors so people can identify with them - icebreaker."

Stowe walked to the board and offered her hand to Thorn.

"Whew, the Chanel No. 5 is overwhelming. Probably went heavy due to a travel day."

Beaumont sat down on the corner of Stowe's desk and exhaled.

"Arline Thorn, Detective," Thorn said. "Nice to meet you. These are Agents Clark and Hudson."

Both men nodded.

Diagram of Death

"Pleased to meet you," said Clark, standing nearly straight up before returning to his seat. Hudson glanced up at his colleague as though he were ignorant to Clark's gesture, then shook off the distraction to remain focused.

"Likewise," said Stowe.

"So we're looking at a pure hedonistic, pleasure-seeker," Hudson said. "All about the sexual gratification."

"Well, you could throw in the possibility of the thrill-oriented excitement," Stowe said. "He's not mission-oriented or visionary. I don't think he's hearing voices, nor is there profit involved. Maybe it's all about power and control, but what difference does it make really?"

"Crunching this data is vital, Ms. Stowe," Clark said. "At the Bureau, we believe this is how most crimes are solved."

"Your studies show that nearly 61 percent of serials only kill two to four times," Stowe said. "If you believed that you wouldn't be here."

Clark and Hudson shifted in their seats. The other men – even the county and state police reps – sat taller and looked at Stowe with admiration.

"It's true. But you may have an unusual situation here," Thorn said. "The next group – 27 percent – kills five to nine."

"And twelve percent kills 10 or more," said Stowe, her sarcasm sharpening. "I've memorized everything the FBI has published on rapists, and one of the 'proclivities' of those documents is the term 'questionable reliability.' It's peppered throughout."

"Harper, please," said Beaumont.

"I'm not trying to be disagreeable, Chief. I'm glad to get the help, believe me. We all know every rapist is different - but categories have to be created for FBI studies and documents. I mean, did you create a 'Body Disposal Flowchart' yet? These aren't prostitutes or 'clients' being killed - and I know surprise attacks fall below 17 percent on the primary approach-scale. But when we catch this stealth son-of-a-bitch, who knows what your parameters will look like afterwards."

"If we don't have to plug him full of holes when we catch him," Clark said. "Have you I.D.'d home owners with military records? I'm sure you know 35 percent of studied-offenders served in the military."

"I do. And, we did," Stowe said. "The problem is, the high cost of the real estate in Ocean Oaks typically excludes young owners, unless they've inherited. Most owners are over 65 and seven out of ten have served. Another stat-buster."

"Well, we've got one surprise for you, and it's not good news," Clark said. "We expedited your national search based on DNA from blood and semen – tapped CODIS. Even had some cold hits. With your four here apparently this man has killed a total of 19 women – that have been found."

"Jesus," said Beaumont.

"Did the data show anything else?" Stowe asked.

"Every murder, the first dating back to over twenty-five years ago, occurred within 30 miles of a Navy base," said Hudson.

Stowe walked to the table and sat down. Thorn did the same.

"That ups the stakes, Harper," Beaumont said.

"Sure does. I'll tell you what else. Ninety minutes ago I had a man with his face pressed to my window checking me out in a towel. By the time I grabbed my gun and threw on a T-shirt he'd disappeared. That's why I was late. I was trying to pick up his trail."

"Could have been anybody," Sneed said. "Since the house was for sale, maybe it was a neighbor wondering who'd moved in."

"Or just a Peeping Tom," said Hudson.

Diagram of Death

"Or you may have become his next target," said Beaumont.
"That's just what I was hoping for."

CHAPTER 17

The drums of fear and discontent were beating Thursday as though invaders were approaching the shoreline. A town hall meeting was scheduled inside the gates of Ocean Oaks for 7 o'clock, in the parking lot outside of Hilton Head Fire and Rescue Station 2 on Lighthouse Road. The shaded stretch of asphalt was quite long. It also abutted a tan, stucco-styled strip mall that included a real-estate office, popular eateries including Truffles Cafe, and a beach-bike rental shop. It also had parking for a hundred cars. Centrally located, many of the attending home owners were able to walk or bicycle to the gathering.

Though fewer than four of ten Hilton Head residents officially claimed a religion, both the Catholics and the Baptists had a representative near the portable microphone provided by fire chief Bud Holt. Joining Lester Beaumont and Mayor Ralph Sneed were Father Francis O'Malley and Reverend William Janson, both considered respected members of the community. LaDonna Reynolds, Sneed's former campaign manager, now his marketing director and sexual façade, stayed close to the Mayor's side, as did her assistant, Chuck Bradford.

For every hundred in attendance there were ten law enforcement officers, half in plain-clothes. By the time Sneed switched on the mic, there were over five hundred concerned citizens packed into the area, including Harper Stowe. A "Friday Zone Assignment Meeting" of these LEOs was scheduled immediately following. Most of the 50, all those in uniforms, circled the group's perimeter. Stowe, still undercover and dressed in running apparel, a dozen others, plus the three

Diagram of Death

FBI agents, were moving around among the attendees, looking and listening for anything suspicious.

"Do you think he's here?" Reynolds asked.

"I would be, if I were going to try it again," said Beaumont. "He might think he'll get a tip on logistics."

"Surely the trails will be desolate this time tomorrow," Sneed said.

"I think we'll be surprised," Beaumont said. "It'll be mostly groups, but individuals too. Too much ignorance, too many curiosity-seekers."

"And too many with 'it couldn't happen to me' complex," said Rev. Janson. "Bullet-proof. Someone like that almost *deserves* their fate."

The group stared at Janson. There was no backing away from the faux pas.

"I – I only meant to stress that this takes community cooperation," Janson stammered. "Certainly no one actually…"

"Chief Beaumont, couldn't you just close down the trails for the evening? Wouldn't that be prudent?" asked Father O'Malley abruptly, trying to deflect the attention from Janson – known as Preacher Bill to his congregation – a strongly-built man in his early 50s who had suddenly become a riddle to the group. "How could anybody justify keeping them open?"

O'Malley had spent just over 50 years in the state, the last 23 on-island in the church parish house. He was 85, slight in build, with an Irish accent that occasionally also took on a Southern distinction, an odd contradiction that brought joy to anyone who came in contact with the man. It hurt him that he had more vacationers coming to Mass than regular attendees, but he still went about his days in a pleasant and openly-optimistic manner.

"Oh believe me, there were advance complaints. Including from the Ocean Oaks Board of Directors," Beaumont said. "Dozens of families will be riding their bikes to and from The Parrot Perch and Bay Harbor on their final night of vacation, grabbing their last-minute souvenirs. Their money is what makes this world go round. Ocean Oaks wants a cop by every palmetto and yet wants them unseen… an obvious impossibility on both counts."

    Stowe had only one acquaintance at *The Beaufort Tribune*, a young copy editor named Allison McGrath, and she recognized her from a distance by her blond hair and blue plastic-framed glasses. She'd met Allison through Chuck Bradford, a neighbor in her condo complex, the down payment for which, he confided to Stowe, a graduation gift from his parents. The township "paid squat" to employees like Bradford. Allison and Bradford had graduated together the previous spring from Georgia Southern in Statesboro, an hour and a half northwest by car from Hilton Head. As Father O'Malley finished a prayer and Mayor Sneed began his opening remarks, Stowe approached her about something she had on her mind. As Harper walked Allison's way, she caught Rhett Richardson watching her from the media gallery, which had grown to well over thirty members. She was flattered by the attention. She lifted her chin a little higher and returned his gaze with a hint of a smile.

    To Stowe, Allison and Chuck were the typical college, plutonic "best friends" still sizing each other up for a love affair. She knew Bradford wanted more. He'd turned down better jobs in Atlanta to follow Allison here. They seemed to spend more time together than most married couples. Bradford had shared tidbits with Stowe about their relationship. In college they had always been there for each other. According to Chuck, one or the other seemed to get jilted at least once a semester, Allison famously on one occasion at South City Tavern, a Statesboro fixture. A drunken, crying fit ensued in its massive back yard. Her vulnerability was a vestibule of hope

Diagram of Death

for Bradford, who worshiped Allison and her delicate features: her milky complexion, blue eyes, and petite figure.

Due to the *Tribune's* deadlines, Allison worked into the evening every other day. Because of his need to occasionally attend evening events on the island, Chuck had a little freedom in his marketing job - at LaDonna Reynolds' discretion. Thus over the last year, Stowe would spot the two going off for brunch or a late dinner on a week day, sometimes both on the same day. Stowe would have occasion to speak to Allison as the pair came and went from Bradford's, and she knew from Allison's comments and her level of respect that she was aware Stowe was a cop.

"Hi Harper."

"Hello, Allison. Didn't expect to see you here." The noise of the crowd and the p.a. caused them to lean closely together.

"It's the newswoman in me. Still hoping for a reporter's job."

"I assume since you're here now, you'll be working late tomorrow night?"

"That's right," she said, genuinely flattered that Stowe remembered such a detail about her job. Stowe never forgot a detail, important or otherwise. Her intention with Allison was a breach of professionalism, but, knowing that all available manpower would be inside Ocean Oaks' gates, heightened circumstance dictated it.

"Can you do me a favor, Allison?"

"Of course."

"It *has* to be confidential," Stowe said. "Tell no one. I need you to watch and text me when Tyler Bishop leaves the newsroom tomorrow night."

"What? You don't think..."

"No. Not really. But just in case this happens again, I want to be able to eliminate him as a suspect. If he leaves early, we'll pick him up within the gates. You understand."

"Yes, I do. Ok, you can count on me," Allison said. "Can I tell you something else?"

"Sure." Stowe had her hand on Allison's back, their heads close together, but she stared out at the crowd, studying faces. Beaumont took the microphone. In an effort to possibly receive a lead based on geographical history someone might have of a neighbor, relative, or friend, he shared the news brought by the FBI.

"We learned today from the Federal Bureau of Investigation, that our killer has been linked to a number of west coast murders, in close proximity to Naval bases, over the past twenty years. If that raises suspicion or rings a bell with any of you concerning Ocean Oaks or Hilton Head residents you know, please don't hesitate to contact our office as soon as possible."

As Beaumont began his safety message, a number of women shouted out questions or statements, some in angry tone, about why the culprit had not been caught already.

Harper Stowe watched her boss, but leaned in to listen to Allison.

"Mr. Finney has extended tomorrow night's deadlines. Told the pre-press, press, and distribution managers that we'll likely be making a late run. He's waiting on the story. The plan is to leave a hole on top of page one for now."

Stowe was taken aback by the news, but didn't show it. Publisher Ray Finney's actions were about as glaring as blood on snow. If it happened during regular hours, sure, blow it out. But to hold the paper *hoping* it happens… amazing. It was moments like these that she wished she was free to kick ass.

"Is the story going to run there if nothing happens?"

Diagram of Death

"No. We're going to pull a feature from the Sunday paper if the news is good… the 'no-rape slash no-murder' story will go below the fold."

"That son of a bitch. Well, let's just pray there's nothing bad to give him."

CHAPTER 18

Windbags one and all, without a clue of what you're dealing with. I stand amongst you, I walk and talk freely amongst you. I listen to the frantic talk, I hear the fear that I have caused. You are so blind, I can warn, I can give advice, I can send you where I want you to go... where it is... "safest."

Yes, you linked my past to my present – my random dots sprinkled around the map. Impulse moves and mercy killings. Impetuous, youthful, chalkboard killings. Admittedly sloppy attempts at love, and yet, here I am still. And, it hasn't brought you to my door. Nor will it ever. My future is secure.

I see my new neighbor in the crowd. What an exquisite beauty. God's perfection, that one is. She is special somehow. I will save her till last, even if I must break protocol. She will be the completing piece.

I watch her occasionally as I move around in the darkness after midnight. When everything has shut down, when cars are scarce and can be heard a mile away, when headlights give twenty seconds of getaway, when in spring the gators eerily croak their mating call, when in summer the mammoth sea turtles walk the beaches to lay their eggs and return to the water, when the sight of stars in the comforting black makes me feel as though I am again at sea, I enjoy walking the paths. I am the only one who does. I am alone and in my kingdom.

CHAPTER 19

Harper Stowe's second weapon, which she wore in an ankle holster when the job called for long pants, was a Kimber 1911. Thin and lightweight, the gun holds a .9 mm clip, and was certainly capable of stopping a human.

As the clock approached midnight, she was sitting at the breakfast nook, rolling one of the gun's bullets around in her fingers. She stared at it, transfixed, contemplating scenarios for the next evening, positive images, in which she would take this unknown combatant down. She studied the bullet's tiny cap, a dormant cylinder waiting to be brought to life by a gun's hammer and the explosion of gun powder. Stowe didn't believe for a minute that this man would stop, despite the incredible odds against him escaping capture.

Knowing now what the FBI had shared, she realized that he was obviously more adept at his craft than she had originally assumed. Her department had never given this animal a nickname, but the FBI – specifically the cynical Jeff Hudson, "Stumpy," if Harper had to give *him* a handle – deemed it necessary and appropriate. The "Ocean Oaks Slasher" had been gaining ground around the Chamber of Commerce and with residents. The FBI boys felt it was too common. After an hour of ping-ponging suggestions, due to the Navy base proximity of the cold cases, Hudson came up with "Nimitz," in reference to World War II Fleet Admiral Chester Nimitz. Chief Beaumont, also a former Navy man, opposed due to the lack of respect and quickly departed. Hudson, continuing to show his colors, immediately turned the tag to "Numb Nuts" in the office. By that time, Stowe and Arline Thorn were so annoyed with Hudson, and Paul Clark's indifference to Hudson's gall, they both took their leave of the men.

Thorn had ridden with Stowe back to her Ocean Oaks stakeout before the Town Hall Meeting. Their conversation was cordial, informational. Stowe found it refreshing Thorn didn't play the expert card. She was lifetime federal law enforcement and at 44, her retirement was within reach… maybe eight or nine years.

"They get us out early when we've put in the time," Thorn said.

"You deserve it at that point I'm sure," Stowe said.

"They don't much want you after 55. It's been interesting work. Something different every time - something unique and memorable."

"You ever wake up screaming?"

Thorn laughed.

"You should consider going federal – you're young enough still. They take you to the criminals."

"After this one, I'm not sure I'll want to be in that pressure cooker every time out."

"I can see that. I liked the way you handled the – quote – gentlemen in that first meeting. You can cut the mustard – as they say."

"Thanks."

"Anyway, you'll look back on this case as one in a long string of wins."

"Do you really think so?"

"I do. He'll screw up. I will say, it all *does* stay with you. Not just the gore. Of course that. Those idiosyncrasies you've come up with that are just his, you'll remember everything in detail… even dream about it. I wasn't one hundred percent honest before."

"That's not a pleasant thought. But I believe you. I've already started with the dreams."

Diagram of Death

"Sometimes they help, if you remember them. This guy, he's got to know if he sticks to these Friday evening-deals, odds are he's going to get caught. So he'll probably stop. He's shown he can move on. Or he's just completely lost his mind, in which case - he's going to get caught."

As Stowe thought on about the case, she felt she – the computer, everyone – was missing a pattern. Could he be completing some puzzle with his kills, maybe even on a national scale? Some dot-matrix of the female form, or the points of a crazed symbol, like the Zodiac? She thought of the movie "January Man." The unsub used windows in consecutive buildings as musical notes on a staff to play out a line of the song "Calendar Girl." There were others. Who thinks of these things? Not the normal mind, certainly. But she also knew not to dismiss him as crazy. She wondered now if she was finally winding down for sleep, or was she just feeling defeated?

She was startled by "knock, knock, knock" on her door, followed by two more. Her heart seemed to rise into her throat. Her nerve endings tingled. She thought of the man who'd looked in her window.

"It's Rhett, Harper."

She walked to the door, .9mm in hand.

"Say that again?"

"I said it's Rhett, Harper."

She flipped the porch light on, opened the door partially, and looked out. He held up a brown bag with commercial markings.

"I thought you might be hungry," he said, his eyebrows raised in question. "I had a feeling you didn't take time to eat today."

"That's presumptuous."

"But am I wrong? I wasn't going to knock if the lights were off. It's just a sandwich…turkey and cheese from Low Country Market over there."

She opened the door and let him in.

"That was thoughtful of you."

"It was no problem. I had to go out – I was having trouble sending. Spotty internet over there. I was hungry too."

"Come over here and sit down."

She returned her primary, a Glock 19, to the table, near the sleek, subcompact 1911. Richardson chose the seat closest to her, as though the items in front of her were a project to be dually worked on.

"Wow. Weapons check?"

"No, not really. I was just sitting here thinking about tomorrow."

"It's going to go well," he said, pouring out the contents of the bag. He slid packets of mustard and mayonnaise her way. "I wouldn't think there'll be anybody for him to choose from out there on the trails."

"Besides me."

"Besides… no, that's not what I – you'll be watched, right? Constantly?"

"There'll be zones I'm running through. Some heavily covered. Some less. I hope I draw him to me."

"You gonna have that with you?" he asked, pointing at the smaller pistol.

"The 1911? You bet I will."

"Then you'll be good. Armed and dangerous. It's a little different-looking."

"Yep. It's a Kimber. A little newer on the gun scene comparatively – out of Arizona."

"Looks like it'll do the job."

"It'll do if I can get a shot off. Depends on how it goes down. It's a big place. He probably knows it better than

Diagram of Death

anyone. And there's an element of surprise he seems to have mastered..."

"Harper. You'll be good – great," he said, squeezing mustard out of a packet on to a bun. "This all ends tomorrow."

She looked at him. Her blue eyes glazed. *This all ends tomorrow.* A vulnerability was present he'd never seen in her. He halted his food prep and looked into her eyes.

Then as quickly as it had come, she shook it off, like shedding a wet raincoat.

"You're right. We'll have so many men stationed, there's no way this guy will shake us – if he's even stupid enough to go out there."

Richardson took a small bite of his sandwich.

"Please eat," he said, as he chewed. "Is there no pattern to the previous murders that led to any suspects? You'd think anymore..."

"No. Not yet, anyway. I swear, I *hope* this guy finds me. I want a chance to groin-kick him once for every vic."

Richardson stared at Stowe, swallowing slowly.

"Then pistol-whip him 'round his forehead and face till he bleeds just shy of dying. I don't want him to miss his liquid sword."

She pushed herself away from the table, stood, and begin to pace the floor.

"I don't doubt you're capable of..."

"Oh, you don't know the half of it, there, my handsome cameraman," she said, reaching and lightly pinching his cheek. "I'm Mel Gibson with attitude. *I'm* a lethal weapon."

He watched her return to her pacing.

"Yeah, and you're making me feel like Leo Getz... Harper, you're pressing. I mean, I, of course, believe you're capable of everything you say, and I certainly wouldn't want to test you on it, but..."

He stopped. He realized now that she'd been contemplating her own death before, her own mortality. In her mind, this could be her last night on earth. The impact resonated so strongly with Richardson he nearly choked on it. He let the conversation go silent for a long minute before he spoke again.

"Wait. I get it. Come here, please. Sit down and relax."

She double-backed to her seat, began opening a sandwich wrapper, playing with the paper, with no real intention of eating. Harper looked deeply into his eyes.

"It's ok to be afraid, isn't it? About tomorrow night? Won't it bring out the best in you? Like you said, you'll have a battalion watching you."

She put her fingers to his lips.

"Don't say any more," she said. "You don't need to say anything."

Their emotions were laid open like a wound. Their chemistry seemed to mushroom. The draw was powerful... overwhelming. They leaned into each other and kissed, long, slowly.

"I don't want to be alone tonight, Rhett."

"I won't let you be."

CHAPTER 20

Harper Stowe and Rhett Richardson allowed themselves a voyage to a place they'd not yet been: the unfrequented island paradise of spontaneity. They found solace in the unmistakable attraction they felt for one another, in the heat from the flames of letting go, deep in their lungs from the warmth they were breathing and the flesh they were touching, the euphoria and power of being absent of outside realities.

When they fell back to the pillows, satisfied and exhausted, neither had ever felt such tranquility. Harper was curious and full of a sense of personal exploration.

"So, tell me more about being from such a large family," she asked, her head lying on his shoulder, her hand lightly rubbing his chest. "I'm envious."

"Envious? Of what, the crazy? The backseat stench?" he laughed.

"Oh, I'm sure there was third seat AC."

"True. I'll admit, we were blessed as a family. There were plenty of bathrooms… plenty of space. Maybe too much. We all had our own rooms so privacy wasn't an issue. If there were any petty jealousies, they were over the quality of devices, you know? Phones, Ipads, ear buds, video games, TVs… pretty spoiled. We certainly weren't hurting. We love each other though. We made it through unscathed."

"It must be gratifying to know you've got a bond – you'll always have a bond - with three adults out there - that you can take pleasure in their happiness as they advance in their careers, as they marry and have kids. You're close, right?"

Oh yeah. The baby is Hank. He just graduated from UNC with a finance degree. He's back in Charlotte… followed in the footsteps. Katy is two years out of school, Wake Forest, and is working in marketing in the Winston-Salem area. Kim, she's just two years younger than me, she's down in Orlando. She's a human resources exec for Disney. She's big-time bright – speaks four or five languages."

"Either sister married?"

"Kim is serious with a guy, uh, Steve Manning. He's a college administrator down there, Central Florida I think. We're expecting an announcement sometime."

"Oh, wow, a wedding. That'll be fun."

"It will. It'll be great. My parent's first kid-wedding."

"Are your folks pretty social?"

"Oh yeah. We have a church, but Dad gets more deals done by way of cocktails than NASDAQ reports. It'll be a party no doubt."

"I tend to be hot and cold with weddings. Depending on who the couple is."

"I'm indifferent at best. I've been to a half dozen of my friends' weddings in the last few years – no seven - been in four. That's never cheap. It's not like they do them at the bride's hometown church anymore. Got to be in the islands or some five-star resort. Good times though."

"Same. I've had to buy, I don't know, seven or eight bridesmaids dresses through the years between my high school and college friends. Always expensive, never reusable. You can't even give them away as prom dresses, not with what the kids wear these days. That'll be my one goal if I have a traditional wedding."

"Guns and ammo?"

Harper punched him lightly on the shoulder.

"No, jerk. More, uh, contemporary… dresses my girls can re-wear socially."

"That's cool - and will be appreciated I'm sure. So, you said hot *and* cold?"

"Oh, I don't like to even think about, much less say it out loud."

"Come on."

"Well, okay. This is embarrassing. I've actually had a couple of grooms – drunk grooms - hit on me the night before their wedding. Rehearsal dinners and such."

"Did you rat'em out?"

"No. Of course not. But what a path to start down. One of the two is divorced already. So maybe I should have told her."

"And that was after she or her parents spent what, upwards of twenty-five, fifty grand?"

"At least, I swear. I had a cousin get married in the Smoky Mountains last summer. It was pretty highfalutin. I'm sure my aunt and uncle had to take out a second mortgage for it. But she was gorgeous."

"What's her name?"

"Jenny Lancaster. Was. Jenny White now. Or Lancaster-White. I'm not sure what she decided about that. That's my mom's side. Mom was a Lancaster."

"You said the other day you were the pampered only child of a lawyer and orthopedic surgeon. Which is which?"

"Dad's the surgeon. Mom's the lawyer. She's in the prosecuting attorney's office. Doesn't care for the criminal element."

"Ok, I see where that came from."

"I've learned it from her. She had… a traumatic experience as a child. She didn't actually witness it but…"

As she said it, Harper sat up in the bed. Rhett, saying nothing, but sensing the gravity of what was to come, did the same and turned towards her. There was just a small amount of light in the room, shining through the partially-opened bedroom door from the kitchen and living area. He could just make out the contours of her face.

"Her grandfather was a policeman, small town, southwest of Atlanta, before Atlanta was its own state. Routine traffic stop, he was gunned down by a man… just passing through. A criminal on the run, heading through town for Texas. Completely random. There were enough witnesses to where he was eventually tracked down and caught."

"Oh man. What a waste."

"Mom was seven at the time. He was her everything. Her favorite grandparent. Her Pa Pa Lanny, they called him. He sang songs to her, she said, played the guitar when he was off, at family get-togethers. It cut her deep."

"So that was her way of fighting back?"

"Mm-hm. Of honoring his memory, she said. She's known her whole life what she wanted to do. She wanted me to do the same, to go into law. But I always had this course, and it was *actually* following in his footsteps, which she really couldn't argue with, though she did anyway. His name was John Thomas Lancaster. Went by J.T. Tall, wiry. A nice-looking man."

"Wow. That's strong, Harper. Great story. What a legacy. And your mom had how many siblings?"

"Two. One of each."

"Either of them do what your mom did?"

"No. She's the oldest… she knew him best. I've seen my mom in action in the courtroom a lot. She's tenacious. Something to see. I wouldn't want to have to go up against her."

"Duly noted," he laughed. "You know, I actually worked in Savannah briefly. Very briefly. I remember hearing your mom's name and reputation. So I'll be stayin' on the right side of the law in Chatham County. Which is not a problem. I've seen some things over there already."

"You'd better just stay on the right side of me."

CHAPTER 21

Jessica Boyd and Kathy Lantz had numerous common traits: they both lived in Ocean Oaks; both were in their early thirties, they were both the second wives of older, wealthy men who were consumed with work; and they both enjoyed running in the early evening. The glaring differences were physical: Jessica was a youthful-looking, five-foot, petite blond, while Kathy was a five-foot-eleven brunette. A former model, Kathy had grown tired of starving herself and was fighting without pills or procedure to keep her figure the way it had been.

At the start of her marriage, Jessica ran in the mornings. The beauty of Ocean Oaks' South Beach was an inspiration. She didn't just jog. She was young and athletic. Her biorhythms kicked into overdrive when she was pushing towards the rising sun in full glide, smooth, seemingly effortless. She was exhilarated by the feel of the burn in her core, in her arms and legs, her shoulders and back, as she went about her day. She would stop between chores and stretch, thinking of her goal for the next morning, how quickly she would complete her five miles, or seven. And, she knew that if she was off the beach and in the shower when Bennett Boyd rose, by 7:15, she might receive some marital attention either there, or just after when she reemerged in her short, silk robe. It was her best bet for lovemaking other than the weekends, because he typically came home from his finance job exhausted and cranky. In the early years, her running impressed him, and he was quick to explore her muscle tone with his roaming hands. It was never spoken, just part of his need for her. She could see it in his eyes, and it turned her on.

Those mornings of playful ecstasy eventually dissipated like a summer shower. She tried for months to keep him interested in the pre-work lovemaking, where a quick rub would instantly make him fully erect, but he said it made him too tired and diminished his work focus. Jessica grew weary of his cold shoulder. She bought a Labrador, named her Lucinda, and with contempt began taking her to walk on the beach about the time Bennett started rummaging around the kitchen for breakfast. She waited till the sting of the afternoon sun died before she considered running, and she did it not for joy but to purge the frustration she felt with her life. She took to the trails for the shade, almost blaming the sun for her waning happiness.

It was only from the familiarity of seeing her there that she struck up conversations with Kathy Lantz. They found that they lived but a few side streets apart. They exchanged email addresses because they both admitted to being on and off the computer all day, and because Dr. Dale Lantz, a strict budgeter with every spare dollar going to the stock market, had given her the option of a housekeeper or a cell phone. She hated cleaning and he, as an on-call surgeon, had to have a landline and the internet. Since she didn't work and rarely left Ocean Oaks, she chose the housekeeper.

So, Jessica and Kathy began the mostly enlightening, sometimes frustrating relationship of being running partners. Three years went by this way. Aside from vacations and infrequent off-island trips the women would communicate a daily start time usually between 5 and 6:30 – barring any scheduling conflicts - and they would run together most week day evenings, and sometimes on Saturdays.

They found they had much in common. The conversations about their husbands alone was enough to warrant occasional afternoon meetings, and thus from their common pain, a friendship took root.

"I'm trying to get Dale to put the crowbar in his wallet for a cell phone," Kathy said one day. "So we can text. I swear that man is so cheap. He thinks he has to have $50 million in the bank to think about retiring."

"I probably need to send Bennett to see your husband," Jessica said. "He's not taking care of himself, drags himself off to work, drags himself home. Unless he's seeing someone else on side, he's completely lost interest in making love. At least he has to me."

"I'm always worried about those nurses flirting around with Dale. That's an easy place to score."

"At the hospital?"

"I should know, honey, I was a nurse until my modeling took off," Kathy said. "That's where we met. Lots of unused storage closets and examining rooms."

"Well, he may be cheap but he has great taste."

"Ah, thank you. Anyway, don't get down. You should get Bennett on some B-12. I'm not sure his heart could handle Viagra."

Jessica shook her head in disappointment.

"He wouldn't want it. That's what I'm saying."

They became so close and so put out by their husbands they discussed the possibility of moving their runs to morning, so if they met in the afternoons, they could also enjoy a post-workout, post-chores cocktail or glass of wine.

After the first murder, another woman, Mandy Tompkins, approached Kathy Lantz about joining the pair for their runs. Mandy Tompkins was new to the community, in her mid-40s, and a running novice. As with any activity, adding a third caused the occasional departure from the set time-range to increase. Also, perhaps because Kathy seemed to embrace Mandy and step into a coach or mentor role, Jessica Boyd became a bit put out or perhaps even jealous of the attention the newcomer was receiving. She was a gracious person, but sometimes it compounded her frustration to slow her pace for Mandy.

Andrew Spradling

The situation came to a head on the Friday of the tenth week. Kathy had emailed Jessica, "On for 6?"

"I need 45 minutes to pick Lucinda up from the groomer. I just got the ready call," Jessica replied, and she headed to her car for the quick drive just outside the gates. The extra few minutes were just because of the late afternoon traffic she would confront – tourists heading out to an early, final dinner of the week. When she turned right on to South Ocean Oaks Drive, she saw Kathy and Mandy together by their meeting spot at the trail. Her window down, she honked the horn of her Suburban, made eye contact with Kathy, and lifted a hand in question. As she drove past she surmised Kathy had already set the start time with Mandy, and thus couldn't comply with her request for the later time - if she'd even waited on her emailed reply.

Jessica was infuriated and hurt. The feelings were pounding in her head. She could think of nothing else.

Once home again she took Lucinda in through the garage, changed her clothes and shoes, stretched quickly and took off with a determined pace. She didn't want to see Kathy and knew the route the pair would be on. She considered just running the beach but decided instead to head towards The Parrot Perch, to the toe of the island, then take a few cut-throughs, one walking bridge, and a couple of side streets to get around to the Barnhart Cove Ruins, then on to Old Mission Road. From there she could again pick up the trail knowing that Kathy would have completed her moderate outing.

Jessica was surprised at herself as she got underway. She was still incensed. The adrenaline was searing into her strides. She was taking in oxygen like a thoroughbred and converting it into energy. This run seemed to be the culmination of the thousands of miles she'd put in over the years. Her form was perfect. She could do no wrong. She

Diagram of Death

would ignore the pain, if it even came. She would be running circles around Kathy Lantz right now.

Clotheslined. Hard on her back. Throat throbbing. Wind knocked from her. Her mouth covered with tape. The taste of adhesive between her lips and the tip of her tongue. Sweat rolling from her forehead into her eyes – stinging, burning. And there he was. No mask, white, ordinary, nondescript. Thin hair. She wanted to suck air through her nostrils but she couldn't reverse the departure of wind - which alone caused panic. She seemed to be drowning. She tried to turn. She felt the sharp edge of a knife blade on her throat. He stomped his knees on to her thighs, pushing forward until he was on her inner-thighs… crushing them. His left elbow was in the dirt by her right ear. That hand held her hair tightly. She clenched her teeth with such force it seemed her molars could explode.

"Hold your hands together above your head – or die," he said, the sharp edge of his knife was poised to slice her neck.

Finally she was able to draw a breath through her nose, her nostrils flailing.

She cursed herself for allowing a petty altercation to cause her to forget today's well-advertised danger. The visuals of the case flashed in her mind. She knew she was going to die, with or without a fight. She overcame her initial fear when oxygen returned to her lungs. She intertwined her fingers and raised them over her head as ordered. His next moves he'd performed many times before: Take the knife from his right hand with his left, then with his right, pull the rope from his shorts and underwear elastic, Miller's knot already loosely tied, slip over her held hands to her wrists, pull it tight. Then he switched the knife back to his right, holding the knot and her hands with his left. Cut off the shorts and panties, in control of victim's arms and legs, drop the knife and pull himself out of his shorts.

Time was thin, and he knew it. He switched the knife to his left hand, elbow back on the ground. As he reached behind himself for the rope, Jessica recognized the opening and struck him in the middle of his face with all the might her leverage and her sense of survival would allow. She broke his nose, but he was only stunned slightly. She grabbed the knife blade with her right hand, forcing it first to slice her skin before her fingers found a hold at the point. She reached for his neck with her left and was able to scratch him with two fingers. At the same time he reared back with his right and punched her face, the flat of his fist finding her left cheekbone. The searing pain caused her to let go of the knife, but she had marked his neck.

"You think you're the first fighter I've come across? I like a fight."

She twisted as hard as she could, dislodging one of his knees. He punched again, regained his knee positioning and once more reached for the rope. He dropped it two feet above her head, stuck the knife in the ground out of her reach, and with both hands retrieved her flailing arms, her right fingers bleeding. In seconds he held both her wrists in his left hand. He slipped the rope over her hands then pulled them secure. He wiped the blood from his hand on her tank top at her breasts. He smiled.

"That was a good try, lady. I'll give you that."

He grabbed the knife, stuck the blade up her shorts till he could see the tip, then he pulled upward, slicing the garment away.

Tears now streamed from Jessica Boyd's eyes.

Next he crossed the blade horizontally under her panties and again pulled. This was not difficult.

"You are a beautiful woman," he said.

Diagram of Death

    She softened her glare. Her last hope of survival was that the man would have a conscience. That he might look into her eyes, feel remorse, and spare her life. As she felt him begin penetration, she instead closed them forever.

CHAPTER 22

Setback? I call it opportunity. Not the best time to get sloppy, I admit. I admired the woman's sand... a little dynamo. She was so focused on her run, she was the easiest take down yet. Luckily, she ran with a water bottle. When I dotted my i's and crossed my t's - with my knife - I had a few decisions to make. My nose was throbbing and I could feel the scratches on my neck. I wanted no part of my skin caked under her nails. Not that I don't leave DNA, but I wanted no additional forensic detail – or the cops to find a reason to go house to house looking for scratches on locals.

It was completely dark. So I dragged her forty or fifty feet into deeper brush. One at a time, I stuck each of the fingers of her left hand into her water bottle, plugging the hole and shaking till I was sure there could be none of my skin remaining. Just to be certain, I dragged her another twenty feet to the edge of a tidal creek. I submerged her hands, arms, and face. Just before I took off, I could see flashlights approaching from a distance. I made my getaway in the opposite direction between two unoccupied houses. Back to my own secluded pool area – privacy I've paid landscapers tens of thousands for. I had to act quickly. I lit my grill and stripped, burning my clothes, my socks, and the rope. I dove into my pool with running shoes back on, and with the knife. I washed it and myself, allowing the chlorine to work its magic. Now for the unplanned damage control. After pulling on my swim trunks, at least one pair of which I keep outside for just such moments, I entered my house to find my wife passed out, as always, pill box, wine bottle, and glass beside her couch. In a tiny trio of decorative wall mirrors I could see my eyes were blackening from the woman's two-handed, potato-punch. I took a large

Diagram of Death

sirloin from the fridge, grabbed a bottled-rub, salt and pepper, ran it all out and threw the meat on the flame. With my lucky knife, I cut the steak in half and laid the knife by the grill. Back inside, I picked up my wife, carried her to another mirror, took her hand, lined up the scratches, and with her four manicured fingers dug deep into my neck. Still carrying her, I grabbed her wine glass, walked outside and heaved her and it into my lighted pool. As she sank I could see when she awoke and started trying to save herself. I jumped into the pool and pinned her to the bottom with my foot. When I was sure she was dead, I pulled her up, yelled 'Victoria' and with my own arm thrashed and splashed for a bit. I lifted her body on to the deck, got out of the pool, ran into the house and called 911. Four minutes later when paramedics pulled into my driveway, I was on my knees trying to revive her. Steaks burnt to a crisp. My statement, given later at the station through moans of sorrow, frustration, and regret: "I was in and out of the house prepping and cooking dinner. I came back out after running in for seasoning - found her in the deep end, trying to save herself – frantically thrashing. She couldn't swim. I jumped in to help her. She was panicked and disoriented. She scratched me and twisted and I guess somehow elbowed me once right on the bridge of my nose as I tried to grip her so I could pull her to the side. That shot dazed me. I lost her after that. She went down. I never should have bought such a large pool with a deep end, but she always said she wanted to learn to swim. I hoped that if she did learn, she would lay off the prescriptions and alcohol a bit – take better care of herself." With that, I broke down in inconsolable tears. It was a damn great acting job for an unfortunate circumstance – bringing paramedics and cops to my door. But, I had an ace I left back with Little Miss Half Pint that will keep 'em looking the other way for a good while.

CHAPTER 23

The Jessica Boyd crime scene was a vigil. Between law enforcement officers, residents, and media there seemed to be enough people to join hands across Hilton Head Island. Harper Stowe had been running from the Bay Harbor area back towards Mission Road when the murder occurred. She was less than a half mile away when she heard the first siren and ran towards it. In addition to the LEOs, a crowd of over one hundred well-behaved citizens had gathered to watch from beyond the yellow and black tape.

"We need to get these people back in their homes," Stowe said. "And get these agents working outward looking for any kind of clue for the direction of his flight."

"I'll take care of all that," Chief Lester Beaumont said, pushing the "end" button on his cell phone. "But you don't need to be here either. Not if you're going to stay undercover. At this – "

"I *am* staying undercover."

"Ok, walk with me over towards the residents, we'll throw up a little smokescreen. And quit pointing like you're running the show."

As they walked alone, Stowe looked over to where Jessica Boyd's body remained. The flash of the police force photographer was illuminating the scene every few seconds.

"Is she in the water? He's never done that before."

"I'll have someone drop off the full report to you in the morning," Beaumont said. "Walk with me. Damn, you won't believe this. Thirty seconds after the body was found, a 10-32 comes in."

"A drowning? On the beach?"

Diagram of Death

"No, over on Dalton Road. It's off of South Beach Lane. I just got the call."

"A pool?"

"Yeah, the husband tried to save her – 10-51, 10-50 – that's the early scuttle anyway."

"Drunk *and* on drugs?"

"And D.O.A. The husband went in, tried to pull her out. She was frantic - went nuts on him. He lost her. Couldn't revive her. He's pretty shook up. They're bringing him to the station while they gather the body... Ok Miss Stowers, one last time, you saw no male running from the East as you approached the area?"

Beaumont lifted the yellow tape for Stowe.

"No sir. I didn't see anybody," Stowe said. "Good luck catching this man, and thank you."

"Thank you for your help," he said.

As she walked away she heard Beaumont begin to address the crowd. In her peripheral vision she saw the media gathering. Rhett Richardson was among them, his camera shouldered. That was another large group that would be much tougher to disperse and it burned her... they could be standing on the unsub's foot prints. She could feel his eyes on her, which she admitted comforted her. She thought of the night before. The morning. Him holding her. So much passion, no awkwardness, no finality. She had no regrets – except tonight's conclusion. Failing to become the man's target caused this. She felt no relief. Instead, more anger. More rage.

Two women from the media group jogged towards her, followed by their cameramen, having seen her exchange with Beaumont, hoping for anything to report. Richardson remained in the group, respecting her space. She waved her hand then held it out, as if to say "Don't approach me."

"I didn't see anything," she said. "Nothing. I don't know anything."

Those words rang so true to her. Her body language showed it. Her shoulders slumped. She was feeling defeated. She walked into the darkness of the path that led to South Beach, her shadow stretched out before her. She knew all the trails so well now. Despite putting in at least 10 miles earlier, feeling stiff and sore, she began to run, thinking about her exchange with the boss. A drowning on Dalton? She put behind her the noise of generators that lit the crime scene, the hordes of law enforcement, media, and onlookers.

The drowning continued to infiltrate her thoughts about the case, her knowledge of statistical facts pounding as rhythmic as her footsteps. *There are very few drownings here per year, and they're usually caused by unseen riptides. More than half are children. An adult drowning in a pool is an aberration. Most residential pools have a deep end of no more than five feet. Grown adults can typically hop themselves out of danger.* That fact, along with the timing, made her immediately suspicious. Knowing the husband was likely at the station answering questions, she took the next turn on the trail, and in a few minutes arrived at the accident scene, a brick rancher in thick cover.

She could see Assistant Coroner Cindy Lewis through the house's kitchen windows. She knocked on that room's door to alert her, tried the knob, pushed the door open and entered.

"Detective Stowe, you startled me."

"How's it going here, Cindy?"

"They called me out to babysit the scene, with all Hell breaking loose - took the body a few minutes ago. I'm to wait here till they bring the husband back."

"Who was leading from your office?"

"Tom Wilson is."

"Call him. Tell him I'm here, and to give you a heads up before they bring him. Tell him if he can to stall a little."

"Will do, Harper."

Diagram of Death

"Were you here at all with the husband?"

"They were just taking him out when I got here. Tom told me a little. Said he was back and forth in and out of the house trying to cook dinner. She was asleep on the couch last he saw, till he walked outside and found her thrashing in the pool."

"Ok. Please, make that call while I look around. If you didn't know, I'm working undercover… staying in Ocean Oaks. I don't want to be seen as a cop by him – seen at all for that matter."

The parameters of probable cause seemed to hover in the air between them, but they both let it go.

"We need a break."

"10-4, Harper. Do your thing."

Stowe walked through the kitchen and dining area and absorbed the layout of the house. She could see the couch in the living area from kitchen door and she could see it from the sliding-glass doors that opened to the pool deck. *There's no way he wouldn't notice his wife staggering out the door. That's weak.*

On the pool deck, she located the grill, walked to it – eight paces from the door – and opened its lid. Two small steaks smoldering-black. She turned the propane tank handle to the right, and listened for the pop as the burners extinguished themselves. Only then did she turn the burner knobs to "off." A thought struck her. She walked back to the kitchen. Nothing else out on the counters or in the sink or microwave that would be considered prep items. Unless he was serving crackers with the meat. A bag of mixed-greens salad sat in the refrigerator. *That could suffice, if he was he pressed to answer.* She went back to the couch and stood, thinking. On one end-table sat an empty wine bottle and a box of the sleep aid Melatonin. She wondered what she might find in the victim's medicine cabinet. She walked down a dark hallway. She was briefly overcome with a rarely-experienced chill, goosebumps tingled her neck and shoulders. Stowe located the master bath. Its vanity and dressing area were outside the bathroom. She opened the mirror and was not surprised to see a buffet of prescription pill bottles, both uppers and downers. All typed neatly to her: Victoria Wainwright. Nothing visible for the man of the house.

Stowe stepped into the bedroom, flipping on the overhead light and fan. The room was neat, and clean. Noticeably absent were any pictures of the victim or her husband. The room had no life to speak of, nothing that represented unity, bond, or even theme for that matter – and certainly not love or family.

Stowe got a sense that her time might be running short. She wanted to see the garage. She walked with haste back to the kitchen.

"I was just coming to find you, Harper," Lewis said. "They're on their way."

"Ok. Thanks. I just want to pop out here real quick."

Through the door off the kitchen she nearly stumbled over a pair of running shoes, drenched, sitting in a circle of standing water.

"What do we have here?" Stowe said. "These things are huge."

"That was mentioned," Lewis said. "Said he was wearing them when he went in the pool after her."

Stowe lifted the left shoe's tongue: size 16. She looked around the two-car garage which held one car, a newer model Ford Expedition.

"Why do people think they need these huge 4-wheel drives down here?" she said out loud.

On the side opposite the vehicle, there were two beach bikes, the smaller one looked unused - brand new in fact. On the full wall past them, a peg board with hooks neatly held

Diagram of Death

smaller hand tools, wrenches, pliers. There were a couple of saws, some woodworking materials, glue and glue gun, sandpaper, a stack of three rolls of duct tape, two partially used. Meticulous, neat. There were eight drawers, four on each side of the work bench. She wanted to look inside all the drawers, but she knew time was short. She opened the first, which held plastic containers of finishing nails and screws.

On the wall to the left of the tools, a framed certificate indicating distinguished retirement from the United States Navy issued to Lieutenant James Edward Wainwright. To the left of that, a map of Hilton Head, the waterways and surrounding land. Below that, a 2-foot-high spool of nylon marina-boating rope. She stood back from it and stared.

"No fibers left behind with that," she said. She looked around. "What else in here says 'I've got a boat?' "

She took a few steps towards the garage door. The SUV had a trailer hitch. In the trash can, a box that once held a boat's fish finder.

"Harper, I think I see the car just up the road," Lewis said, through the opened door.

"Ok, I'm out," Stowe said. "Thanks, Cindy." Stowe departed as she'd come in, through the kitchen door. With no time she stepped across the driveway and in to the bushes and trees. She wanted to see the man.

James Wainwright stepped out of the front seat of the police cruiser. He was noticeably taller than the average man, Stowe thought, based on his chest, shoulders and head appearing well above the roof of the car. Otherwise average-looking, non-descript, thin, sandy-brown hair parted to one side and falling onto his forehead. Someone you would hardly notice, and not look at twice. Except for his height maybe. He was not thin, but not overweight, soft somehow and unintimidating. He was dressed in swimming trunks, a short-sleeved, button-up beach shirt, and well-worn, brown loafers.

On his neck was a white bandage, secured with medical tape. The bags below his eyes were blackened.

Stowe thought of the man she'd met fishing on the beach. He talked about shoes, the size of one of the local's feet. What was it he had said? "I think I could use his shoes as water skis." She wanted to see the facial renderings he said he'd help with. *That would only prove he was a runner. But, it would prove he's a runner.* She looked at her watch. It was nearly 11 p.m.

CHAPTER 24

The glorious pink of the pre-dawn sky in no way reflected the hangover of dread, disappointment, and fear Hilton Head Island's inhabitants were waking up to on Saturday. By the time the sky turned blue, the exodus of weekly tourists was again underway, as more potential suspects – and relieved potential victims - packed up and checked out.

Harper Stowe had tried to sleep but couldn't. After her visit to the drowning victim Victoria Wainwright's home, she showered and prepared to report to headquarters. She wanted to hear and evaluate any and all evidence as it came in. She knew though that a two hour nap would serve her well so she laid down, but too many thoughts blitzed her brain: *What's with all the contradictions from the previous murders? Jessica Boyd was left in water. She was moved twice after the abduction. Why? For deeper cover? Had a potential witness happened by? Had Jessica Boyd left clues about the murderer? Had she been able to fight back? Mark him perhaps?*

She had stood in her driveway to appreciate the darkness 4:30 a.m. provided. A cool ocean breeze swept across the island, the rustling of the leaves the lone sound she identified. It was like the equation of music, beginning with silence and building. Only one desolate lane, Royal Fern, separated Slack Trimmer, her street, from Dalton. She hadn't realized that fact when she was inside the Wainwright's home, conducting her unethical and thus-far secret walk-through. Back out to the main road after watching James Wainwright's exit from the police cruiser, she was surprised when she reached her street so quickly.

Andrew Spradling

This is the killer's element. He's most comfortable in the darkness. She walked down her street towards the beach, past two houses, to a path that led between the homes to Royal Fern, across it to the next path, and then to the Wainwright's. Stowe walked softly. At one point, she startled a grazing deer, the "Chssht, Chssht, Chssht," of its frantic hops decreasing as it disappeared into thicker cover. *How do deer make it to an island?* She stood staring at the Wainwright's home... darkness in the darkness. Only a hint of starlight proved the house was there. And yet, she couldn't shake the feeling that she wasn't alone. *Could this man, this James Wainwright, have pulled off these murders? Murdered his entire adult life?* She wanted to remember this feeling, this absolute awareness, this nocturnal awakening, of functioning in the dark.

    She moved past Wainwright's home and made her way to the beach, her concentration so on the case, she was practically unaware of her own movements. It was then she again witnessed the nuclear explosion of pinks and oranges that became dawn, and with it came new hope. The inspirational sight motivated her to attack her work, to overcome this evil combatant.

    At the station, Stowe found the sketches by local artist Ted Lamar. The HHPD had too small a budget and too little need to employ its own artist. The nearest SC state police sketcher was in Columbia. Thus, Ted Lamar was used in a pinch. He was retired federal Drug Enforcement Agency, so Beaumont and Stowe both felt he was qualified to handle the person-to-person contact and questioning necessary, and his sketches were excellent. He had retired to Hilton Head to join the art community just across the bridge in Bluffton, sharing a retail display house in Old Towne with four other artists. There were at least six similar houses in Bluffton's Old Towne that sold paintings along with other Low Country finds, making it

Diagram of Death

the current rage and one of the trendiest spots for art on the southeastern coast.

She found Lamar's renditions of the subjects on her desk. She realized per his note he had also sent them to her phone while she was running, just before the murder. The first was definitely the sharp, handsome features of Tyler Bishop, which reminded her she hadn't heard from Allison McGrath during the evening run. *Did that mean he'd stayed late at the office? That he was no longer a suspect? I'll have to track down Allison.* The second was most-likely this James Wainwright, but in a poll not everyone would agree. They weren't strong leads. All the sketches really said were that these men sometimes run in the evenings. But given the circumstances, feeling she could almost hear the community outcry, she'd take them.

She thought back to her conversation with Allison McGrath. At 6:30 a.m. a co-worker brought in a dozen copies of *The Beaufort Tribune*. She stared at the paper, its Saturday headline read: **FIFTH VICTIM DOWN**. The subhead: *Perp Again Escapes After Slaying.* The picture showed the crime scene, crowd and all, Jessica Boyd's body covered by a police tarp. They even had her identity in the story. An inset photo, one with no journalistic integrity, showed a distraught Bennett Boyd at the scene.

Bennett Boyd had arrived home at 8:45 to find no hint or clue as to where Jessica might be. Her car in the garage, her dog in the house. His level of community awareness was low, his reading of newspapers equally limited. *The Wall Street Journal* garnered most of his attention. Still, even he knew of the murders. He paced the floor of their kitchen, tie loosened and pulled with no regard to one side of his collar. As he searched for a note or some notification of her whereabouts, through one of the front windows he noticed a helicopter flying, roughly three hundred yards away. A search beam shined down. He walked out on to the front porch. He was temporarily mesmerized by the uncommon sight... confused. What did it mean? Then the dots suddenly connected. He was horrified at the possibilities.

He left the house walking in a panic. He crossed the street and approached the paved path with a glaring sense of unfamiliarity. But he did not hesitate, even starting to jog into the darkness. Visuals of Jessica pounded at his mind, happy pictures, moments filled with contentment. They weren't new, he admitted to himself. There weren't recent good times to imagine. She'd almost become a stranger to him. He thought of his indifference, of those mornings she yearned for him and he was in too big a hurry, that it made him too tired at the start of his day, to accommodate her. *"Please, Lord, this can't be happening. Give me another chance. Give me another chance to be a better husband to her. Wait. You're over-reacting. You don't know it's her. It could be anybody. She could be assisting. Maybe she saw something. That's more like Jessica. She ran too well to be taken down by some psycho. She's an athlete. Alert. Strong."*

Occasionally there was dim lighting from homes along the path, otherwise he was in darkness. Alone with those crippling thoughts about Jessica. He thought and pictured her eyes, face, and smile, about the line of her back, the shape of her 5-foot body. He thought about her wit in their good times. How she would belt out lines from songs he vaguely knew. He became cognizant of his breathing. He was out of breath - panting. He slowed to a walk. He could hear the shuffling of his shoes, mostly dragging along the asphalt. A feeling of dread paralyzed his chest. He was able to see the lights now, hear the generators.

As he approached the scene, in the group of spectators he noticed someone he recognized – the statuesque Kathy Lantz - standing with another woman he'd never seen before.

Diagram of Death

As she began walking his way, to halt his progress, he could see that she'd been crying. His resolve began to wither.

"It's not," he said. "Tell me it's not her."

"Bennett. I'm so sorry."

"Tell me it's not. Tell me."

"I... I can't," she said. "We had a ..."

"A what," Boyd said, his eyes now wide yet vulnerable.

"A miscommunication," she said. She looked past him to the group of police. She waved them towards Boyd and her. It was Chief Lester Beaumont who approached. "She went off on her own... I'm so sorry..."

"Mr. Boyd? Mr. Boyd, I'm Chief Beaumont. Please sir - we had a car coming to your home. Sir, please, step over here. Away from this crowd."

"Is it her?"

"Sir, please."

"Is it Jessica?"

"Sir."

"Tell me!"

"It is. Mr. Boyd, but you don't want to see her this way. Trust me. Please, let me take you..."

Boyd stepped around Beaumont towards the crowd of cops between him and his wife. The group of onlookers went silent, the media all had their lenses on him. The officers formed a wall to stop him, holding his arms and shoulders as gently as possible yet firmly enough to get the job done.

"I just want – I just want another chance," Boyd said, under his breath. He'd given up the fight to get through. "Lord, it can't be her. It can't be my Jessica."

"Let me take you home, Mr. Boyd. We talked to her running friend, but we have just a few questions. Please, sir."

"Ok, ok," Boyd said. He leaned his head and shoulders to one side, to see past the law enforcement in front of him to the form of his wife's covered body. "Take good care of her."

A sobering calm befell the entire area, as Boyd turned, his face drained of all emotion.

As he began walking away someone said, "We'll be there for you Mr. Boyd."

"God be with you," said another.

"Keep the faith," said a third.

"That's right," said yet another. "You'll be in our prayers, sir."

The whole crowd began offering encouragement. The sound rose into the evening sky.

"Wait. One thing I want to do," Boyd said to Beaumont, changing his course, moving towards the media.

Beaumont and his crime scene team delivered their evidence to the graveyard shift at the office and had gone home for a short rest. Only in studying the newspaper did Stowe realize that the husband had come to the scene, a major drop of the ball by HHPD, not dispatching immediately to their home. In the picture though, she noticed that Boyd, obviously upset, was speaking. Then she realized why. In a boxed sidebar a headline read: *Husband of victim offers $100,000 reward for information leading to arrest.*

CHAPTER 25

Mayor Ralph Sneed was due to meet with Chief Lester Beaumont at 9 a.m. Saturday, along with the FBI and Harper Stowe, followed by an emergency Chamber of Commerce session at 10. Stowe was studying the forensic analysis reports when Beaumont dragged himself into her office, looking much like a grandfather who'd worked a 20-hour day - until 4 a.m. - before grabbing two-and-a-half-hours of sleep. Lead FBI agent Paul Clark seemed much fresher because he rarely slept anyway. When he left the crime scene he found an all-night gym and worked out for two hours followed by a 30-minute power nap.

Stowe was getting punch-drunk because she hadn't slept at all. Though she didn't believe or trust it, the information she'd just acquired had spiked her adrenaline momentarily. She was ready to burst as soon as Sneed closed the door behind him.

"He left a hair - a pubic hair. It was stuck to her side by her right hip," Stowe said. "The DNA test shows that it's possibly from an Asian. But I don't think..."

"Well that narrows the pool by 97 percent," Clark said.

"Listen, this guy is smart," Stowe said.

"Asians usually are."

"No - that's not what I'm saying. He's jerkin' our chain - the guy is leaving false clues."

"You think with everything going on, with police literally every 250 yards, with the damned cavalry coming down on him, this guy took the time to plant a hair he'd brought *with him*. Do you really think he's that precise?"

"I think he's every bit that precise. Maybe that's why he hasn't been caught in what, nearly 35 years?"

"I think you're half-baked," Clark said. "You're bold, but that might be part of the problem."

"Well, thanks. Coming from you that means less than nothing. Listen, I don't need you coming down here from…"

"Agent Clark, Harper. Cool it now. We're all exhausted. Let's try to be civil," Beaumont said.

"What are the chances of that hair staying on her after being dragged through the weeds and palmettos like that?" Stowe said. "I'll tell you something else. That 250 yards might as well be two miles if he's surrounded by 25 yards of cover - which he was."

"Not at first he wasn't," Clark said.

"So, uh, what's the next step here, folks?" Mayor Sneed interjected. "I have to report to the Chamber about what's going on."

"No, you don't," Beaumont said. "Not *exactly* what's going on. Nobody is ruled out as a suspect."

"Oh you think someone on the Chamber of Commerce is behind all this? Come on, Lester."

"Well, not really, but it's not impossible," Beaumont said. "And we don't know who they know and talk to - who their neighbor might be. Loose lips sink ships."

"This is all bullshit - irrelevant rhetoric," Clark said. "You people are back to square one."

Stowe slammed her hand on the two sketches on her desk, then she picked them up. Beaumont stood and watched her. She took a deep breath, then exhaled.

"Did anybody report seeing a male running alone? How did he get to his spot? Did he sneak to it – or wait there all day," Stowe said. "We need to pull everybody back in."

"To see if they saw an Asian running?" Clark asked.

"Or one of these guys," Stowe said, presenting the two sketches to the men.

"Who are they, Harper?" Beaumont asked.

Diagram of Death

"That one is Tyler Bishop, if I'm not mistaken," Sneed said.

"That's right, Mayor," Stowe said. "He raised your suspicion, did he not? During your interview?"

"He did. Said the rapist used a rope when it was never reported – or confirmed to my knowledge."

"I just got word he left the *Tribune* newsroom with enough time to get back to Ocean Oaks. I got it from a copy editor," Stowe said. Allison McGrath *had* texted Stowe, just later than she'd hoped. Knowing cell reception was bad in the newsroom, McGrath had intended to walk outside and resend her message. Before she could, the news of the murder caused the pace at deadline to frenzy.

"Who is the other man?" Sneed asked.

"It could be the husband of the drowning victim from last night," Stowe said. "I believe it is. Talk about a situation rife with suspicion."

"The man lost his wife Harper," Sneed said. "Have some compassion."

"You're viewing him as a voter and a citizen, Mayor," Beaumont said. "Try to think like a cop."

"I'm no odds-maker. But what are the chances of two unrelated and suspicious deaths occurring practically simultaneously, within a half mile of each other in Ocean Oaks," Stowe said.

"It's never happened," Beaumont said. "But it's not impossible."

"I will say, in my experience, two deaths like these would most likely be linked somehow," Clark said.

"Your saying that this man raped and killed Boyd, then ran home and drowned his wife?" Sneed said.

"Yes. Think about it… maybe he had to," Stowe said. "Maybe Jessica Boyd got the drop on him somehow. I mean, he's marked. Did you see him Chief?"

"No I didn't," Beaumont said. "How did you see him?"

"I was going to tell you later. I stopped by their house on my way home from the Boyd crime scene. I just waited and watched when they brought him back from the station. I was hidden."

"And?" Beaumont said. His face showed no emotion but he was proud of his lead detective's tenacity.

"He was marked up. Black eyes. Scratched on his neck."

"That's all in the report, Harper," Beaumont said.

"I know. And we all know – everybody knows - that someone drowning can abuse the person trying to save them. They drill that notion into lifeguards-in-training. But this woman was average height, thin, and a lush. And Wainwright looked to be about 6-7, at least 250. It just doesn't fit to me. He could have thrown her out of the pool if he'd wanted to."

"That doesn't prove a thing," Beaumont said.

"I know. But think about it. Only one way easier to get away with murder – take your mark hunting and have yourself a gun accident."

The three men stared at Stowe, saying nothing. She raised her hands, shoulder height, palms up, as if to say "Am I wrong?"

"We need to investigate Tyler Bishop – see if he has alibis for any of these five Fridays. But I'm gonna keep my eyes on this Wainwright."

•

Diagram of Death

CHAPTER 26

Saturday. This is a day-after like none before. It's usually the only day I don't feel a pounding need sexually, so typically it was the only waking 16-hour span I didn't resent my wife and her... frigidity. My efforts didn't mean much, never amounted to progress. I'd make her some brunch, try to get her excited about doing something... anything, potting flowers, a hand of cards, a movie, even a short walk. "We can take your wine to the beach, my love. We'll keep it in a cooler. I'll pitch the tent, take the chairs." Nothing. "How about a boat ride? I'll take you out in the lane, we'll talk to the dolphins, feed them some popcorn shrimp. You liked that once." Once. Nothing. She couldn't be reached. My boat is shelved in dry storage like a jar of pickles. Not anymore. I will now return to the water. With her life insurance cash I may trade up for a real boat. Hell, maybe I'll sell the house, buy a yacht, rent a slip at Bay Harbor, and hang out with the millionaires. Wouldn't be the first time I've lived on a boat.

The house is silent. I love it. I have a call or two to make. Cremation, no service, a loving obituary. She had no family, no friends. I had her wine shipped in by the case, two a month. Maybe they'll send a card. Otherwise, I expect no correspondence. I had a few Navy buddies, but I let them slip away. No matter. I regret killing the young girl last night more than I do Victoria. If I have any regret at all. Victoria. How pretentious. Never Vicky, or Vic. Always Victoria.

The girl last night was beautiful. Her running form exquisite. She had an energy about her. I'd seen her before out there. She wasn't a mother, I could tell that too. Did she want to be? Did I rob her of that? It couldn't be helped. She was a cog in my wheel. A shining light in my masterpiece. I hold her up to the gods.

Which leads me to the new neighbor. She's flawless. A classic, like Grace Kelly, Michelle Pfeiffer, or Charlize Theron. In real time I guess a Jennifer Lawrence or Margot Robbie. I have just three to go. I'd like her to be the last. But if time gets short, or the heat turns up, she's certainly the most convenient. Since I've possibly drawn police attention to myself, I may have to abandon the time table.

CHAPTER 27

Harper Stowe awoke from a four-hour nap Saturday afternoon to the sound of an incoming text from her mother saying she'd just arrived at Harper's condo. It was not a planned visit, and typically Muriel and Carter traveled together on the weekends if they left Savannah.

"Are you coming home soon? Or would you have some time if I come to where you are? The station?" Muriel asked.

Stowe had a list of leads and follow-ups pertaining to the case she wanted to get started on. She hadn't seen her parents since Easter. Her sporadic phone calls to them had become less frequent in the past eight weeks and they all three knew and understood why. Their family operated under a professional courtesy. If her mother was trying an important case it would be the same for her. Carter was always busy. Each weekday he was prepped for surgery by 7 a.m., so his routine was basically clean living, early to bed and early to rise. In the afternoons he had office hours for new patients and to check the ongoing progress of current patients.

Stowe was groggy. After staying up through the night and into the morning, the nap did as much harm as good. Minutes passed as she thought of the best way to handle her mother.

Another text came in: *"?"*

Stowe knew her mother had driven the backroads into Bluffton, still at least an hour with Saturday traffic, to see her. She had the utmost love, respect, and admiration for her mother. Both were pragmatic to a fault. They'd always been open and honest in their conversations. Stowe assumed she may have something to discuss about her father. His health perhaps? Why else would she make the drive unannounced?

"Do you have your key? I can be there in a half hour. I'm going to get a coffee, want one?"

Knowing she would get out on the trails later she dressed in running shorts, a tank top, visor, and sun glasses. She left her toes free though with a pair of everyday sandals. She left the neighborhood quickly, with the top down on her Mercedes coupe. Outside the gates of Ocean Oaks she turned left into Starbucks. The store was near-empty as the late afternoon temperature spiked in the high-90s. She ordered two beverages and thought about the heat. The top would be going up, and the air conditioner on, as she began drinking her much-needed caffeine.

"You're not hitting the road are you?" a voice said.

She turned and was face-to-face with Tyler Bishop. Her mind had gone domestic - on to family matters. She was taken aback. Her face flushed imagining that he might be the cold killer.

"I'm sorry if I startled you. Didn't I speak with you in my parking lot the other day?"

It was a rhetorical question for Bishop. Exchanging words with Stowe was unforgettable to any man.

"Uh, yes, we did talk."

"So are you off?"

"Off? No, I have another week... with my family."

"I wouldn't run alone anymore."

"Yeah, I guess it was a bad night. It's shocking."

"It really is. I think everyone is numb. Course, I guess women are safe for a couple of weeks."

"Oh yeah, the pattern. I read about that. Not sure I'd trust it."

"Well, I don't blame you, not with your life. The guy has been like clockwork though."

They each seemed to be studying the other, trying to read if the conversation was finished and, in Bishop's case, if

Diagram of Death

bringing up the murders with a woman - a blond runner possibly in her thirties – was insensitive. Bishop found Stowe immensely attractive despite his love for his wife, and his proceeding efforts at an affair. Stowe was searching for a question to clear Bishop of the crimes - or implicate him - without sounding cop-like.

"So, where are you from?" he asked.

"I'm up-state. The Greenville area. Simpsonville," Stowe said. She was improvising as she spoke, having not taken her Carrie Stowers-façade too far in her own mind. One of her South Carolina track teammates was from Simpsonville. If he quizzed her on the top three local eateries there she'd be exposed as a fraud. "Are you visiting?"

"No, I live here."

"Oh. I thought I picked up on a little bit of Yankee," she said, with an intentionally-flirtatious tone.

He laughed.

"I moved here from New York. I didn't realize I brought it with me."

Stowe glanced at the wedding ring on the hand that held his cup.

"Too young to be retired I assume, unless you're filthy rich."

"Far from it. I'm the political editor out at the *Tribune*."

"Interesting. I saw that paper this morning. Did you write any of the murder stuff?"

"No, I have a Sunday column. I turned it in at six on Friday and got the hell out of there for the weekend. They were fully-staffed… in case."

Dread pierced her body for an instant. He would've had plenty of time to return to Ocean Oaks. Stowe also felt he was bragging about his column, which had her considering his egomania or narcissism. He was polished. Trying to gain trust. *Maybe it was him. Maybe he did it.*

"Here you go Ma'am," a staff member said as she sat two cups on the counter. "Have a good one."

"Thanks. You too," Stowe said. She put a couple of dollars in the tip cup. She was thankful for the buffer. "Well, this is me. I guess this is it... until next time?"

"Tyler."

"Nice to meet you, Tyler. I'm Carrie."

"Yeah, it was nice seeing you again as well. I hope we run into each other another time," he said. "Closer to home."

"Well, I'm definitely finding my way to the sand."

"Maybe I'll see you there."

He held the door for her and they went to their respective cars, both watching the other while trying not to reveal they were in observation mode.

Stowe thought about Bishop and this James Wainwright as she drove to her actual home. They seemed as different as night and day. Bishop appeared refined and well-adjusted. Could he be the killer? There was a hint of testosterone, of machismo, assertiveness, that made it seem possible. There was no question he was hoping to see her again, one way or the other. Between his wedding ring and the other possibilities she was repulsed and angry. To rid herself of that feeling, she thought of Rhett Richardson and where he might be. He most-likely would have cleared out of his rental, unless he was willing to pay full price for the upcoming week, if it was even available. She would call him after she talked to her mother.

Muriel Stowe was resting comfortably in one of Stowe's matching high-backed chairs when she walked in. She'd already made herself a cup of tea, and was flipping through a *Southern Living* magazine with little interest while she waited. Muriel didn't intend to stay on-island. She and Carter had a dinner party to attend at seven-thirty. The double-

Diagram of Death

shot of caffeine couldn't hurt as she managed the backroads back to Savannah, keeping herself out of I-95 traffic.

"Hi Mom," Stowe said. She leaned and kissed her mother's cheek. Muriel smiled.

"Hello, young lady." She gave Harper time to set the drinks on the coffee table between them and seat herself.

"That's quite becoming," Muriel said, raising an eyebrow to Harper's hair. In her haste, Harper had forgotten about her color and style switch. She pulled off her visor.

"Oh, thanks."

"I saw you on the news last night at the murder scene - as a resident. I can only think the worst."

Since she could remember, Harper had known her mother as the toughest of the tough, razor sharp, uncompromising in her beliefs, both as a lawyer and in the civic, social, and religious aspects of her life. As a teenager and young adult, Harper watched her try criminal cases unflinchingly as an Assistant District Attorney, saying what needed to be said to and about hardened criminals who put zero value on others' lives and property.

Muriel had Harper nearly swayed to the law over law enforcement. "You know I respect and admire what you do Mom. You're amazing," Harper said at the time, at Christmas break, a year and a half before her graduation from USC, plenty of time to prepare for the LSAT and begin applying to law schools. "But I want to be part of the first wave. I want to solve the crime - find the criminals. I want to make the busts. I want the action. You're honoring your Pa Pa Lanny, and I want to too. But I want to do it my own way."

In her grogginess on this Saturday, Harper hadn't considered that her mother had figured out that she'd gone undercover. But she wasn't surprised. Still, she wasn't prepared for the discussion. The past four days had been a blur of activity. And in truth, she thought there was no way the unsub would escape Friday night.

"You're undercover?" Muriel said. "Just say it."

"Yes, I am."

"It isn't enough to be tracking one of the most horrific serial killers ever, oh wait, *rapist* and serial killer, and you're letting yourself be used as bait?"

"Mom, please don't look at it that way."

"What other way is there to look at it, Harper?"

Harper sat gathering her thoughts. Muriel had much more remaining in her arsenal.

"You know, your father and I worried each and every day – each and every shift – before you made detective. There's just so many things that can happen out there when you're dealing with the public – dealing with criminals – as this family well knows. You can't see it all coming at you. Pull someone over for a bad taillight, you don't know what they're really up to. They could shoot you down on the street."

"Mom, I…"

"No, wait. When you made detective, I was relieved. Your father was relieved. At least you are in control of the situations you walk into. In our minds you're safer. But now this."

"Look, I admit, the way you say it, it sounds bad," Harper said. "But Mom, I've seen all these victims, these vibrant, beautiful women. I've talked to their grieving husbands and looked into the eyes of their crushed, heart-broken children. It's so sad, it's gut-wrenching. They're out there running, completely trusting their environment – and they've paid the price…the greatest price."

"So you're willing to be the next victim?" Muriel said. "You're willing to make that sacrifice? Well, I – we – are not ready to lose our baby, our only child. Have you thought of that? Have you thought of us?"

Diagram of Death

Muriel Stowe was two syllables from a good cry. Harper had never seen her close to that condition. Ever.

"I *have* thought of that. But Mom, you know and I know there is nobody - *nobody* - on this island more capable of bringing this man down than me. You've got to have some faith in me."

"I do have faith in you, Harper. You know that. And I know how capable you are – if you aren't blindsided. I know you can take anybody in a fair fight. I love that about you. But this man isn't going to square off with you. He's not going to fight fair. He'll take your head off when you're the most vulnerable, and put you in the dirt."

"That's a grave account, counselor. Is that figuratively or literally in the dirt? Or under the dirt?"

Muriel tilted her head and smiled. She let out a breath of laughter that could have been mistaken for a sob. Her eyes widened before she blinked, erasing evidence of a tear.

"I'm sorry, child. I am," Muriel said. "I have experience in this area, you know. There's been a 24-year gap in police fatalities at home, and they're operating in a warzone. It's freakishly lucky. I don't know how you expect me not to worry."

"Mom, I know you're going to worry. I'm sorry you have to. And I'll admit, I thought no way this son-of-a-bitch was not getting caught last night. I thought it would be over today. But I've got it narrowed down. I think I'm closing in."

"That's good news. Just please be careful, Harper. I won't say 'Don't take unnecessary chances' because you already are. I'll let you in on a little secret. I didn't tell your Dad about this. He was already asleep last night."

"Thanks, Mom. No, that wouldn't have been good for anybody," Harper said. She relaxed into her chair. "But if you're interested, I do have some news about another man…"

CHAPTER 28

Ralph Sneed was a novice as a mayor. But as a former corporate executive – and even more as a day-trader in his own wealth management - he could sense panic like feeling the early winds of an incoming storm. He knew panic could cripple his island.

After meeting with Chief Beaumont, Harper Stowe, and the FBI Saturday morning, he attended an emergency session of the Chamber of Commerce. Sneed had walked through his office in route to the meeting. Calls were coming in ten-a-minute. Concerns, worries, fears, tips, complaints. He knew the same was happening downstairs at the Hilton Head Police Department.

Five minutes after Sneed joined the group of twenty, publisher Ray Finney had the old-timers whipped into a frenzy about a few cancelations he had received on his Ocean Oaks properties. He was waving around Myrtle Beach's *The Sun News*, its bold-type headline reading "Ten Weeks of Terror Plagues Hilton Head."

"This is an obvious ploy to steal back some of our traffic - those sons-a-bitches. Completely unethical," Finney said, his voice rising. He of course failed to share the news of his own delayed deadline from just twelve hours earlier, or the fact that, despite the additional cost of holding his trucks, or in hopes of making up the loss, *The Beaufort Tribune* printed an extra ten-thousand papers to restock the boxes leading out of town through Saturday afternoon. Neither fact would surprise anybody in the room.

"We're not terrorized," he went on. "We're *dealing* with our maniac. It's plenty safe if you just stay together. It's not like we're in the middle of a turf war for the drug trade."

Diagram of Death

Mayor Sneed watched from the corner of the room, seated, leaning against tinted glass that weakened the glare of the sun-soaked day. They were meeting in the conference room of First Trust Bank. Sneed had been slighted – outright offended - in the past by Finney. He was just taking all the information in for now.

"Here's the key, and I don't think I have to point this out to anybody," said Ronny "Tank" Welch, mammoth owner of two bar-and-grills, the more successful of the two within a hundred yards of Ocean Oaks' gates. "His sixth victim – thirteen days from now – that's July 4th week. If I don't blow it out July 4th week, I'm dead in the water."

"I'm with you there," said Steve Lester, owner of Sound Paddleboards and Kayak Tours. Lester was young, tan, and half the weight of Welch, all of it from outdoor fitness. "I won't survive if my July starts slow."

The owner of Low Country Books, Chelsey Wilcox, early fifties, elegant, attractive, always in a sun dress, was even less optimistic about the future.

"I live on a shoestring anyway. These past two months haven't helped at all," she said. "I'm ashamed to admit this. I prayed all day yesterday that this man would be shot down – so that the media could blast out that it was all over. I think I'm going to have to shut my doors."

"Folks, folks, I think what you're sensing is a knee-jerk reaction just hours after-the-fact," Sneed said, standing, finally too frustrated by the remarks to keep quiet. "You all know my PR manager LaDonna Reynolds. She can attest that this same thing happened two - and four - weeks ago, but ultimately the public's insatiable need for proximity to the situation prevailed. Sales stayed solid overall."

"Sneed, my cancelations were from families that booked with me every year," Finney said. "You think I'm going to be able to reach out and bring in new business – find new clients in a week who are willing to pay three, four, eight grand?"

"Mr. Finney, I've been sitting in our office all morning fielding calls," LaDonna Reynolds said. "The real-estate offices are getting calls from potential renters I'm told – curiosity seekers. There's even a club that dissects murder cases looking to spend July 4th week here. I feel certain we can direct some renters you're way."

"I was going to hold off on this," Sneed said, stepping closer to Reynolds and putting his arm around her. A few members expected a wedding announcement, Sneed's duplicity successfully intact. "LaDonna is going to handle the distribution, but I'm donating eighty-thousand dollars to run the Hilton Head Island promotional commercial the Chamber had made two years ago. We're going to run it regionally from Atlanta to Cincinnati and eastward in."

The buzz in the room went silent. Even the ultra-conservative Ray Finney could not complain.

"That should help, Mayor," Finney said. "On behalf of all the members here let me offer a sincere thank-you."

A chorus of "Hear-Hear," "Yes," "Wonderful," and "Thank-you," filled the room.

"We're changing a bit of the dialogue," Reynolds said. "I've already talked with four cable stations. It will be up and running by Tuesday. We're going to run it for a week until July 1st."

More approval was vocalized.

There was one topic Sneed failed to address, mainly because he wasn't exactly sure how it would affect the situation. It wouldn't commercially, except it could possibly help with the rentals. More likely it would be a crop of extremists living in the backseats of their cars. Sneed knew it was information he needed to share with Lester Beaumont and Harper Stowe, a definite headache for the HHPD. He'd taken

Diagram of Death

one call personally in his office. It was the State Commissioner of Insurance. Due to the announcement of the Bennett Boyd reward of one-hundred grand, and a moderate offering from the F.B.I., thirteen bounty hunters, a.k.a. fugitive recovery agents, had applied for sponsorship in South Carolina.

CHAPTER 29

Harper Stowe's first attempts at tracking down Rhett Richardson early Saturday evening were unfruitful. She left a message or two. A moment of doubt concerning her Thursday "End of Her World" behavior entered into her thinking, but she pushed it away. She refused to second-guess herself. She was too strong-willed.

The connection is real. The feelings are real. And he is one good-looking man. She thought.

Harper was still at her condo. Her mother had taken her leave after an hour long "bull session" about the virtues of Rhett Richardson and a few other more trivial subjects. Muriel was pleased to hear her daughter discussing a man in a romantic sense. The men they usually talked about were either criminals or co-workers.

"I'm glad I can report to your father that you're dating," Muriel had said. "And a man named Rhett to beat all… You know, we haven't ruled out grandchildren. That would be a blessing."

"Mom. I'm making no promises," Harper replied, smiling. Her genuine smile was striking, but as elusive as swift justice. "Even if we do stay together, I'm not sure our professions are conducive to parenthood."

"Well, a mother can hope, can't she? I'll talk with Carter about buying a house on Fripp. It would be easier on everybody if all the grandparents were on the same island."

"Oh Mom, please. Anyway, you could take a boat from here to Fripp. It's probably only eight miles from one island heel to the other.

"But not from Bluff Drive, dear. From our dock on the Skidaway it would seem like forty miles. All of our time would

Diagram of Death

be spent on the boat, worrying about the tides, darkness, storms, gas."

"Well, Momma, *if* we get married, and *if* we have children, and you don't want to travel by boat or car from Savannah, by all means buy a house on Fripp. Make sure it has at least four bedrooms because we'll need a place to stay. Rhett comes from a large family so who knows how many people will be at the in-laws on a given weekend."

Harper laughed about the conversation as she walked aimlessly around her living room and kitchen. She was deciding whether to give up on finding Rhett for the evening and head back to Ocean Oaks for a run and surveillance, or wait a while longer in hopes of a great dinner and better company.

She sat back down and noticed a promotional map on the coffee table. She'd been picking them up since the first murder. Studying them in spare minutes, waiting for something new to pop into her thinking. At least a dozen were piled up in her backseat. Strange now to think: ten weeks, five murders, solid investigation. She felt she knew so much more now than she did then. And yet, no arrest.

Harper opened the map, which presented Hilton Head Island in the shape of a shoe, toe to the left. Daufuskie Island was the only other landmark, above the shoestrings. Promotional advertisements lined three sides of the map with an index on the bottom. She took a pen and made a heavy dot on each murder site. Harper tossed the pen back on to the table and stared. One ad, no logo nor color, said simply, "Come Worship!" and had a list of churches on the island. That reminded her of the story that Chief Beaumont told her about the bizarre faux pas of Rev. William Janson at the town meeting Thursday, while she was in the crowd playing concerned-newcomer. He described an *"it couldn't happen to me"* complex. *"Someone like that almost deserves their fate,"* Lester said he'd said.

Very ungodly, she thought.

Harper called the office and requested a background check on Janson. As she was finishing the call, Rhett Richardson beeped in.

"I'm back out at the Marriott," he said. "I walked over to Coligny to pick up a few things. I was hangin' with some Colignyites. I guess I couldn't hear my phone."

She knew Coligny well. A circular strip mall a half mile outside the less-used North Ocean Oaks Drive gates, it was a haven for those unwilling to pay astronomical Ocean Oaks' prices for a week in the sand. It is a Myrtle Beachesque, beach-trinket destination – shark's tooth necklaces, sun glasses, fishing gear, towels, T-shirts and hats, for the vacationers staying at the Hilton Head Marriott Resort and Spa and other hotels on the southeastern side of the island.

"You can make friends anywhere, can't you?" Harper said.

"Yeah, I can – and I didn't even have my camera to loosen them up."

"Would you like to spend some time cheering up a lonely woman? I could make you dinner or we could try another place – off the beaten path so to speak."

"I'm definitely up for either. You call it."

"Well, why don't we just go out? I'm not in a mood to face a Harris Teeter for supplies. I'm not in Ocean Oaks, by-the-way, I'm at my actual home. You can pick me up and I'll give you the real-life, quick tour."

Fishcamp on Broad Creek was indeed out of the way, all but hidden on unlit Simmons Road, not far from the Cross Island Expressway Bridge. The thoroughfare was named after "Cap'n" Charlie Simmons, Sr., part of the Gullah/Geechee Nation, who moved both people and product to and from

Diagram of Death

Savannah before there was a bridge. The black man piloted sailboats in the 1920's and then owned one of the first motor boats in the area, tripling his exporting of anything from butterbeans and watermelon to shrimp and oysters - even cows - to market in Savannah. The first bridge to the mainland wasn't built until 1956.

"See that? Two months short of a hundred when he died in '05," Harper said.

"Quite a story. Imagine how much the island changed throughout his life."

The couple read the story on the wall as they waited for their open-air table. Able to access her closet for the first time in days, Harper chose a form-fitting yellow dress that caught the attention of every patron in the outdoor area behind the restaurant. A recording of Van Morrison's "Into the Mystic" completed the vibe.

"Let me just say – before anyone else does – that you look stunning," Rhett said. "Makes me feel inadequate."

"I think I got a little excited about the idea of an actual date," she said. "There hasn't been a whole lot of that in the past year. Oh, and you look just fine, by the way."

"Thank you kindly. I think it's interesting though. That dress is the same color as your front door at Ocean Oaks, Ms. Carrie Stowers. That's how I recognize your house. Is that some kind of coincidence?"

She laughed.

"Well you know yellow is supposed to be inspirational," she said.

"Oh, I'm inspired."

"And it's intellectually stimulating – it fills you with vitality."

"Uh-huh."

"It's also the color of love. Yellow roses mean love."

"Really."

"That reminds me, when we sit down, I have to tell you about the conversation I had with my mother today. You won't believe it."

They were in such proximity and so connected emotionally, he leaned and casually kissed her, then he took her right hand with his and spun her, finishing with his left in her right, in a dance position, his right hand on her back. Harper looked at him without speaking, overcome with a sense of déjà vu concerning her parents and the way they showed their love. She'd never mentioned it to him – it was completely spontaneous and authentic. The hostess approached them, and she slid her arm through his and they followed her arm-in-arm to their table, again drawing looks.

The entire evening went this way: candlelight, good wine and seafood, a breeze off Broad Creek across the wide lot, through the sporadicly-growing live oaks, sweeping the day's heat out to sea. From a distance they could see the faded yellow reflection of the moon glistening on the black water as they finished their meal.

Back at her condominium they sat down on her couch, with nothing more in mind than relaxation.

Rhett narrowed his eyes at the map. He'd always studied them through his childhood, as his parents relentlessly searched for the right place to purchase a beach house. He had intricate knowledge of the coast from Jacksonville to Wilmington. But this was something else, something more. He was visualizing something *in* the map. Something else from his youth. Something from the wall of his father's study.

Harper noticed his fixation.

"What is it, Rhett?"

He reached and rotated the paper about 45-degrees counterclockwise. Then he stood and looked down at it. He picked up a pen and sat back down.

"Can I write on this?"

Diagram of Death

"Oh, sure. Like I said before, I've got them all over the place."

Using a magazine as a straight edge, Richardson began drawing lines from one murder site to each of the others. Each site began to take on the illustrated point of a star.

"With the map turned to true north, your dots in my mind form the points of the Navy Oak Leaf. A Lieutenant Commander's insignia. Except there are three missing. Here, here, and here," he said, drawing circles around the new marks. "What do you think?"

CHAPTER 30

"Twice he's had charges dropped for sexual assault. Once in Lancaster, Pennsylvania, which was where his career as a minister began. He was from that area. The second in a small town in North Carolina – Salisbury. Just north of Charlotte. The rumor on the dropped charges was intimidation," said Pete Waters over the phone to Harper Stowe. Waters was Hilton Head Police Department's newest detective, and as such assigned weekend research duty by Harper, which gave her a twinge of guilt occasionally, but not this time. Rev. William Janson was looking more and more like, if not her third suspect, along with Tyler Bishop and James Wainwright, a person of interest.

"He's been working his way south: Baltimore, DC, Charlottesville, then all over the Carolinas. This looks to be his eighth church – quick exits. And get this Harper, he was dishonorably discharged from the Navy – conduct unbecoming. He'd been stationed at the Navy Shipyards in Philly, he was kicked out just before they closed it down in the '90s. And that's not 50 miles from Lancaster."

"Great work, Pete," Harper said. "Do we have a physical address on him?"

"Yeah, DMV has him right by Island Baptist Church. He's in the Parrish House – 1232 Wisteria."

Harper looked at the clock – 8:02 a.m., Sunday morning. Rhett Richardson handed her a fresh cup of coffee just after she hit "end" on her cell. She was wearing a flimsy tank top and shorts, sitting at her dining room table, map folded out. She scribbled notes on a legal pad. He sat in the chair next to her, but pulled it out far from the table and faced her.

Diagram of Death

"Thanks," she said, and took a sip. "I think it might behoove me to go to church this morning."

"Hey, it's not a sin if you're in love."

"That's not what I meant."

"I know. I was just playing."

"Were you?"

"Was I...?" he said.

"Playing?"

Attempting to confuse Rhett's line of thinking during conversation was becoming an amusing game for Harper. Sometimes he'd come up with a great response. Other times – like the first night he approached her - he'd back out of the topic hoping to start over.

"Not about the love," he said, and he turned to her. He reached and ran his fingers through her hair at the back of her neck. She tilted and slightly turned her head from the tingle she felt as his thumb gently brushed her ear. He sensed her pleasure. She turned to him and they kissed.

"Can you really?" Harper asked.

"Really what?"

"Love me already. You've not known me a week."

"But I can. I do. Besides, it's been a hell of a week."

"That's just from being thrust together in a perilous situation."

"For you. Is that why you love me? Don't answer - I didn't mean that."

"Don't worry. I'm not going to throw this away," she said. "You've been growing on me since the beginning – that awkward introduction. Last night, when we danced, I think that sealed the deal. I've never been so at-ease – so comfortable - with a man in my life. My father dances with my mom that way. As I watched them when I was young, all it said to me was love. Maybe that's idealistic."

"I don't think so. It's real. I feel it so strongly, it..."

"Takes your breath away?"

"Something like that. My heart is soaring... I have an emotional purpose... a reason for living."

"As do I."

"I don't want you getting hurt - or worse – before we get to the road we're going to go down together. I want to protect you."

"That's unnecessary."

Rhett frowned.

"So, church. This Janson. I remember seeing him at the town meeting with the old priest. Not a small man. Do you want me to go with you?"

"No, I don't. I need to be alone. I just want to get a better sense of him. I haven't decided how to go about it."

"Take the altar call, after the service. Put yourself on the prayer list or whatever – make up something – you wayward soul."

"That's an idea."

"Yeah, a good one. Unless he has some assistant pastor handle it. But I doubt it when he sees you walking down the aisle. Just don't let him take you home for Sunday dinner."

"Don't worry."

"I do worry," he said. "Let me ask you a question – on the ends and outs of law enforcement. If you've got three suspects in mind, can you not just haul them in and get blood, urine, semen, whatever you need?"

"You don't watch much T.V., do you. There're crime shows – law enforcement shows - on twenty-four hours a day."

"Do cops watch crime shows?"

"No, not really."

"I understand the law as it pertains to journalism. But this is a whole different can of worms."

"Here's the thing. These are *my* suspects, but not necessarily official suspects. This is tricky. I have no proof, no witnesses, really no probable cause. I mean, this guy is good - except for leaving his DNA. He leaves fake clues. A pubic hair - possible Asian - on Jessica Boyd? He probably got that off a urinal. So, we have to build a case. Unless the man is caught in the act – that was the goal Friday. Your epiphany last night could help pinpoint his attack sites. But, I'd have to have a warrant to gather that evidence. Especially after…"

"After what?"

"Oh… this has to be between us only. I'm trusting you."

"You know you can."

"I was in Wainwright's house after the Boyd murder. Nothing conclusive there. Some enormous tennis shoes, soaking wet, in the garage. The report said he was wearing them when he went in the pool after his wife. The garage. I – I think he owns a boat. So much was happening that night."

"So get a warrant."

"No judge would grant it unless I can establish probable cause - hard evidence. Unless the suspect would volunteer it."

"I'd volunteer it if I was innocent. You could at least eliminate suspects that way."

Harper looked at him, saying nothing, then her gaze drifted towards the windows. She was imagining the scenarios. What if she asked the right man? What would his reaction be?"

As she quietly thought, Rhett finished his coffee, stood and walked his cup to the sink. He didn't want to interrupt her strategizing. As he turned their eyes met again, Harper's expression indicating she'd returned.

"Well, I'm bummed. I checked my email and messages while you were on the phone. The BBC doesn't want me back here till Tuesday July 4th week. And ESPN can use me for regional coverage at an amateur golf tournament, outside of Gainesville."

Harper's shoulders dropped slightly. His presence had been a wonderful reprieve from the intensity of the case. Then she smiled and looked directly into his eyes.

"Well, I'm going to be quite busy anyway, Mr. Richardson," she said. She stood, pushed her chair in, and took him by the hand. "Now, I have two appetites this morning. The second can be taken care of at the Hilton Head Diner. Care to join me for the first?"

CHAPTER 31

Victoria Lynn White Wainwright, 54, of Hilton Head Island, South Carolina, died Friday, June 26, at home, due to a tragic pool accident. She was preceded in death by her parents, Judith and Victor White, of Pompano, Fla., formerly of Washington, D.C., and her sister, Rebecca White Fisher of Chester, Va. She is survived by her loving husband of 32 years, James E. Wainwright, at home.

Victoria was a member of Island Baptist Church, past-president of the League of Women Voters (LWV), a member of the National Organization for Women (NOW), a member of Women Impacting Public Policy (WIPP), a member of the Ocean Oaks Garden Club, and a member of the Ocean Oaks Wine Tasters Society.

Victoria loved life and lived it to the fullest. A graduate of Georgetown University, she was politically active for women's causes for many years. She was happiest at home tending to her plants and vegetables, and cooking gourmet meals. She also enjoyed boating, golf, tennis, music, and reading, especially her Bible. She was the love and light of James' life. Knowing Victoria now walks with the Lord in heaven is what sustains him.

There will be no service. Victoria's ashes will be scattered to the Atlantic Ocean, which she so dearly loved. In lieu of flowers, the family suggests donations be made to the National Alliance for Mental Illness (NAMI). Porter Funeral Home is in charge of arrangements.
- The Beaufort Tribune

What a crock. I could hardly control my laughter when I wrote it. She had her moments early on, but those days went

Andrew Spradling

wayside quick. I was aboard a ship much of the time, being in D.C. lobbying for the damned feminists drained her of mind and spirit – made a drinker out of her.

Onward and upward, I always say. Saturday I traded for a 34-foot '04 Cabin Cruiser Express – eighty grand, minus fourteen for my little fishin' job. I can live on it if need be. And I can entertain on it out to sea – you just have to be a little more creative with the blood-letting. Believe me, the boat is a carrot most of those little rabbits will bite on.

Just one last order of business before I fly the flag at half-mast, before I fire three volleys, give her a hand salute, and dump her ashes. Her Pastor called to comfort me, though I think it's been a couple of years since she attended a service. My accountant suggested a donation to her church to drop my inheritance just below the next tier of taxation. I'm willing. After that, my masterpiece - and any collateral damage I inflict - will be my focus.

CHAPTER 32

"You know, I was just shootin' off back there – at your place," said Rhett Richardson. "I wasn't really thinking."

"You're kidding," said Harper Stowe. She picked up her glass of orange juice as though she was about to have a sip. She could back him into another verbal corner if she so chose. "I never said I was going to do it."

"But you acted like it was a good idea."

"It was a thought."

A smiling, black waitress named Darleen approached with two platters. "Eggs and fruit?"

"That's me," Harper said. She sat both their meals in front of them.

"Think you're good then, Honey? See anything else you need?"

"Just more coffee when you have time, please," Rhett said, without taking his eyes off his food – the Big Breakfast. He still had the appetite of a teenager. "Thanks."

Hilton Head Diner – brick, bright, and upscale, it even had a bar - was booming, and noisy.

"This place has a "Happy Days" feel to it," Rhett said.

"Next time we're out for breakfast I'll take you across the bridge to the "Squat and Gobble." You'll feel right at home."

"I'll bet."

They'd just beaten the morning rush, but the place filled up behind them. Harper wore a strapped, sky-blue dress. *Man, those shoulders and arms are anything but domestic. Tanned and toned*, Rhett thought. Harper arranged her plate just as she wanted it, then unrolled her silverware. Rhett was spreading strawberry jelly on his toast. He could see her mind was back on task.

"Look, there was no way I was going to fabricate a lie with a minister by taking the altar call," Harper said. "That would be pretty tough to forgive."

Rhett looked at her, silently chewing, letting her words sink in. *"Ascribe to the Lord the glory due to His name. Worship the Lord in holy array."*

"That's impressive."

"Is it?"

"Do you often quote the Bible?"

"Depends on the situation. Church doesn't come up that often. Look, I was in a Rorschach moment, Harper, at your place – first thing that came into my cabeza."

"I understand," Harper said, picking up a grape. "So you agree there's some weight to that moment in a church?"

"I do. You're approaching the altar of God."

"Yes.... Well, had I done that, I would have been uncomfortable with the whole situation," Harper said. "My deception would have been with the members, the preacher, and God. A lie to beat all lies. I can come up with another way. Besides, there's no telling who will be in this service – people in the community who know me professionally. It's tactically risky. I'll just meet him after."

"You could just say you're distraught about this situation in Ocean Oaks. That's enough – and the truth."

"I'll come up with something. You're right. That's not bad. So this is serious to you – pulling, I'm assuming a Psalm out of the air like that?"

Rhett stopped again. He smiled slightly, shaking his head, thoroughly impressed with Harper and her knowledge.

"Twenty-Nine, Two....We haven't talked about this," Rhett said. He watched his fork as he used it to push food around his plate. "I went to Liberty U., private, Christian, in

Diagram of Death

Lynchburg, Virginia. My parents didn't want me mainstream, at a party school. I guess I picked up quite a bit of scripture."

"Was there a problem?"

"Oh, you know, the affluent, in high school around Charlotte, probably having too good a time with my Country Day classmates. Nothing major. The folks just didn't want it picking up steam at UNC, NC State, or Duke."

A man at the next table lowered his opened newspaper enough to glare over the top disapprovingly. They both noticed him.

"The good thing about it, bouncing between Virginia Tech and UVA – and sometimes down to Raleigh-Durham - I worked as many football and basketball games as I wanted for ESPN. I've been working for them for over ten years."

"Couldn't you just get on full-time with them?" Harper asked.

"Doing the games are fun but that's not going to bring me the *real* stories I'm looking for – we talked about that before."

"Oh, right. The conspiracy theorists."

"No," he said, suppressing a smile. "The conspirators."

Harper laughed. As she did, she looked back at the man with his newspaper. He'd folded it, flipped it, turned the pages at least a dozen times sitting there, completely ignoring his wife, who quietly drank her coffee. Harper leaned towards the paper, focusing on the page facing them. It was the obituaries.

"What are you doing?"

"Hold on. Victoria Lynn White Wainwright," she said. "It's the obit of the woman who drowned Friday night. That was fast. Especially since it was an accident."

Harper used air quotes for accident.

"I mean, think about it. He didn't get back from the station till late Friday night. She's at the morgue waiting for an autopsy, he's calling the funeral home Saturday and putting together the obit.

Five minutes later the man folded up the paper, dropped it on an empty seat at his table, stood and walked away, leaving his wife behind to calculate a tip. Harper stood.

"May I?"

"Oh, sure. He just picked it up at the register."

"Thanks." She sat back down, shuffled through until she found the page.

"Loving husband… Island Baptist… no service. Island Baptist?"

She looked at her watch.

"Let's finish up. I don't want to be late."

CHAPTER 33

It was impossible for Harper Stowe to be inconspicuous at Island Baptist Church. Tucked away behind its own shelter of live oaks, pines, and palmettos – like most buildings on Hilton Head Island – the tiny chapel was located out an old fishing road towards Broad Creek, the land donated to the church by a long-departed member. The structure was wood, painted white. Atop it sat an old-fashioned steeple. Its parking lot was a bed of pine needles. Inside, there were but twelve rows of pews, separated by the middle aisle. She slid into an empty spot to the right in the eleventh row.

Detective Pete Waters had reported back to Harper with a little more information on Reverend William Janson on her drive from breakfast to the church. Lancaster, Pennsylvania, was a community largely comprised of both Amish and Mennonites, and he'd apparently been shunned by both, unwilling to repent of his sinful behavior. When the Navy discharged him dishonorably, he had nothing to return to in Lancaster County.

As the organist began to play "This Is My Story," Harper watched the members end their conversations with hugs and handshakes, and begin making their way to their seats. Consumed with the case for the past ten weeks, she realized it had been at least three months since she experienced fellowship and worship at her own church. A cleansing seemed to take place from the beginning, when she was greeted at the door by an older gentleman, probably a deacon, as he handed her a bulletin. She thought of Rhett Richardson, his story about attending college at Liberty University, and the look of sincere regret in his eyes as they parted, saying he would return to her on Tuesday of the next week – the 12th week.

Andrew Spradling

As the last of the congregation sat, James Wainwright entered and made his way to the front. He approached Rev. Janson as Janson stepped down to floor level to meet him. They shook hands, shared a few words, then Wainwright took a seat in the front row and Janson returned to the pulpit. Stowe's internal antenna was abuzz. After a quick good morning and welcome, another gentleman led a tiny choir of six and the group of fifty or so in "Holy, Holy, Holy."

"Let's bow our heads in prayer," Janson said.

"Heavenly Father, we thank you for this opportunity to gather today in this humble house of worship, to praise You and Your Son, Jesus Christ. Bless us this day, Lord, give us strength to overcome the temptations this world brings to our doorstep, through our televisions, our computers, and our cell phones. Keep us worthy, Lord. Help us in our fight to remain pure. Forgive us our sins as we continue our march to Glory. We ask in Your name, Lord, Amen.

"We have a guest today, and we want to make a special announcement before our next hymn," Janson said, stepping back down to the altar before the congregation. He now spoke without amplification but was easily heard. Harper found it difficult not to fidget in her seat. Her senses were ablaze with anticipation, her ears perked. Janson went on. "Some of you may know, there was a tragic accident Friday evening. I am saddened to share that we lost our church sister, Victoria Wainwright, who no longer suffers, no longer wants, who walks the streets of Glory with our Lord. Her husband, Lieutenant James Wainwright, retired, is here with a special gift to honor Victoria, and hopefully enhance our worship experience in the future."

Wainwright joined Rev. Janson, who put his hand on Wainwright's shoulder. Janson stood at 6-foot-2, but Wainwright was at least a half-head taller and noticeably larger in stature. Wainwright, his features half-masted to grimace,

Diagram of Death

pulled a check from his jacket pocket and the pair held it together.

"We have spoken many times about better-utilizing our land just behind the church and its beautiful view of the water. In the name of Victoria, to honor her memory, we will build an outdoor sanctuary – a gazebo, garden, and courtyard - behind the chapel. There will be a plaque placed there to share the story of this generous gift in her name. We want to humbly thank you, James, for being here today and delivering Victoria's wishes to us."

Wainwright released the check and raised his hand to the congregation. His mouth upturned slightly. A chorus of "amens" and "bless yous" followed. He then lumbered to an empty outside aisle seat, farther back in the church, on the opposite side of Harper.

"Let's all stand and welcome our neighbors as we sing 'Nearer My God To Thee.' " With that cue from Janson and now in greeting-mode, the congregation began to sing. Wainwright turned inward to shake the hands of those who approached. Overtop their heads he spotted Harper Stowe, also receiving handshakes. He stood transfixed. His eyes couldn't leave her. Harper noticed his gaze but continued greeting worshipers. The members who approached Wainwright last realized his distracted indifference and turned away, put off.

As Janson began his sermon, Christ's disciples and the storms they faced, the words passed Wainwright's ears without registering. He was thinking only of the woman in the blue dress – his new neighbor. By turning his legs inward towards the center of the room he was able to watch her through his peripheral vision without constantly staring. Harper was aware he was watching, but assumed he was seeing her for the first time.

What is the deal with this guy? Could he really have been so callous as to meet with the funeral home, write or help get the obit written, have her cremated, plan this with the church, and all twelve or fifteen hours after his wife's death? Could he be that cold-hearted? Did the county not perform an autopsy? Maybe the church project was planned or being planned – or was in her will. Maybe I should ask Janson these questions. No, don't blow your cover. Two sexual assaults swept under the rug? Stay the course. Test your instincts. See if there is something with him as well. And, it's interesting, not a word mentioned about Ocean Oaks and the murders. No special prayer, no message of safety. Could that be denial of his own actions? Or worse yet, misdirection?

When Janson's message was delivered and the service ended, Harper quickly approached him at the altar.

"Rev. Janson, my name is Carrie Stowers," she said, shaking his hand. Using both of his, he continued to hold hers throughout. Wainwright, having removed his sports coat during the service, piddled at his pew, pretending to gather his personal items, as he watched their greeting and conversation.

"I live alone in Ocean Oaks and I've been so distraught – terrorized - by this whole situation. It's all I think about. I'm considering moving, but that's no quick solution. And of course financially I'm upside-down on the home I'm afraid to leave."

"I understand your dilemma. There is no easy answer with this person on the loose. Do you have family in the area?"

"I don't. I closed on my place just after the first murder. I've only lived here a month and a half... moved here for work. It's really affected me. I can't get good sleep. I've met my neighbors, but who can you trust? I'm hoping you could... pray for me, maybe put me on a prayer list? Please."

"My dear, of course we can do that. All of that. Rest assured the Lord will be watching over you. Have you found your church home here on the island?"

Diagram of Death

"No, not yet. I've visited a couple of other churches though."

"Let me ask you, Carrie, have you given yourself to the Lord – as an adult?"

"No, sir, I was baptized as a baby."

"I believe, we believe, to be right with God, you must make the decision to serve our Lord once you're fully-grown," he said, his tone soothing. He was nearly stroking her hand now. Still, Wainwright watched. He focused on Janson's hands, growing agitated. "Do you know of the Anabaptists?"

"No, but…"

"A long time ago Menno Simons followed the movement, brought it across the big pond. Infants can't make the decision to follow God. You must surrender yourself as an adult. Only when you walk with the confidence of your salvation will you walk fearlessly in this life. If you need to make a baptismal decision, we could…"

"I feel like my salvation is safe. It's my throat I'm worried about. I notice you didn't mention the situation at all today. I was surprised at that."

"Well the Wainwright's gift took the time I tend to use to remind the congregation that worldliness interferes with their relationship with God. We tend to downplay current affairs," Janson said. His left hand moved to Harper's arm, as he began to attempt to turn her towards the altar. "Though it probably *was* an oversight to not mention the situation in prayer and the latest victim – Jessica Boyd I think. Perhaps we should – Oh - Mr. Wainwright."

"I don't mean to interrupt – I'll wait."

Wainwright's body seemed to loom over the meeting, blocking the light from the rear door. Harper recognized a Wainwright-imposed tension in the situation.

"No, it's all right. This is Ms. Carrie… Stowers, correct? James Wainwright."

"Hello, sir. I'm very sorry for your loss. Tragic."

She pulled her hand from Janson's and shook Wainwright's. Touching him caused a chill to run up her spine. The size of his hand made hers look like a child's.

"Thank you… very much. Rev. Janson, I just wanted to let you know if you needed anything more for the project to just call. I know some contractors as well."

"That's very generous but we'll probably build it ourselves. I have some men here who are handy with a hammer. It'll just be a matter of purchasing materials. Your generosity thus far is more than adequate."

"I see. Fine then. Just know I'm willing."

"I just realized you two have something in common," Janson said. "You both live in Ocean Oaks."

Wainwright looked down at Harper and smiled. He tried to summon a little charm.

"Well, that's an interesting coincidence – and a pleasant surprise."

Diagram of Death

CHAPTER 34

I've never killed a man. I guess out of respect for the jobs they do, mainly. The noble beast. The provider. There've been a few that've made me consider it. Irritants on ships. Tight quarters – that's no place to be with the loudmouths. The uncouth, uncivilized, disrespectful nimrods, talking incessantly about the girls they've bagged, the size of their junk, the tattoos they have - or worse yet - want, the whiskey they'll binge on, the rules they'll break. So undignified. So filthy. They waste every dime they make. Never think of the future. I, at least, did that. I have the home, the boat, the security. There was one other man, my immediate superior, Frank Monk, due for a good flogging – minimum. He was the one. The one that kept me from becoming a Lieutenant Commander. That's all the billet I wanted. Just the next step higher. The LC's got the insignia. That thing caught my eye as a child, somehow. I would draw it on my notebooks, doodle it in my notes. But Monk kept up with the tests, the hurdles, the less-than-glowing reports. He wanted to keep me where I was. He once told me he couldn't trust my motives. I could never figure that one out. I did my job. All I did was my job. He's still climbing the ranks. Down at Jacksonville. That might be the first trip the boat makes. There are millions upon millions of men in America. They die every hour. Bar fights, muggings, car wrecks, drug deals gone bad - prescription drugs no less. Victoria left a bathroom full of 'em. Yeah, I might have to pay ol' Frank a visit – tie up loose ends. He was a gambler. Not just a parlay card player. Used to straight-line college football games... multiple bookies. There's an angle for you. Unless things come to a head here. One thing's for certain. I don't ever want to see that damned preacher again. There are

Andrew Spradling

certain traits you can sense in a man. Certain… appetites that can't be hidden. Maybe I should respect his brash pickup moves. Maybe I should envy his ability to communicate. But he was up to no good, I could see that. I better never see him around Carrie Stowers. That could be his undoing.

CHAPTER 35

Once she was away from the bizarre scene at Island Baptist Church, Harper Stowe - driving her convertible Mercedes, top down - admitted to herself she felt a longing for a Sunday dinner at the home of her now-deceased maternal grandparents, Jackie and Buck Lancaster, with her mom and dad, the cousins, aunts, and uncles. Muriel Stowe had both a sister, Gwenie shortened from Gwendolyn, and a brother, Jack. The siblings had seven kids between them. In her youth, Harper looked forward to Sunday afternoons as much as anything. She and her cousins would run, play, and fish on Grandpa Buck's lush Savannah lawn which abutted the Skidaway River.

Regular church attendance was a practiced family obligation. Those dinners afterwards were often the only time of the week Harper's parents could relax and laugh together. Carter Stowe genuinely loved Muriel's siblings and their spouses. He had been a late surprise to his aging parents, and they had long-since passed. Grandma Jackie sensed a yearning in Carter to embrace the family, so she would tirelessly put the work in to make Sunday dinner as often as possible.

Harper, approaching the gate at Ocean Oaks, could almost smell the golden brown breading of her Grandma Jackie's chicken frying in hot Crisco, feel the comforting warmth of her chicken and dumplings in her belly, visualize the texture of her roast beef, carrots, onions, and potatoes, and feel the weight of her homemade yeast rolls in the palm of her young hand. Anything Grandma Jackie made always seemed to be the best Harper had ever eaten.

"The most important ingredient I put in every meal is love, my dear," she would say, touching Harper's cheek. "There are no shortcuts."

That child learned as much as she could from Grandma Jackie, but recipes known and not practiced were much like love that's unrequited, there is danger of it fading into the oblivion.

As Harper approached her pseudo-home on Slack Trimmer Road, the nostalgia was clinging to her like the heat. But she had work to do. She decided to go for the trifecta in terms of contacting suspects.

I'll see if I can track down Tyler Bishop this afternoon... on the beach. He saw my car at the coffee shop, so it would make sense that it be parked near one of the other buildings close to his – rather than walk the two miles with my chair on my shoulder and look to him like I was staying somewhere else. I could throw my running shoes in the car as well, in case he heads off to the trails. That is, if he's even home. This might be a work day for him. It's worth a shot. He said he had the weekend off.

Harper had packed a black bikini and an off-white suit cover. As she dressed she touched the small cross she wore at the end of a thin, gold chain. A gift from her parents when she began working in law enforcement, she wore it daily. Only when dressed for a special occasion that called for specific jewelry – a rare occasion – did she take it off. She decided, as she again reminisced about the Sundays of her youth, to keep it on today.

There were a couple of old, low-setting beach chairs in her garage, some books on shelves in the house. Apparently the woman who owned the place was a big supporter of local talent. She had a few dozen books with "Local Author" stamps on the covers. Stowe bypassed the Pat Conroy section, because she, like all book-loving southerners, had long since read them,

Diagram of Death

and chose "*Jericho Cay – A Bay Tanner Mystery*" by Kathryn R. Wall. Harper chuckled.

"A female Private Investigator? I can get into that," she said aloud.

Half an hour later, Stowe was parked at Bluff Villas on Land's End Road and walking through the dunes out to a part of the southern-most beach on the island called "The Point." The Point was the headwaters for dolphins to cruise the channel between Daufuskie and Hilton Head Islands, by Windmill Harbor into Pickney Island National Wildlife Refuge and out to the bay at Parris Island. There wasn't much going on there, but from her seat in the sand Harper could see people moving about Daufuskie in golf carts, a few others lounging on the beach. She guessed the divide to be about a half mile or 3,000 feet.

Harper was six chapters into the story, getting sunburned and hungry, and was about to give up on Tyler Bishop when she noticed him approaching from down the beach. He'd just finished a run. He wore running shorts and shoes, a watch, and athletic sunglasses. He carried a hand towel and a water bottle, nearly empty. Sweat dripped from his face to the dark hair on his chest. Watching his steps through the sand, he hadn't noticed Harper yet.

"You look like I did that first day we talked," Harper said, loud enough to cut through the wind. "Tad warm?"

"Oh, hello Carrie," he said. He smiled, obviously elated. "I didn't see you there."

"Have a good run?"

"Pretty good. Took the trail down, beach back, about five miles," he said. He peeked at his watch with a satisfied head-bob. "Really good actually. Where's your family?"

"Oh, they're not much for the sun, you know? A bit older." She wanted that subject to stay vague.

"Yeah, I understand. My wife has yet to come out here."

"I hear that happens a lot with folks that move to the beach. Too busy to enjoy it."

"Do you mind?" he asked, pointing to the sand.

"No, go ahead."

Bishop laid his hand towel on the sand beside Harper, poked his water bottle in next to it, turned, and dropped himself onto the cloth. Legs bent, he threw his forearms around his knees and grabbed his right wrist with his left hand. He looked out at the water, as though the waves were giving him the courage for his next subject.

"I was really hoping I'd run into you again."

"It must be fate."

"What do you do for a living Carrie?"

"Oh, I'm in banking – personal finance. Pretty boring really."

He nodded his head slightly.

"I was hoping you might be in counseling or psychology. My wife… Donna… she's going through some changes."

"Women do that. Is she your age? In her forties?"

He glanced at Harper with a quick smile.

"Ouch. I'd hoped you'd think I was closer to your age."

He raised his glasses into his wet locks, as though, with such a solemn and important subject on the table, he didn't want to hide his eyes. The move wasn't lost on Harper's cynicism. She could see his pupils shrink from the blinding sun.

"It's not that. She's… I'm afraid she's becoming a shut-in. She doesn't want to be around people. She fears it. This situation, nobody within twenty-five feet, she'd be uncomfortable."

"What's the term for that, demophobe?"

"Right. Well, ochlophobia is the proper term for crowds. Ran us out of New York. But I thought it would be better here."

"If you don't mind, Tyler, why are you telling me all this?"

"I don't know. I can't talk about it with the people I work with. Maybe because you're essentially a stranger. Because you're leaving. I guess I just need to say it out loud."

"Ok. I get it. Has it changed things… inside your home?"

"No. That's all the same for the most part. But we have a daughter who will graduate next spring. I don't know if Donna will even be able to attend her commencement. It's gotten bad lately."

"Do you think the murders have made it worse?"

"It's possible."

"Were you in town when all the murders took place? Could she have felt, I don't know, unprotected?"

"Yes, I was," Bishop said, shaking his head. No wait. Actually, the second murder I was in Columbia. I went to a political rally for that schmuck hoping to replace Lindsey Graham in the Senate. Waste of time. But that one was the shocker – Barbara Robinson."

"I heard about that one."

"That's when we knew the first one wasn't random. People were freaking out. Donna was a mess, wanting to move. You can't trust him sticking to the type of victim he's choosing. Donna didn't want to let Erin out of the house. I remember I talked to her on the phone for half the trip home that Saturday. At least an hour and a half."

Stowe felt relieved Tyler Bishop absolved himself with an easily-verifiable alibi. He was headstrong and a bit arrogant – probably hitting on her and willing to cheat on his wife - but not a killer. Harper's focus immediately returned to Janson and

Wainwright. The conversation went cold. She realized she needed to respond and searched for a pacifying repost in regards to his wife's condition. Bishop abruptly shifted gears.

"I can't believe you're a banker, Carrie," he said, glancing her way again, this time without his sunglasses, stealing a not-so-discreet eye-full of her body. "I would have guessed physical therapy or fitness expert. You look like you could kick the shit out of everyone on this beach."

Having had enough she stood, stuffed her book in with her cover in the seat's pocket, folded the chair, then patted him on his shoulder as she began to walk away.

"Yeah? Remember that. I hope your wife starts feeling better soon."

CHAPTER 36

If apprehension was the animal Harper Stowe most wore on her sleeve, the unknown vehicle in her driveway upon her return home to Slack Trimmer Road – an older-model, silver Buick with a hunter-green replacement hood – became an elephant. She considered driving past, turning around and leaving, but her cop's instincts wouldn't allow it. She pulled in beside the car and immediately recognized the driver to be the preacher, Rev. William Janson. He was sitting behind the steering wheel reading a book she presumed to be the Bible.

She thought back to the church visit, from which she was only four hours removed. *I gave him the golden ticket – the visitor's card. Filled out nicely, address and all. Thank God I put my cover back on before I drove home – after that parting shot on Tyler Bishop. That would not have looked appropriate. What's he want already? Rhetorical question. You know what he wants.*

She looked at Janson and smiled – threw up her hand in a wave. He reciprocated then turned as he opened his door. As he stepped from his car, Harper grabbed her Kimber 1911 out of the middle console and placed it in the only place she thought it wouldn't be detected due to the length and moderate looseness of her cover, the front of her bikini bottoms. She exited her car quickly, meeting him at the front bumper of his.

Her mind was a weapons flurry. *I am not letting him in the house – no matter how rude. Where did I leave my primary? I spent the night at the condo with Rhett – after meeting Mom there. It must be back in the bedroom – I don't think I left it on the table. But he's NOT going in anyway.*

She instinctively twisted her lower back a little, stretching. She dropped both hands, extended her fingers, made fists, and released. Without even realizing it, she positioned herself in front of him with her left foot forward – from the waist down she was in fighter's stance.

"Ms. Stowers, How are you?" He reached his hand out to shake. Stowe took it, and shook his, but then pulled hers away quickly as he was beginning to reach with his left to again pet hers.

"I'm fine, Reverend Janson."

"Please, call me William. We're not as formal as it might have seemed. It looks as though you were able to relax a little at the beach."

"Yes, well, I needed it. I was able to do some thinking," Harper said. *Where do I go?* "And… I have some friends just up the road who are on their way. They're going to help me try to get this place in shape – paint a little. It's unfit for visitors. I'm embarrassed to say I'm still living out of boxes."

Janson looked down at Stowe and smiled ever-so-slightly. A body-gesture expert would suggest he didn't believe her. He then glanced at the porch and front door.

"Those two chairs will do nicely," he said. "I love the heat."

"Ok. That's fine then." They walked the curved sidewalk to the two wooden, slanted chairs - painted canary yellow to match the door.

"I know this is a quick turnaround, but I just didn't like the way our meeting ended today. I felt I shorted you on some proper guidance."

"It was fine. You gave me a lot to think about. Well, between your sermon and after."

"Before we were interrupted by Mr. Wainwright, I was going to lead you in prayer. I thought about the situation out here a great deal after you left. Have any support groups been started?"

"I don't think so. I haven't heard of any."

Diagram of Death

"Well, Carrie, is it ok if I call you Carrie? A support group would give everyone – other women in the area - an opportunity to discuss their feelings and concerns. Maybe form a little coalition for activism… or at least awareness. I'm amazed the last murder could even happen. This place should have felt like a ghost town – or a police state. Anyway, it could be very helpful. I'd be willing to sit in. You certainly shouldn't leave the Lord out of it."

"I agree. It's not a bad idea. I'm sure it would be helpful to other local women as well."

"Here's my card. It has all my numbers on it. Let me know if I can be of any service."

"I don't know where I'd start," Harper said, taking his card. "I know very few people here."

"Just think about it. I'm sure the Ocean Oaks board could give you some direction as well. Maybe your friends that are coming would have a few ideas. If you knew more people around you, maybe it would make you feel a little safer."

"It's true."

"If you'll allow me, I'd like to pray with you. And then I'll take my leave. But I hope I hear from you, Carrie. You're a ray of sunshine in this abysmal situation."

Both Stowe and Janson leaned forward and bowed their heads, each clasping their own hands.

Across the street, in the heavy shrubbery between two houses, James Wainwright lowered into a crouch. His blackened eyes narrowed. He viciously slammed to the ground a rock he'd picked up while approaching his spying position. He began writhing his hands, though he was as unaware of doing it. He was in need of an outlet, like a pressure cooker with no jiggler to release its steam.

CHAPTER 37

The rhythm of the beach bike on the trails is hypnotic. Riding allows me to drift away into my own world. But it's not quiet, per se. The pedals squeak. The chain clicks. The fat tires on the asphalt hum constantly. There are disruptions... bumps in the road. Hitting the brakes for people, passing other bikers with children in tow, wayward children on their own bikes, the occasional tree the trail was actually built around – some close enough to catch your hand grip. But it can be a symphony when you're feeling good, when you're at your top speed, making the rounds. Eight points are easily reached – less than three minutes apart. They've been there in my head for years. Points on the map: Royal Fern, Barnhart Cove Road, Lighthouse Lane, Twin Pines Road, Painters Woods Court, North Live Oak, Turtle Lane Drive, South Beach Lagoon Road. They've been marked on paper, electronically, and hardwired in my mind. I can circle the perimeter from site to site, or I can cross to each point, back and forth. That takes an extra minute, some occasional cut-throughs from one street to the next. Twin Pines Road, North Live Oak, Painters Woods Court, Royal Fern, Lighthouse Lane, Turtle Lane Drive, Barnhart Cove Road, South Beach Lagoon Drive. But it's all an imprint. Call it a blue print for the victims. I couldn't leave it now – unfinished - if I wanted to.

  So Jansen couldn't wait long, the son-of-a-bitch. He'd been sitting there nearly an hour when Carrie showed. I think his interest goes a little deeper than prayer. The girl is amazing. No way he was getting in her house. I've got a plan for him now. Simple in its execution. But I'll have to speed up my deal. I won't be able to wait till Friday-week. There's too much at stake now. So gullible, they're even trusting my

Diagram of Death

timetable. Back to sleep for twelve days. This'll throw 'em all for a loop. In fact, I believe I found number six. Just stretched out reading on her pool deck, blind to the traffic, music playing loudly, good greenery for cover, all alone. Much easier than taking down a runner. That's another good thing about the beach bike. It's ok for a man to have a basket to carry around the essential tools - knife, tape, rope – wrapped in a friendly beach towel.

CHAPTER 38

The call came in earlier than all the others – 6:25 p.m. Sunday evening, but daylight. Solid daylight. So brazen – to everyone privy to the initial call, which was few. It was like a low blow slipped in by a cunning prize fighter. Female, mouth taped, murdered, presumed raped – undoubtedly raped. Naked from the waist down, only twenty feet from the rental home's back exit, the sliding glass doors leading to the pool. She was found just off the painted concrete and brick deck in the grass. Tricia Newcomb, 33, blond, mother of one, from Cincinnati, Ohio. Discovered by her husband, Vince, who had been just outside Ocean Oaks' gates at the Harris Teeter, stocking up on groceries for the start of their vacation week. The daughter, three years old, napping inside, never awoke until the father returned.

"Is it possible we have a copycat?" Lester Beaumont asked. Harper Stowe, the three FBI agents, and a small crew from the Coroner's Office were the only other people at the scene. The murder was so unexpected. So caught off guard were the Ocean Oaks' residents, the Hilton Head Police Department was able to shut down the street with a couple of city waterworks trucks, and establish a perimeter around the house on Turtle Lane Drive. The extra space allowed Stowe access without fear of being seen by media or curiosity seekers – her undercover status still intact.

"We'll know soon enough," Stowe answered. "Give us a quick turnaround?"

"You bet, Harper," said Assistant Coroner Cindy Lewis. "Have to extract a sample here first."

"Well, one thing seems to be missing. Unless they find it somewhere on her body... no fake clues," said Paul Clark, leader of the FBI group. "There's nothing here – looks like pure impulse."

"Or a trigger," Beaumont said. "What would trigger a serial killer who's been on a set time schedule? To go – what – twelve days early."

The group went silent. Thoughts of her suspects and the peculiar day they provided raced through Harper's head.

Janson. Was that an act? Did he want me in the house or the back yard to rape me? Could his failure be the trigger? What if Tyler Bishop lied – to everybody? He could have lied to his boss and his wife, checked into a local hotel, watched that political rally on Facebook live, or seen news clips of the highlights, called what's his name, Ford Pennington – he'd already have his number - and say "Hey I'm sick, I couldn't make it but..." and ask his questions over the phone, put a Columbia, SC, dateline on the story he would send to his editors by email, drive into Ocean Oaks for a run, get his rocks off on Barbara Robinson, sleep like a baby in the hotel, talk to his wife on the cell phone the next day for an hour and a half, bitching about the Saturday traffic on I-95, then lie to me about the whole damn thing. That's not thin. Then I piss him off at the end of our little beach session so he goes off looking for someone. If it's big Wainwright, I don't know. He seemed perturbed at church. Maybe he saw me with Bishop... or, no, Janson. Or both. Can a serial get jealous?

"Look at this. Bicycle tire track," said FBI Agent Arline Thorn, standing just off the front corner of the pool deck. The imprint was in fine, sandy, dirt. "Looks like he might have just quietly leaned the bike up against the house. Snuck up on her. Don't see any footprints."

"That's different," Stowe said. "But the bike may not necessarily be his. The track could have been here before – from the last renters. It hasn't rained for days. Still, we should get a crew out there asking people if they saw anyone suspicious riding."

"Right. I'll make that call, Harper," Beaumont said.

"Well, damn, I don't believe it. This is new," Cindy Lewis said, putting what looked like a turkey baster in a plastic bag. "No semen. He either used a condom or didn't finish."

"Or he was interrupted," said Arline Thorn. "And if he was interrupted, would he have slit her throat?"

"He had to slit her throat," Stowe said. "Eliminate the witness."

The group again went silent, this time collectively pondering many scenarios, including the likelihood of putting a condom on under these extraordinary conditions.

"I can determine if he used one back at the lab," Lewis said.

"Maybe he put it on first. Before the abduction. She was probably right here in this chair," Stowe said. "It would have been easier than the normal take down."

"If it *was* possible for this guy to get a condom on, it could be his fake clue," Paul Clark said. "He knows it would throw us into uncharted waters."

"Confusing the hell out of us is what it's doing," added Agent Jeff Hudson. "And I agree with you, Paul. What better way to throw us off? Hell of a lot better than leaving part of a workboot shoestring or an Asian pube. This gives anonymity. You can't even say for sure if it *is* a fake clue."

"Because it might be somebody new," Stowe said. "Or it could be the perfect way for the husband to off the wife. The condom being their birth control with the baby in the house. She could have seen the sex coming, but not the blade."

"It's a possibility, but I doubt it," said Clark. "He seems pretty shook."

She turned a map around to the group with six dots marking the murder sites.

Diagram of Death

"I came up with this yesterday. Well, a friend did," Stowe said, glancing at Beaumont. She touched her pen to one dot. "Here is today's murder. Does anybody see what we may have come up with?"

"I think I do," Beaumont said. "Is it a Navy cluster?"

"I believe so."

"That means there are only two more spots, right?" Beaumont said.

"Possibly. If this is what he's really doing," Stowe said.

"Only two more murders?" Cindy Lewis asked.

"Well, we don't want any more murders obviously," Stowe said. "But if we could narrow down his attack sites to these two remaining areas, it would certainly help with surveillance. Even if we have to start doing it around the clock."

Beaumont stepped close to Harper.

"Do you know more than you're telling us?"

"We need to talk, Boss."

CHAPTER 39

One of Reverend William Janson's passions as a teenager in Pennsylvania was baseball. Growing up in Lancaster County his loyalties and devotion extended to the Philadelphia Phillies. When James Wainwright walked into Janson's office at Island Baptist Church mid-Monday morning, he found a slugger's paradise of autographed black-and-white action photos of Mike Schmidt, Steve Carlton, Pete Rose, Greg Luzinski Manny Trillo, Lonnie Smith, and Tug McGraw.

"Good time for that club," Wainwright said. "Are you from Philly?"

"Just west. Yeah, my Cardiac Kids."

"They won the World Series in what, '79?"

"No, that was the Pirates. It was 1980 when we won our first Series."

"Oh, that's right. See a lot of games?"

"Some when I was a kid. My dad took me a few times," Janson said. "I saw more around that time – when my buddies and I could drive ourselves."

"Sounds like good times. Did you play too?"

"We played. But between the long winters and our devotion to the Lord, it wasn't easy to rise above the pack," Janson said, glancing from Wainwright to the photos then back again. "Your visit is an interesting surprise. To what do I owe the pleasure?"

"Well, Rev. Janson, I have a big favor to ask. I probably should have mentioned it yesterday, but in truth I didn't think of it."

"I see. Please sit down. What can I do for you?"

"Well, this is kind of embarrassing, but I'm sure you've heard it all," Wainwright said. He removed his sunglasses,

Diagram of Death

revealing his still-blackened eyes. "I'm taking my boat out to open water to spread Victoria's ashes. Before, in my mind, I'd presumed I would want to be alone. But, well, I've never been an overly-devout person – like she was. I'm feeling now, to do her life justice and to respect the Atlantic, I need, a more spiritual person – maybe, I don't know, I just don't want to do it alone. Could you maybe come out with me and say a prayer when I commit her remains?"

"And you are doing this when?"

"Right now."

"Oh. Oh, goodness. I…"

"I knew it was a longshot – and an imposition - but I'm feeling this *need* for closure with her. I know you didn't know her, but she loved it here… before she kind of slid. I'd hoped you'd be free. We could also talk about a new smart TV and a video system for the church kids. Seventy-inch?"

"It's just that I have this paperwork and deposit to tend to."

"Oh, couldn't that wait a couple hours? Please. I packed a lunch. It's a beautiful day. … I can have you back by one o'clock - if necessary. If you change your mind out there and aren't in too big a hurry, I've got some fishing poles on board. We could get to know each other a little better."

An hour later, Wainwright throttled down on his newly-purchased, used 34-foot cabin cruiser, soon to be christened "*Last Chance.*" Having negotiated Broad Creek and the channel, it was now pointed dead east.

"I won't take us out too far. Just enough to get us through the traffic," Wainwright said loudly over the high-pitched roar of the engine, the swish of the boat cutting through the water, and the cooling wind. "How about a soda?"

"You get out here a lot?" Janson asked, seated facing Wainwright, who stood behind the Captain's chair with his left foot in the seat, leaning his left arm on his left knee, as his right hand drove the boat. Janson popped open a can of Pepsi and took a sip.

"Look at this," Wainwright said. His hand opened to the space between the chair and the wheel. "I'm going to have this modified – farther back, bigger, and higher. I couldn't sit here if I tried. Anyway, no, I don't. But I plan to much more now. You're always welcome to join me."

"Thanks. I appreciate it."

The conversation died briefly as Wainwright tested the engine's capacity. The craft was cruising at thirty-five miles per hour.

"What's with the two anchors?" Janson asked. Both a well-worn, rusted anchor, and an obviously newer one set on either end of the open area of the deck, each with yards of synthetic rope attached.

"It's just a good idea out here, once you get your bow-anchor secured, throw the second one out off the stern. That way if you're fishing, the boat doesn't continually turn into your lines."

"That's pretty smart."

"Yeah, well, it's a passion of mine. Victoria never really wanted to be out here – even though she knew I loved it. I'm retired Navy. But, unfortunately, I had to keep an eye on her most of the time."

"We make sacrifices for the ones we love. That's too bad, though," Janson said. "I don't want to pry, but having knowledge helps with prevention. And if I'm going to say a prayer…"

"It was pills and alcohol. Took hold while she was still working. Eventually, she couldn't function at that capacity."

Wainwright pushed the throttle forward a quarter of its arc, the boat slowing to half its speed, the engine noise decreasing accordingly. The vessel was already so far out only the tree tops of the island were still visible. A feeling of isolation overtook Janson.

"She became an alcoholic. I tried to get her help, but she gave up on me."

"How much farther?"

"Oh, just a bit more. Nice isn't it?"

Janson didn't answer.

"Part of the 'puzzle of you' came together for me in your office," Wainwright said, making air quotes as he spoke, his tone sarcastic. "When I realized you're a die-hard Phillies fan. Baltimore's just as close to Lancaster as Philly, were you not an Orioles fan, too?

"They were great early – if you cared to follow the impure American League. How did you know I was from…"

"And the Pirates – just a little farther west?"

"A little too loud and colorful for my taste," Janson said. He was distracted now, wondering when he told Wainwright exactly where he was from. "Schmidt hit his five-hundredth homer off those bastards."

Wainwright laughed.

"What do you think of Lonnie Smith? He was on your wall – a rookie in '80, right?"

"Hit three-thirty-nine in a hundred games that year. Could have been one of the greats. Wasn't his fault they traded him to the Cardinals – the only team better than us in '82 – won it all. Stupid. Then he wins again for the Royals in '85 – against the Cardinals. Three rings. Drugs got him, though. Wouldn't have happened if he'd stayed with Philly."

"Uh-huh."

Wainwright pushed the throttle into neutral and turned the engine off.

"The Phillies hit a rough patch in '95, right? After coming out like gangbusters?"

"Yeah, 37-18 start. Then they went 3-16 in early July, lost eight in a row in August."

Wainwright studied him, slowly nodding his head.

"You were in the Navy then weren't you?"

"Uh, yeah, I was. How did you…"

"I did some checking on you, Preacher. I have some good sources in Navy personnel."

Janson stood but held firm, his eyes narrowing.

"That's when you raped the girl, right? Was she your first? And all because the Phillies set you off that August?"

"Start this damned boat and get it headed back to shore," Janson said, his arm jerked violently as he pointed at the ignition key. Wainwright's tone remained calm.

"I assume if the Navy knows about two, there's a lot more. You just didn't have the guts to shut'em up, did you. Did you."

"I said start this boat," Janson said. He closed the eight feet between himself and Wainwright quickly. Janson pulled his right fist back to punch.

Wainwright faced him, showing Janson the blade in his right hand.

Janson stopped, relaxed his right arm but raised his left fist, his eyes wide. He had avoided confrontation his whole life, instead using his strength to overwhelm the women he'd raped.

Who is this man? What in the hell have I got myself into? Lord, please be with me. Help me.

"Did you intend to rape Carrie Stowers?"

Janson's expression turned from fear to confusion.

"No. I just wanted to help her. I've put all that behind me."

"Don't lie to me, you fuckin' coward. I can tell it's still in you."

Diagram of Death

"No. It's not. It's been like twelve years since I..." Janson said, retreating from his incriminating past. "I thought maybe... maybe I'd get to a point where I could ask her out."

"Ask her out?" Wainwright said. He laughed. "Right."

With a quick thrust of his hand, Wainwright jammed the five-inch blade between Janson's third and fourth ribs, puncturing his lung. Janson's eyes widened. Wainwright watched him. A slight smile upturned. As Janson's legs became untrue, Wainwright shoved him back into his seat.

"That's bullshit, Preacher. Admit to me you were going to rape her. If you do, I'll get you to a hospital."

Oh my God. Lord, help me with this psycho. I don't want to die. Just tell him the truth.

"Ok, I was – at first. If I could get her inside, I was. She's perfect. I couldn't help myself. But as we talked..."

"Sorry, Preacher. She's out of your league."

Wainwright stepped to his left and with irreverence to his previous statement again put the knife in Janson, this time with an underhanded motion to Janson's right side. Janson tried to block the move, but he was sluggish. Wainwright left the blade in.

Forgive me for my past, Lord. For what I have done. Forgive me of my trespasses.

Wainwright reached for the rope tied to the older anchor.

"She's part of my plan, Bill. Is it Bill? Preacher. I couldn't let her be a part of yours. You should *not* have gotten in my way."

As Wainwright spoke, he was already down on one knee wrapping the rope around Janson's ankles, then between his legs and the ankle bindings a few times for good measure. He then tied it off to Janson's belt after pulling it under and through. Janson exhaled slowly, which gave way to the gurgle of rising blood. He spoke in a whisper.

"You're the serial?

"I'm afraid so."

"And... your wife?" Janson whispered.

"Means to an end. Mind if I stand you up?"

Wainwright pulled Janson upward by his pants and belt at the sides of his waist until he was leaning against the rail. With the knife handle suspended horizontally he shoved Janson backwards over the side of the boat. He squatted, picked up the anchor, stood, and threw it in just seconds later.

Wainwright looked around. No one in sight. He examined the palms, then the backs of his hands. He did the same with his forearms, and then his clothes. He bent and studied Janson's seat and the boat wall and floor behind and below it. All clean.

"Amazing. Not a drop of blood anywhere."

He walked to the starboard side of the boat and looked over. No sign of anything or anybody. He started the engine, pulled the throttle down and turned south.

"Think I'll do a little fishing before I head in," he said as the wind began to blow strong through his hair. He inhaled the salt air through his nose and deeply into his lungs.

"Oh, I almost forgot."

Wainwright walked to a bag sitting on the bench seat around the boat's stern. From it emerged a silver-plated urn. With no words or thought of ceremony, he tossed the entire contraption, lid tight, into the Atlantic Ocean. It sank quickly through the boat's wake, and out of sight forever.

CHAPTER 40

"I think I'm being used by two of my suspects in a little game of tug-a-war," Harper Stowe said. "And my third suspect – married, of course - was trying to hit on me yesterday at the beach."

It was Monday morning. The investigative team and Chief Lester Beaumont were back at Hilton Head Police Department headquarters. A briefing of the Tricia Newcomb autopsy findings was forthcoming.

"You had verbal contact with all three of your suspects?" asked Agent Paul Clark.

"I did. It's been an interesting couple days – wedged between the two murders," Stowe said.

"Pete Waters told me you had him digging deeper into William Janson's background over the weekend." Beaumont said. "Is that part of this?"

"Yes it is," Stowe said. "He was accused of raping two women. One in Philadelphia, the other in North Carolina, but the charges were dropped. So he doesn't register - wasn't on our sex offender's list."

"Well - that's hot," said Clark. "We should have been on him all damned day yesterday. Might be one less dead body."

"Hold on now. And I'm not saying we shouldn't. Just hear me out," Stowe said. "I go to his church yesterday morning – Island Baptist. And who shows up there but James Wainwright – the husband from the drowning Friday night. He's making this big donation in his wife's name - *and* her obituary was in the Sunday paper. I mean, this guy had a busy Saturday for a widower twelve hours into his grieving."

Stowe told the group her story about Wainwright fixating on her during the service, how he interrupted her meeting with Janson afterwards in domineering fashion, and how Janson then showed up at her home later Sunday."

"What the hell did he say he wanted – other than to tie you up," Clark said.

"This was his reaction to my ruse at church – before Wainwright stepped in. We sat on the front porch and talked about a support group," Stowe said. "We prayed, and then he left on his own. It was creepy, but I never felt threatened at all."

Beaumont had begun to fidget in his seat as she spoke. When she followed with the Tyler Bishop beach exchange, he stood and paced the floor, his fatherly affection for Stowe subconsciously outweighing his presence and position as commanding officer.

"So the trigger I mentioned at the crime scene last night could have been you – or the unsub's reaction to one of your conversations?" Beaumont asked.

"A most beautiful trigger," said Agent Arline Thorn, looking directly at Harper. "I can buy into that."

The group transcended into silence, considering the hypothesis put forth.

"It's… a possibility," Stowe said.

"But for which one?" asked Beaumont.

"Studies are against it being Janson," said Clark. "It's a big leap for a rapist to become a murderer if they weren't one already."

"He seemed to me to be a man's man, despite his profession," Beaumont said, recalling the town meeting the previous Thursday. "I understand what you're saying though. It takes a different breed to use the knife the way this perp has."

"Well, I thought at first Bishop had given me a solid alibi for the Friday of the second murder. Said he was out of town - in Columbia at a political rally. Filed a story from there. I bought it at first, but I got to thinking about it – he easily could have pulled all that off from here. I think he was lying. I'm going to call the candidate. See if he remembers."

"We should send some crews to check hotel tapes," Beaumont offered.

"That's eight weeks back. Even digital surveillance is kept only thirty days. A few days more if motion detectors aren't set off much," said Stowe. "Waste of man hours."

Assistant Coroner Cindy Lewis entered the office, just as Stowe was finishing her Bishop update.

"What did you find out?" Beaumont asked.

"There's no doubt that a prophylactic was used," Lewis said. "Definite traces of the lubricant. So, there's not a single shred of evidence pointing in any individual's direction on this one."

"And no condoms were used in the other five murders," Stowe said.

"He just keeps gaining ground," Clark said. "If it was our guy and he's discarded his schedule – he could be out there right now searching for his next vic."

"I'm afraid I have some more bad news, Harper," Lewis said. "We found no D.N.A. under the fingernails of Victoria Wainwright. If there ever was any, it apparently was thrashed out – left in the pool. The water and chlorine washed her clean."

"Or he could have been lying about Victoria scratching him," Stowe said. "Could be the reason Jessica Boyd was dragged to the edge of the water."

"So you like Wainwright for this thing?" Clark asked Stowe.

"I haven't seen the proof yet. But I just don't believe this drowning scenario," she said. She looked at Beaumont. "I think we need to get tails on all three of these guys immediately."

"Oh, shit. This is all we need," Beaumont said, holding up his phone. "Text from the front desk. Mayor Sneed just led twelve bounty hunters into the lobby."

Diagram of Death

CHAPTER 41

The first time I saw it, I laughed right out loud. Nearly spilled my celebratory Fat Tire. Really? Right now? A commercial promoting Hilton Head Island? If that's not bringing the lambs to the slaughter – the sheep to the wolf – the pie to the party - I don't know what is. I think maybe I'll send a thank-you letter to the township administration, or the Chamber of Commerce. Maybe to the Mayor himself. Mayor Sneed, I believe. What's his game? Appeasement? I could put it in a nice thank-you card: "I'd like to offer my sincere gratitude for keeping the numbers up. The rental houses filled. The trails occupied." Though I have but one more to find before I... meet up with Carrie Stowers. Of course, that'll be a big surprise. For all they know, I'm shootin' for a hundred. Seems like their money could be better spent elsewhere. But, what do I know.

I will say this. I got a kick out of disposing of the preacher. Wasn't much to it, really. I thought he'd put up a little fight. So gullible. What did he think I was taking him out there for, sell him baseball cards? Did he really believe that Victoria's ashes bullshit? A rapist posing as a preacher. What's the world coming to? Almost as bad as a priest. Thought he could lay claim to Carrie. Thought he could woo her? My girl? I've got to admit, that's the maddest I've been for a long time. Enough to get me off my schedule. Picking an off-day made that conquest all easier as well. She was just lying there alone, couldn't hear, wasn't looking, never saw the fight coming - a choice after my own heart.

I won't rush this next one – no reason to. I want to reestablish a lay of the land – see what kind of net the cops are casting. I'll keep my eye on Carrie. But for now, think I'll enjoy a day or two on the water. I've got my Dish Tailgater

Andrew Spradling

sitting on my roof and a 50-inch on a swivel I can see from my deck. Satellite T.V. at sea, fresh fish, a cooler full, and Carrie Stowers on my horizon. What could be better? Maybe as the sun sets, I'll write the mayor to thank him.

CHAPTER 42

"I see some familiar faces among you runners," Chief Lester Beaumont said, addressing a room full of bounty hunters in the Hilton Head Police Department briefing room. "Good men who have helped us in the past, and who have been well-rewarded for their service. However, there is little I can tell you right now; likely a white, middle-aged male, perhaps posing as a runner or a cyclist. This latest murder – if it was our perp - puts an end to schedules and timetables. The best advice I can give you is to be out there with your eyes peeled for suspicious characters. Be ready to intercede at the drop of a hat. There's no skip-tracing technology or people searches to be utilized here. We know nothing. Less than nothing.

"Because of what I just told you, since your bond agency paperwork has been properly filed with the Department of Insurance, here represented by Theo Lopez with Mayor Sneed, there's just one last thing we'll ask of you. Because of all the extra law enforcement in the area, we are requesting you line up for headshots."

A collective groan arose from the group. Beaumont smiled, but remained all business.

"We're providing sheets with all your names, numbers, and faces to be carried at all times by LEOs," Beaumont continued. "I'm sure you don't want to be mistaken for the unsub – might get you shot. Let me stress one thing: this Boyd-reward might tempt you to go a little rogue, a little cutthroat. Don't let it. Don't get greedy. Act responsibly and in cooperation with all agencies represented or there will be hell to pay boys. I mean that. Any questions? No? Good luck, and, the camera is just through that door to your right."

A Beaumont hand gesture got the group moving in a begrudging shuffle towards the area in the next room, a coalition of lottery-seekers. One of the bounty hunters lingered. Chuck Breckenridge, 6-foot-3, thin, early fifties, short brown hair, lined, tan face, a former Special Forces Marine and a veteran bail bondsman of over twenty years. He turned his back to the exiting group as Beaumont approached him.

"Whatta' you have for me?"

"You remember Harper Stowe don't you?"

"You kiddin'? Does a Gator bite?"

"I'm giving you two names and two areas – so you can watch her back. She's undercover… short, blond hair now. Goes by Carrie Stowers. Chances are this will bring you closer to the perp than anything else you can do. We think she's caught this guy's eye, whichever one it is."

Beaumont discretely pulled a folded slip of paper from his trousers pocket and then shook Breckenridge's hand, passing it over to him.

"There should be tails on these guys by dinner so you may want to focus on Harper. I put her address on there as well – but she runs miles and miles every day trying to draw him in."

"Oh hell."

Beaumont smiled.

"I think you can handle it. Since you're doing me a special favor I won't take my normal cut – just five."

"Such a caring boss. Five percent of a hundred grand is pretty good for doing nothing – plus whatever the FBI has scraped together to throw in."

"It's not for doing nothing – and you've done quite well for yourself on – what now – a dozen times on the inside track?"

Breckenridge gave a condescending smirk.

Diagram of Death

"So, you gonna tell her? She's damn good. I don't want her doubling back on me. I fear her more than this loose butcher – she'll be on the trigger."

Beaumont went silent in thought, staring at a high corner of the room to his right.

"For now, no."

"That's gonna piss her off."

"You just hang back. It's like a jungle in there. You'll be well at home."

"So, what's with the areas then?"

"Oh, you'll love this. We think the guy might be completing the eight points of a Navy cluster."

"Another flipped-out blue boy. Jesus, what is it with you guys, Beaumont?"

"I don't know, Chuck. You tell me."

"Got to be the confined spaces," Breckenridge said, walking away to join his comrades in the picture line. "I know it would irk the shit out of me."

CHAPTER 43

Harper Stowe was now depending on her colleagues more than ever - and she was overwrought with distrust. When the meeting broke, three plain-clothes teams of six were assembled and assigned to pick up and stay on the trail of Tyler Bishop, Rev. William Janson, and James Wainwright. This blanket, around-the-clock surveillance, along with a few dozen other law-enforcement officers continually dispatched and moving about Ocean Oaks, twelve lurking bounty hunters, an escalation of public awareness, made another murder seem impossible.

Still, the perp's murder of Jessica Boyd on Friday, with a battalion of badged-marauders on high-alert – and with her running alone through each zone as bait - made Harper remember that anything was still possible. The juxtaposition between a potentially violent death or her finest hour caused a surge of conflicting emotion.

Fight it off and stay focused.

With these ops launched and underway Stowe took an hour to attempt to confirm or disprove Bishop's alibi, a Ford Pennington political rally, the weekend of the second murder.

Ford Pennington's strong suit as a senatorial candidate was his media presence. A youthful-looking 57-year-old former Air Force Captain, Pennington was a corporate lawyer savvy enough to keep most of his business dealings behind a closed curtain and out of public scrutiny. But he would, on occasion, wisely make announcements when his business benefited the public good.

Connecting with this former Gamecock, who had spent much of his Air Force career at the now-closed Myrtle Beach Air Force base, wasn't difficult.

Diagram of Death

"I know Tyler Bishop, Detective, yes," Pennington said, via telephone. "He's done his best to rattle my cage a number of times. I've done nothing to the man, but every time he mentions me it's as if I murdered his dog or something. Do you know him?"

"Yes. Well, I've spoken with him a few times."

"I don't know why Ray Finney felt the need to bring some damned Yankee down here to get involved in our politics. A disgrace is what it is."

"I appreciate your position, Mr. Pennington, but I have a specific question about Bishop I'd like for you to try and remember."

"I'll do my best."

"This would have been eight weeks ago on Friday, April 26, in Columbia. A rally you held there. Do you remember that night?"

"Oh, of course I do, Ms. Stowe. A great night. Had hundreds of students and alums straight from Five Points. You know there's a boom going on downtown. Unbelievable energy – near seven thousand people in new housing there now."

"I've heard that. That's great. What about Tyler Bishop. Do you remember him being there?"

"Oh, darlin', takes no thought. No, he was not there. He made such a production about it with Rebecca, my campaign manager. I had to speak with him by phone ten minutes before I was supposed to walk on stage. She said he was quite the prick about it, pardon my vulgarity. I almost blew him off, but his early scathings concerning some of my positions had lightened up a little, so I wanted to stay to the good, you know?"

"Do you remember what time you took the podium?"

"I do indeed – 6:30. We wanted folks loose from happy hour yet with plenty of time to still enjoy the evening. We had a dinner afterwards for contributors."

"Was there anything specific that you talked about?"

"Oh, except for a little bit about being back at USC it was just the same old stuff. Which side of the fence on this issue versus that issue and why. I have to tell you, I get so tired of that part of it. Has no bearing on the job I'll do in Washington."

"Did you – or someone on your staff - read his story the next day?"

"I did. He fudged it – like he was sitting in the front row. He could *seeeee* the sweat," he said, stretching the "see" and imitating the vocal stylings of a southern preacher the entire sentence. Stowe envisioned Pennington with one hand raised and shaking. She laughed.

"What a piece of work," he went on. "I told Rebecca to call about him. I don't know if she did or not. It was a complete misrepresentation. So he had a flu bug or something, why didn't he just bag it? He could have caught me out speaking twenty times since then. Must've been desperate for a column."

"Right. Why indeed."

"Is there something I'm missing, Detective? What's all the hubbub?"

"Just checking whereabouts, like I said," Stowe said.

"Well I know there's more to it than…"

"I would appreciate your confidence in this matter, Captain."

The line went silent temporarily. Pennington appreciated the Mission reference and the fact that Stowe had done her homework. It also took him to a time in which the understanding of implications were highly-important and best not discussed.

Diagram of Death

"No problem, Detective Stowe. If I can ever do anything else for you, just let me know."

"Thanks and good luck in your campaign. I'm a Gamecock too, by the way... ."

"Well, that's good to know. I sensed something great in you. Go 'Cocks!"

Stowe left her office in a rush to share the news with Lester Beaumont. She wanted to inform him, then hustle back to Ocean Oaks for an evening run. With Tricia Newcomb's murder on Sunday breaking the every-other-Friday pattern, each excursion she made was to be announced and monitored, her cell phone a mandated permanent fixture on her for tracking purposes by other LEOs.

She was more determined than ever to bring this man down. And if Bishop had lied about the trip to Columbia, there was at least a chance he was the killer. Why else deceive in such a way?

"There *are* other reasons to lie – at least to the paper – if he's not the killer," Beaumont said. "And of course, he doesn't know you're a cop. He was trying to impress you – pick you up. Would that impress you?"

"Covering a political rally? Not so much. Might... interest me. Not impress."

"We'll just have to check him out. He could be double-dipping somehow, maybe a job interview with another paper, a cooler-air weekend destination, or, of course, maybe a girlfriend. I'll call Judge Prescott and see about getting his phone records subpoenaed. Maybe they'll show something – give us a lead."

"People wouldn't believe the complexities, would they? Of an investigation? It's exhausting. What's happening with the tails?"

"Glad you asked. Bishop is still in his office. We're set to move on that one," Beaumont said. "Wainwright can't be located at the moment."

"Probably flown to Cancun to party."

"Here's the strange one. Janson's car is at the church, but he's nowhere to be found."

"Missing?"

"Looks like a possibility. Or he fled."

CHAPTER 44

    The next twenty-four hours was a smooth desert - as if after a conquering sandstorm. Neither was there water, nor an oasis offering hope. For Harper Stowe, a day of quiet was a relief. Between catching up on reports and delegating assignments she got in three moderate runs from Monday evening to Tuesday afternoon, with not more than a glance from a male passerby. In fact, she sensed a disconnect, or covering of emotion. Cold faces. A lack of friendliness. Personalities like stone.
    Men covering up what, fear? Fear of what, suspicion? A chance of being questioned. Of being apprehended?
    An All-Points-Bulletin had been issued for Rev. William Janson as a person of interest and possible suspect. No information was forthcoming. Reports were in that Tyler Bishop had gone straight home from work Monday evening. He emerged Tuesday at 9:30 a.m. and returned to the newspaper. No word yet on his evening activities. James Wainwright's whereabouts were also still a mystery.
    Stowe had cut her second run short Tuesday to clean up and attend the visitation and memorial of Jessica Boyd. Bennett Boyd remained devastated by the loss of his young wife. The details, as he learned them, added to his misery like extra lashes from a whip.
    He hired Keith Family Funerals to handle the arrangements, and chose the Inn & Club at Bay Harbor for the event's venue. Bennett Boyd gave Keith an open checkbook, no expense too great for the memorial, and the funeral the following morning. Since The Inn & Club was promoted as the number one luxury hotel on Hilton Head Island, it seemed his bill would likely match his hundred-thousand-dollar reward. A

banquet room with floor-to-ceiling glass, stained wood trim, fine tapestry, typically used for weddings and receptions, with views of golf courses, the Atlantic, and the Bay Harbor Lighthouse, was utilized for the mid-week event. Some of his friends in attendance requested dockage for their yachts, and he put Jessica's parents, the Dunlaps, her siblings, and their families in rooms for their three-day stay.

The event was a gut check to the community. Jessica Boyd was thus far the only local victim. All others were from far away areas of the country. Each had been transported home for burial. As the first local ceremony, the media had it on their story rosters. Bennett Boyd was even allowing a few minutes to be videoed for public awareness and as a reminder that his reward for apprehension of the killer was pending.

Stowe attended as Carrie Stowers, a concerned woman from the neighborhood and a fellow runner.

"I'd seen Jessica on the trails many times, Mr. Boyd, I'm so sorry for your loss," she told him. "She was obviously a friendly, wonderful woman. I wish I'd been able to get to know her better."

"I'm sure she felt the same," he said. "So you live here, in Ocean Oaks?"

"Yes. I'm on Slack Trimmer, off of South Beach Drive."

"Please be careful – safe. Jessica's running partner is just over there. You should talk to her – run with her," Boyd said, looking over at Kathy Lantz. Kerri Thompkins, the late-joiner to the running trio, was with her as well.

"The man is the devil. And you resemble Jessica – taller is all. Look at Kathy. He wouldn't have picked her – because her hair is dark. I just – I just don't know what this world is coming to."

"Mr. Boyd…"

Diagram of Death

"Jessica was a fighter. She was all Tae Bo with Billy Blanks before the PX90 stuff was out. I'd get tickled watching her, her tiny body, kicking and shadow boxing. She'd do an hour a day sometimes then run five," he said, his voice growing louder. "I hope she gave that man a fight. I hope she tried to punt his balls through his throat. I know she did."

Stowe glanced around the room. All eyes seemed to be on them as his tirade escalated.

"Well, again, my condolences. It was a pleasure to meet you."

Stowe met and offered sentiments to all of the Dunlaps as well, but her eyes and mind were back to work. Boyd's comments returned her thought-process to James Wainwright.

So, Jessica knew how to throw a punch… what-do-you-know. Then five minutes later there's big James with his black eyes and broken nose and scratched neck. What if he drowned his wife for a cover-up? Knee-jerk reaction to getting his butt whipped. But here I am going from Wainwright to Bishop to Janson to Bishop to Wainwright. Where is the proof I need? And where is Wainwright?"

As she finished with the family, Harper looked around the immense room. It was lined with men she assumed had no business there except to catch a killer. In the clutch that matched her charcoal dress was the folded sheet with the headshots of the bounty hunters. She wanted to speak with Kathy Lantz, but first she needed to slip into the washroom to refresh her memory concerning these "runners" or fugitive recovery agents. To avoid confusion with another possible suspect or suspicious person, or recognize anything else out of whack, she had to have the faces of the bounty hunters down cold. She took one last inconspicuous glance, then retired to the ladies room.

Before she returned, Chuck Breckenridge, who realized she was on to the group, slipped out the side door to the massive, covered porch. If Harper remained at the event, he would continue to watch her through the protection of nightfall and glass. If she departed, he would follow, and then do the same. Watch her through the lonely darkness of nightfall.

CHAPTER 45

Her short drive home from Jessica Boyd's memorial service had Harper Stowe pondering the absurdities of fate, and how, perhaps, a few minutes earlier or later might have made the difference in Jessica living or dying.

If the dog groomers had called for pickup a half-hour earlier, if there hadn't been four pet owners in front of her for the slow retrieval of their animals, if the Friday rush hour hadn't slowed her down at the traffic circles, if she'd stopped at the store for groceries, if she'd been held up at the Ocean Oaks gate, if her mowing service had blocked her side of the garage instead of Bennett's just before she departed, if her running clothes had been in the washer, if she'd just run the beach instead of going to the trails, then maybe, maybe, Jessica Boyd would still be alive. Timing.

It was assumed that the perp had waited in hiding to ambush his victim rather than approach her as a runner, because no law enforcement – including Stowe - had noticed a man jogging alone in the half hour before the murder. But now because of the Tricia Newcomb site, there's the possibility of his also being on a bicycle.

Could he have been riding his bike prior to Jessica Boyd? All the murders maybe? Ditched near the ambush site for a quicker getaway? If Jessica had just run on the beach. Why am I thinking this way? What can it possibly help with this investigation? Every option open Harper.

Stowe had introduced herself to Kathy Lantz as a neighbor but not a runner – she didn't want to have to turn down an invitation to join the group - and learned of the communication mix up that had led to Jessica taking off on her ill-fated solo run.

"It was my fault this happened," Kathy told Stowe and a few others that had gathered around her. Tears streamed down her cheeks. "I just assumed she'd be ready. I didn't wait for her response. It was our routine. Now I have to live with the fact that, not only is she gone, she was upset with me in her last hour."

"You can't think that way," Stowe said. "It's not your fault. Have you watched the news? This is a lifelong serial killer."

"Oh, and not only that. When she drove by and we made eye contact, I could tell she was questioning our start. I knew then she had something to do – I didn't know what. If I'd known she was just picking up Lucinda, we could've waited for her. By then I wasn't even thinking about the damned murderer. I guess because I knew *I'd* be safe."

Kathy Lantz, whoa girl- a little T.M.I. Attention-seeking? Is she one of those who has to be involved in the situation? Has to make it about herself? Look how this affects me?

Something else was on Stowe's mind as she drove. Upon her return to the memorial from the ladies room she knew that one of the bounty hunters – the most distinctive of the group - was gone. His tall, wiry frame, and rough features triggered a sense of déjà vu in her. Yet she couldn't quite place him.

Just after passing through the Ocean Oaks gates her cell phone beeped. Her car's Bluetooth picked it up. Lester Beaumont's voice came through her speakers.

"Harper?"

"What's up, Boss?"

"I just received some new intel. I wanted you to be the first to know."

"What's going on?"

Diagram of Death

"The subpoena on Tyler Bishop's phone records came through. There's a number he's calling quite frequently – not his wife or daughter. Turned out to be a local: single, female, school teacher. He called her five times on April 26th. And the team just followed him to her residence."

"An affair?"

"Looks like it."

"So that would explain his lying about Columbia…"

Stowe leaned her head back on her leather seat's headrest. Her hands were at seven and five on her steering wheel. Defeat seemed to show in the downturned corners of her lips. Night had befallen Ocean Oaks. She slowed her car down. She was having trouble seeing the road.

"Maybe we can start trying to dredge up a witness who saw him there that night – since the guys are just sitting… watching. What else?"

"That's it, kid. Thought you'd want to know. How'd it go at the Boyd memorial?"

"Bennett Boyd told me, and I quote, 'Jessica was a fighter.' All five-feet, one-hundred-pounds of her. You know what that tells me?"

"I think so. Wainwright?"

"We need to find that son-of-a-bitch. Let's talk about it tomorrow."

Stowe turned left on to Slack Trimmer Road. As she approached her house she recognized Rhett Richardson's Envoy sitting in her driveway. It stirred her emotions.

As she put her Mercedes in park, he stepped out of his SUV. She walked to him slowly and all but collapsed into his arms. They embraced, holding each other like long-lost lovers. He'd been gone less than two and a half days. A long minute went by that way. In his arms, holding her tightly, Rhett could almost feel her body asking for his strength. He waited, glad for the positive reception.

When Harper finally broke from him, their lips came together briefly... tenderly.

"I'm so glad to see you."

"So am I, Harper," he whispered. "I could think of nothing but you while I was down there."

"What's your story?"

"Well, I'm back. After Tricia Newcomb Sunday night the BBC wants me here full-time - till this concludes. They even paid ESPN to find a replacement for me in Florida. I'm sorry about what happened – had to be gut-wrenching. I guess it changes everything for you game-plan-wise."

"It does."

They were holding each other gently at mid-arm's length. He took her brevity as a sign the subject was off limits.

"Listen. I've checked back in out at Coligny – at the Marriott. I just wanted to see you for a minute... say hi. Let you know I'm..."

"No, please," Harper said, touching his chest with the palm of her hand. "Stay."

They began walking to her front door, arm-in-arm.

"Ok, I will."

During their embrace, across the street, between two houses and in the cover of darkness, Chuck Breckenridge moved into position. Deeper in the perimeter, James Wainwright surveilled a strange man watching Carrie Stowers and her guest. He became enraged.

CHAPTER 46

The fish were biting: grouper, tuna, threw a little hammerhead shark back. Grilled out there and watched baseball – like Hemingway on "Pilar," I'm a modern "Old Man and the Sea." Except for the big screen. I'm sure Papa at least had a transistor radio. Anyway, drank coffee all morning and beer all day. High living. A steady breeze kept me cool, and my straw hat kept me from burning. The stars overnight were an odyssey of light. Mesmerizing. I felt small... mortal. I didn't want to hit the hammock. My only regret is that Dex, my lab, isn't with me. He died late winter. Near six months now.

So I come home from my first overnight to find my Ocean Oaks world turned upside down. Carrie Stowers has a boyfriend. Well of course she has a boyfriend. How could she not? She's the most attractive woman I've ever seen. Fit. Strong. Beautiful. I can't believe she's not married. But, apparently she's found love. I can tolerate that for the short-term. I guarantee he won't be there when the time comes for me to take care of our business together.

But who is this damned stalker watching her? Why is he watching her? I mean, I understand why he'd want to watch her, get close to her. But what a breach of etiquette. What's his motivation, his intention? Perverts by the barrel. He must be like that conniving preacher. Janson, the Philly cheesesteak. Shark food. If this guy's like the preacher, which he must be, he's gonna die bloody.

CHAPTER 47

The love of a man, or the potential acceptance of it, had been fleeting for Harper Stowe. She came to the force with a steadfast policy of not dating colleagues within the ranks. And police work was her life. There was a real estate developer she'd spent time with when she was still a uniformed patrol officer, but he had an issue with her ever-changing schedule and she began slinging bricks and mortar concerning some of his business practices that skirted the letter of the law. She then heard he'd provided cocaine to two bikini-clad young women on his boat, possibly teenagers, possibly for sexual favors. She never called him back, or accepted one of his calls again. The urge to bust him - versus the acceptance of admitting the rumors were hearsay - was an anvil around her neck for a long while.

A few months later she met a city planner, an engineer, but he was too narrowly focused and yet too "far out" for her gun-slinging pragmatism. But, no more than they saw each other, it took months for her to figure out.

She realized that some men were simply intimidated by her. That's what turned her on about Rhett Richardson. He was not only a confident man, he was a good man, strong, fit, and ruggedly handsome. Other than his occasional twisting of thoughts and words, mostly playfully-prompted by her, he was extremely intelligent. Their Thursday night encounter, the night before she was laying her life on the line, he was wise enough to be tender and gentle with her. She'd since learned he could be animalistic in his lovemaking, as could she now with a partner she yearned for.

When Rhett returned to Ocean Oaks from Florida the night before, Harper was so spent they shared only a bit of

Diagram of Death

conversation before deep sleep overtook her. When she woke refreshed, she knew he would be more stimulating than coffee or juice. Naughty smile on her face, she reached for him and realized, though he was still asleep, he wouldn't object. She took the initiative, and he woke to a vision of loveliness, a pleasure exuded by a gasp, followed by the biting of a lip, her head turned, her eyes closed, her full breasts rising and falling with her arching back and the steady plowing of her hips. He would never forget it, and he would hope and pray for more. She was the honey and milk of his promised land. He was her Eden.

Her enjoyment was far less when she left the Slack Trimmer Road house for a run on the trails. There was too much at stake now – administratively, physically, and mentally. She had to be completely ready for an attack and she was confident that she was, but that added a level of tension to what had been fluent art.

Her cell phone had to be with her at all times as two dozen colleagues monitored her movement through the Ocean Oaks zones. All of her senses were attuned to her surroundings. There were wide-open, danger-free areas where the trails were parallel to roads and water, but along the secluded paths crossing the island, every dozen strides were wrought with life-threatening ambush points.

Typically, her morning runs were shorter and less intense than her evening outings. The first five murders had occurred at dusk, only the last was a bit earlier, between 6 and 6:30 p.m. She needed to be razor sharp then, with maximum energy.

But on this Wednesday morning, Harper had an acute sense that she was being followed. In the turns, she could inconspicuously identify the people behind her using her peripheral vision. There was a man and woman immediately to her rear, but behind them, a male – all alone – followed, some twenty strides behind the couple.

I can't make out the guy's age with the beard, sunglasses, and ball cap. And shirtless. In shape, that's for sure. I could turn left up here towards the Barnhart Ruins and see if he follows. Or in a quarter mile I can turn left to Bay Harbor, or right, back to South Beach – see what he does.

No sooner did she have the thought, the couple veered left to the Barnhart Ruins area. Before, Harper could only hear her own and the couples' shoes touching the pavement. Now she could hear the man's footsteps as well, and his cadence was decidedly faster and getting louder.

It was decision time. Two hundred-fifty yards to make her choice. She increased her own pace, but his was still quicker.

I'll have to slow to make a turn – that's not the issue. It's open there. By the main road. In this last 100 yards, he could think he could drag me behind any number of bushes or into isolated thickets. Here's a fairway with no one on it in either direction.

Her sense of vulnerability was suddenly heightened. She had her Kimber 1911 in a Lycra holster no thicker than her sports bra, strapped to her left side. With each stride, under her loosely-fitting tank top, she could feel it graze her left arm.

I'm not going to pull it. Wainwright's probably the guy, not this beard. You don't know that for certain. I can't pull it till I'm attacked anyway. But what am I going to do? Turn left to Bay Harbor, there will be tons of people along the way on bikes, walking to tennis courts. Turn right, he has a thousand options. You want to give him the option, don't you?

At that moment, the morning sun was casting Harper's long shadow towards two o'clock. Suddenly, with fifty yards to go, she could see the end of his dark form nearing her feet.

Diagram of Death

His footsteps were louder. Her senses were tingling. Twenty feet from the stop sign, she made her decision.

Stop and go back. That's logical for a runner. Let him attack, if that's his plan. I can see who he is. Stop at the sign and go back.

Harper did just that. She ran just past the trail's turn, touched the pole of the stop sign, pushed off and headed back from where she'd just come. The man was close enough to, but he did not touch her. Didn't look at her. He looked to his right, and then leaned into the right turn on the trail to South Beach.

Is that the man from last night? The bounty hunter that disappeared? Why would he be following me?

She made another quick decision. If she continued on after her double-back then she could take a trail that would put her where he was heading. Her mind pictured the sheet of bounty hunter headshots and scanned it.

I want to follow this man. This Breckenridge. Is it Breckenridge?

She began to run. All out. She had flashbacks of her college track career. Southeastern Conference races were always competitive. Any mistake could mean the race. Any mistake now could mean her life.

Fifteen minutes went by. Heart pounding, breathing hard but controlled. She stopped twenty yards from the junction of the two trails. Cognizant of her surroundings – the danger points - she also felt her muscles tightening. She pulled first one, then the other knee to her chest, then she spread her feet wide and stretched as she waited. She felt as though she was one open pore as sweat rolled down the sides of her face, down her body. She found shade. Though there was a thicket of trees and brush hiding her, she had a clear view of anyone approaching from the way he would be coming. She had become the hunter.

Five minutes went by in the late-June morning heat. He never came through. She knew the trails well enough. It would have been a monumental athletic feat for him to have beaten her there.

Maybe it wasn't him. Maybe it was a renter or someone from over at the golf resort who just happened to fall in behind me. Very possible. White men with beards, sun glasses, and hats in a certain age group very much resemble each other. But it doesn't add up. What the hell? Something's amiss.

She pulled her cell phone from its holder on her right hip. Lester Beaumont had texted her. The beep had been muffled in the holder during her all-out run.

Call me ASAP.

She texted back: *Give me 10*. Her sweat dripped on to the phone's clear cover. She wiped it on her shirt, and put it back in the holder. Some 120 feet away, from where she had just come, an HHPD colleague stepped out of the brush. Harper waved him off, and gave him a thumbs up. He disappeared into a thicket. She stepped back on to the trail, walked the twenty feet to the junction, turned right to jog the last half mile back to Slack Trimmer in cool-down mode. She stopped and looked back over her shoulder.

"To hell with it."

She turned around and began running in search of the man she thought had been tailing her.

Chatter among those LEOs on-device, listening to and watching Stowe, went ballistic. Zones north and east of Greenbank Drive, Ocean Oaks' main thoroughfare – which she would likely cross - were not covered this morning.

CHAPTER 48

Chief Lester Beaumont was waiting in the boulevard that had become Harper Stowe's Slack Trimmer driveway. His car was running, air conditioner cranked, when his No. 1 returned just after noon Wednesday from her wild goose chase. He was cool, calm, and collected. She was hot, jumpy, and irritated - and not trying to hide it. Forty-five minutes had passed since she had texted that she would call.

"You put the team in crisis-mode with that stunt, Harper." He'd stepped out of his car to meet her face-to-face. "And you look terrible."

"You are not endearing yourself to me right now, Lester."

"I'm not trying to. What's wrong?"

"Well, one: it's a-hundred-three degrees – in the shade. Two: I just ran nine miles because I thought I was being followed. And three: not by our mass-murdering rapist, but by one of the bounty hunters."

Beaumont looked at his feet like a guilty dog. Stowe made a note of it.

"Yeah, I got the reports coming over here. The team guessed that's what you were thinking. Harper, none of our people were over by the resort. That was unplanned and dangerous."

"The whole thing is dangerous, Lester. Let's not pretend."

"You want off? I shouldn't have to remind you that this was your damned idea. I've got an ulcer from it."

Stowe was pacing back and forth across the driveway.

"I know it was," Harper said in a quieter tone. "I'm just… it's frustrating."

"What?"

"I said it's frustrating."

"Look, get in the car - please. Cool off. Or show me this house we lassoed. You need to rest. Sit. Hydrate. I've got a couple things to discuss. Then you can relax – and don't come into the office today."

Beaumont followed Stowe through the canary-yellow front door. He couldn't hide his disappointment when he stepped into the foyer.

"Well, it's got potential, I suppose."

He followed Stowe to the kitchen and then sat down at the table.

"Yeah, this is a house someone would likely tear down and rebuild – due to the proximity to the beach. I don't think anything's been done to it in twenty-five years – except maybe the paint on the door. That's *got* to be fresh."

Beaumont laughed. But it wasn't authentic. He was distracted. Stowe was pouring cold water from a purifier into two glasses.

"I guess it's ok for entertaining though," Beaumont said.

She stopped and looked up. She sat the pitcher on the counter and turned to face him.

"Well, I guess that answers my first question." She stepped to the table and, as she disseminated his meaning, her restless hands picked up a wooden napkin ring. "You're having me watched."

"Everybody's watching, Harper. You know that."

"You know what I mean. Tailed. There was a man – vaguely familiar to me for some reason – watching me at the Boyd memorial last night."

"No one can take their eyes off you. Get real, Detective. At an event, wearing a dress, what do you expect? You're striking."

Diagram of Death

"Stop with the B.S. The same man was just following me, I believe, on the trails. You know something about that?"

"Tell me about the boyfriend."

She slammed the ring back on to the table, leaned in and pointed at Beaumont.

"You tell me about the man you put on me, Lester. What the hell is that about? Who is he?"

Beaumont stood, in deep thought, and walked around the table to where she had been pouring. He finished what she'd started, handed her a glass, then took a drink from his own.

"Look, I did it for your protection. And I did it for me. Cause most of the time I'm worried sick about you. I couldn't face my family, your parents, or the world in general if something happened to you out here."

"So who is Chuck Breckenridge? That's his name, right?"

"Chuck is a former armed forces associate. Retired Marine. Cold War all-star. Did the kind of shit that isn't written in reports in triplicate, if you know what I mean. The last time we did something together was about nine years ago… about when you started on the force. You may have seen him then. Seems like last month to me. Anyway, he showed up with the other bounty hunters. I figured, if you close in on our guy – or if our guy finds you - Chuck's the best backup you can have."

"You think it would have been wise to tell me, Chief? I could have shot the man."

"I'm sorry about that. I – should have. Everything happened real quick. I made a snap decision and I wanted to give it a day to breathe."

"I see. Well, you know I believe it was unnecessary, but I understand."

"Thanks. And I shouldn't have said what I did about your visitor. I didn't know you had a significant other in your life. You certainly deserve a little down time with everything you've been doing."

Stowe said nothing.

"All right, all right. You don't have to tell me."

"He's a good man. You'll like him."

"I'm sure I will," Beaumont said. He smiled. "Makes me feel parental. Like I should be saving for a wedding or something."

The conversation stalled. Beaumont gathered himself to leave.

"Oh, I almost forgot. Wainwright's back home. Got in last night. We don't know where he came from… where he'd been. He just rolled in. We won't miss him again."

CHAPTER 49

I am a patient student. The gators that frequent the lagoons and tidal creeks in Ocean Oaks are the teachers. I've taken the opportunity to observe and learn from these ancient reptiles and the way they hunt. Her tail a steady source of power, she swims slowly into an area with bank-brush or angled trees that reach down into the green water, maneuvers into it, and lays waiting. An hour can go by. Longer. Her nose resembling imperfect tree bark, her eyes lumpy knots, until a sizeable fish approaches or a pelican struts up hoping for a stab at lunch. Quicker than a blink the prey is seized in her inescapable jaws. Sometimes she'll just hold the fish, as to not alert the other potential catches in the vicinity, only occasionally adjusting her grip. For one is not enough. One is never enough.

Me, I'm hoping for a second passing by my prey. In darkness and my intentionally-thick seclusion I disappear from my pool deck and into the woods behind my home... slowly, each step cautious and quiet. I know the best routes to all the areas of Ocean Oaks. My areas. I stop and crouch where stalker-boy watched Carrie Stowers last night. His return will be the confirmation of his guilt. I become the trees and underbrush. He won't see the first jab of my knife coming. When he reacts to his pain, he'll get the second. Then the throat. Three easy steps.

At first, I thought this man was after me, though that theory would mean that I would be targeting Carrie. It's no stretch to assume that she would be in my sights. She's exquisite. I'll admit I let this man get in my head a little since last night. Is he a cop, predicting my next move? Did I show my hand? I've never written her name. It's all between my eyes

Andrew Spradling

and ears in the gray matter. I've only watched from afar. Except for church Sunday. That was pure torture. Her fragrance was intoxicating. How could this guy know? He couldn't. But it's given me a new perspective, along with the two occurrences I witnessed today. Recon pays. I figured it out. I saw Carrie signal a man who had apparently been watching her on her run. I've seen these cops before out there, worked my way around them. But I thought they were watching the runners at random attack spots. Until today. They were watching her... ever so graceful in full stride. Then I watched her in her driveway talking to that blowhard Beaumont. Chief Lester Beaumont, spokesman for the inept. It all came together then. Carrie Stowers is a cop. I felt somewhat betrayed, but it only makes her being the final stroke of my masterpiece that much more grand. A cop, man. That won't be forgotten. That will make the act live on. Just making a few final adjustments - one surprise. It's good to have compelling thoughts to ponder while in deep cover. Pass the time. And here comes my man now...

CHAPTER 50

    The body of Chuck Breckenridge was found Thursday afternoon by the tree trimmer of a local landscaping outfit as he was dragging cut limbs into deeper woods. Had Breckenridge's throat been slit near the water, the gators may have dragged him into the depths insuring instead another disappearance or missing person like the Rev. William Janson, who had yet to be found. But as was the case, and location, he was discovered first by flies, on a day so hot and humid the blood bath in which he laid had barely congealed.
    Breckenridge's remains were less than two hundred and fifty feet from Harper Stowe's front door, between the two houses across Slack Trimmer and into the woods, though with a direct line of sight to her home. The act of murder was still anything but commonplace on the island, and yet the gathering of these homicide detectives, coroners, and forensic specialists among themselves had become not only exhausting but old hat. The small talk one makes with seldom-seen associates no longer bore repeating. A justifiable silence ensued, until Stowe's team made a discovery that had them scrambling. The only "trophy" reported missing from the six rape victims – the opal and diamond pinky ring of third-victim Tamera Pauley – was found in Breckenridge's front pants pocket.
    Chief Lester Beaumont, with Stowe backing him up, was the voice of reason as the allegations and theories began to fly.
    "Look, I know this man, I know his background. He came here to find the murderer for the reward - and I gave him a specific task to carry out because of his special training."
    "But, can you account for his whereabouts the past ten weeks? You don't really know where he was, do you? His

comings and goings?" said FBI agent Paul Clark. "By definition he *could* be a suspect."

"Not to mention it's mindboggling that you gave an outsider a duty only a fellow-officer should have been assigned," added Clark's counterpart Jeff Hudson.

"You people are missing the point. No, I shouldn't have gone out of office for this. And yes, in a court of law I'd have to say I'm unaware of his location prior to the arrival of all the bounty hunters. But Chuck Breckenridge was the epitome of counter-intelligence. He lived it. He'll likely be buried at Arlington. He's a national hero. I'm floored that he couldn't stop the man we're after. *That's* the worry."

"As if it wasn't a worry before?" said Hudson. "His proficiency with the knife?"

There was a moratorium on speech as everyone watched the deliberate steps of the two coroners making their way out of the woods with the body on a hand-held stretcher. They all stood straight. Beaumont saluted.

"This is all a waste of breath," Stowe said. "If Breckenridge *is* the rapist, who killed him? Why would they? He's toying with us."

"Exactly," said Beaumont. "Another red herring - a false clue. His blood will confirm what's obvious to me."

"It tells us something else," said Agent Arline Thorn. "Again, this man is watching you, Harper. There's no question now. He's drawn to you. And since he did this, maybe he thinks he's protecting you. But why? What's his motive?"

All eyes turned to Stowe.

"I don't know. Maybe… maybe he wants me in his Navy cluster. Would he plan that far ahead?"

"Sure he would," said Paul Clark. "He's yet to make a mistake. You don't get this far error-free without some serious planning. I mean damn, there hasn't been one eye witness."

Diagram of Death

"Well, if it brings contact, that was the whole point of me being here, right?" Stowe said. "That's when we'll take him down."

CHAPTER 51

The lead "Ocean Oaks Slasher" investigators emerged from the woods into the chaos of police cruisers, a departing emergency vehicle, and the corresponding flashing lights and radio transmissions, though an order had come through – no sirens since no life was at stake. Everyone was tired of the sirens, and leery of the tourists hearing them. The media was behind yellow tape on the top of dead-end-by-beachfront Slack Trimmer Road. They learned from a patrolman who met them in the backyards that Mayor Ralph Sneed was waiting to speak with Chief Lester Beaumont. And, they heard Sneed was hopping mad. Such news only irritated the veteran Beaumont.

Harper Stowe stopped at the corner of the house to her right and took two steps backwards. The group hadn't anticipated the media catching wind of this murder scene – at least so soon. Of course, it would only take one rogue police scanner for the entire horde to appear. Stowe had entered the woods dressed as she most often had been on this case, in running gear.

"I can't cross the street to the house. I'll blow my cover," Stowe said, though speaking to no one in particular.

"We could have the mayor back his big-ass Navigator in here to pick you up," Beaumont said. "Nobody would see you then."

Stowe laughed.

"You're displaying contempt for your superior, Boss."

Beaumont grunted. "Maybe I am. He doesn't need to be here. And why does he have to have a car like that?"

"I think he donated the Lincoln to the township. A little tax write off. Sweet ride too – that's two rookie cops' salaries at least," Stowe said.

Diagram of Death

She looked down the street, opposite the madness. All was clear. No one had slipped past the roadblock, nor were any neighbors outside observing the media circus, which had included Rhett Richardson, his camera shouldered. The idea that she'd recognized his form in such a quick glance made her smile to herself. These houses could be sitting empty this week, she thought.

"I think I'll walk the tree line to the beach - behind these homes. Could someone pick me up down at The Parrot Perch in a half hour?"

"I'll do it," Agent Arline Thorn said. "Should someone go with you – at least to the beach?"

"No. I'll be fine."

Stowe disappeared behind the house to the group's left. Beaumont and Thorn hesitated, watching her leave. Agents Paul Clark and Jeff Hudson walked ahead, attempting to embroider importance for the cameras by feigning meaningful conversation with equally benign hand gestures.

Immediately there seemed to be a change in the atmosphere: a shift in the wind, a good bit of cloud cover, perhaps from a storm approaching from the Atlantic. The kind that rolled through in late afternoon then dissipated over the mainland, leaving only a thick blanket of humidity. Stowe felt it too. It was not only weather-related. There was something disturbing about walking behind these homes. A sense of trespassing. A feeling of isolation. An altered perspective of the world from a new view. Looking for faces, Stowe glanced at all the windows of the house she was behind, then ahead to the next one. She heard something move in the woods to her left. Probably a squirrel or raccoon. Maybe a deer. No sound of retreating footsteps followed. Suddenly she wished she was walking in the cover of darkness. She felt exposed and acutely aware that a murder had taken place eighty yards away. The feeling clung to her skin. She heard another sound – a snap of a branch. She saw no movement in the woods, yet she felt she was being watched.

Stowe picked up her pace, and reminded herself she had the snub-nosed .38 under her left arm. She spotted some gray-blue sea between the beachfront homes that T-boned Slack Trimmer. No sand yet. The elevation and the dune grass obstructed it.

Why am I equating safety with the ocean? Get ahold of yourself. There's nobody hiding here.

She stopped. Faced the woods. Shook out her limbs like a prizefighter.

See? Nothing.

She laughed and continued on her way. There was no public access between the homes in this section of beach, but, seeing no one to disapprove, she jogged her way through anyway.

The tide was nearly at its lowest point and now there was no hint of the weather that seemed to have teased the atmosphere just moments before. Her pupils burned as her eyes adjusted to the white brightness. Harper trudged through the loose, never-touched-by-ocean sand to the hard-packed, tan, high-tide-touched variety and turned right. With the strong breeze at her back she walked quickly, still, always, looking at faces, searching for clues.

Between the wind and their music, they don't have a clue about what's going on back there.

After a mile of walking southwest, she reached the island's southern-end turn and began a westward trek. The ever-present wind was now against her – pelting her face along with the occasional particle of sand.

Why kill Chuck Breckenridge? What's to gain? Or prove? What motivation could he possibly have had? Did he do it just to show how far ahead of the game he is? No way he thought that ring would throw us. So, why kill Breckenridge?

Diagram of Death

Stowe turned and walked up the beach to a path that would lead her to The Parrot Perch. As she did, two incoming texts caused her cell phone to beep almost simultaneously. The first was from Beaumont. It read: *been suspended pending invest. N touch soon.*

The second read: *911 call. 7th victim just reported.*

Stowe stopped dead in her tracks. Breckenridge's death finally made sense.

Son of a bitch. He did it just to keep us occupied.

She began to run to catch Agent Thorn for her ride to the crime scene.

CHAPTER 52

Throughout the entire murderous spree, Barnhart Ruins was the most likely spot in Ocean Oaks for such a cowardly act to take place. In Harper Stowe's mind, it hadn't happened there *because* it was the most likely location. The grounds included six secluded acres, off the beaten path. What remained was a mansion-sized foundation overlooking Calibogue Sound, and a few slave quarters or storage shacks. The home was burned by the Union army after it had used William Barnhart's mansion for its headquarters following its invasion of Hilton Head Island. The once-pristine lawn was now jungle with a century and a half of tropical overgrowth.

The Ruins' location was only on the cusp of one of the two remaining Navy cluster points in Harper Stowe's map of the murderer's attacks. But obviously close enough, she thought. The area was still being monitored by a roving patrolman, but coverage was lighter because of the work at the Breckenridge murder scene. The patrolman surveilling the Barnhart Cove area had yet to check in.

"I never, ever, thought, through all this, after all the safety messages, that a woman would come in here alone sightseeing," Stowe said. "It boggles the mind."

"Maybe she didn't know," Arline Thorn said.

"She couldn't have known," Stowe agreed.

"She didn't," said Detective Pete Waters. "I was able to track down her realtor from the information in her little bag. Just got off the phone with her."

"Wait, you were first on the scene?"

"Yes, I was. Well, a married couple found her. They called it in. So, Patricia Oldenkamp had flown in late Wednesday – last night. She was to meet a group of college

Diagram of Death

friends for a long weekend - fifteen years after their graduation from the University of Wisconsin. This was all set up months ago. But because their rental was sitting empty, the woman I spoke with gave them an extra night free. Oldenkamp, who apparently had just gone through a tough divorce, was the only woman able to take advantage of the extra day. Her friends' arrivals are staggered throughout the day. Four are here already."

"And this is how she ends up. What a welcome for them," Stowe said, looking at the ground past the body. The remains from the waist down like all the others, shorts and panties cut away. Her arms were outstretched, her head turned to the right. A significant difference. All the others had been left in their unfortunate random pose, except for Jessica Boyd, who'd been dragged to the edge of the water. There must be a reason. "How old?"

"Thirty-seven."

Stowe turned away, took a couple of steps towards nothing in particular, put her hands on her hips, and looked to the sky.

"I'm so tired of this," Stowe said, turning back to the body.

The two women continued scouring the crime scene, mindful of their foot placement. Detective Waters retreated a half-dozen steps and observed, waiting for his next duty.

"Are these oyster shells she's lying on?" Thorn asked. "They're everywhere."

"The house was made with tabby, an old, lowland masonry practice," Stowe said. "Crushed oyster shells burned to make lime, then mixed with whole shells, water, and sand."

"Moses was to make bricks without straw…" Thorn said.

"Exactly. It forms a building compound," Stowe was now carefully examining the ground all around the body for anything left behind. Many of the random-sized shells had caught and were holding Oldenkamp's blood, often spilling over one shell to the next rather than seeping into the ground. From above, at least from her waist up, it looked as though she was lying on a crimson blanket.

"You think the blood is why he laid her arms out?" Thorn asked.

"I do. Christ-like. Hell, it's a horizontal crucifixion – minus the cross," Stowe said. "This is gonna make the ghost freaks go nuts. They say this place is haunted – paranormal activity at night. I've walked back here before during this time of day... it's a little spooky."

"Compared to this?" Thorn said.

"Sad to say, cause of what we get used to, but yes, there's a definite vibe."

"Did I see 'Toney' on one of the signs? Before Barnhart?"

"It was built by Captain Jack Toney around 1790. Word was, Toney lost it in a poker game to William Barnhart in 1840. Barnhart and his wife raised four daughters here until the war came crashing in. They had to bolt. It's all written out there on the marker. And it's on the National Register."

The sounds of engines, tires, and brakes on the nearby roadside parking area alerted the trio that the rest of the team had arrived.

"The help's here, Pete. Could you try to track down the officer that was supposed to be working this zone for us? Maybe work your way towards the water."

"You don't think...?"

"I just don't know. I mean, you'd think he would have come around by now."

"Will do, Harper," Waters said. He disappeared into the brush to the back of the site.

Diagram of Death

"I know how she was feeling," said Thorn. "Divorced, alone... searching. Vulnerable."

Stowe thought about ignoring the comment, keeping her head down and just continuing to work. But Thorn seemed to be reaching out lately, and for Stowe, getting answers was like breathing oxygen.

"You too?"

"After about three and a half years of doing this - everywhere. He wasn't built for it. Had to have more... others. That was thirteen years ago."

Stowe stared into Thorn's burnt-walnut eyes.

"Has there been anybody else?"

Thorn tried to smile, but failed.

"Not really. I hope yours goes better."

Stowe thought of Rhett Richardson, who forty-five minutes ago was videoing the Breckenridge crime scene, and would undoubtedly be across the road when they left the Ruins. She smiled slightly, despite believing that their work wouldn't lend to a perfect relationship scenario.

"I think it will."

The coroner team of Tom Wilson and Cindy Lewis approached. Agents Paul Clark and Jeff Hudson followed. Behind them was Mayor Ralph Sneed, trailed by LaDonna Reynolds, his P.R. manager.

"Agent Hudson, please tell the Mayor this is a crime scene. No civilians," Stowe said, loud enough to carry to the road. "Not yet."

"Okay, Detective," Hudson said, turning to face the Mayor.

"He has no business back here... we have to safeguard the integrity of the scene," Stowe said.

"Holy Christ," said Lewis, getting her first glimpse.

"You said it," Thorn offered.

"We're going to need a pic from above – bird's eye," said Stowe.

"I'll get my ladder," Wilson said. "Never would have thought I'd need it."

"Why do we need it?" Lewis asked.

"Because this was a departure. Intentional," said Stowe. "Even if it was just his reaction to the pool of blood. It says something."

"Maybe he's reaching out," Lewis said.

"Maybe, he's asking for forgiveness," Stowe said.

"He's made a staurogram with her," Clark said. "It's Greek. The 't' superimposed on the 'p,' forms a ' ⳨.' It was used as an abbreviation for the word cross, and it represented Christ on the cross. But I think it also translated to the word help. This guy's not shallow."

"The guy is riding a blood wave. Four souls in less than a week. Five if it's Wainwright," Stowe said, her reactionary statement hiding her admiration of his historical reference. A mental note was made. "This is not *The Da Vinci Code*, and I don't think he's asking for help."

"Maybe he is," said Thorn. "Maybe he's tired too."

"If I'm right he's got one to go," Stowe said. "I'm going to go look for Pete Waters."

"Wait, Harper," Hudson said, rejoining the others. "The Mayor wants to speak with you privately, he said. "I think he has an offer for you."

"Any media out there?"

"They're getting here now."

"Then bring the Mayor in for me, please. Just over there. Not the P.R. girl though. She can wait."

CHAPTER 53

I guarantee the sons-a-bitches are still sitting in their parked car, watching my house. Serves them right. I left my ride in the garage. I guess they think I'm inside, feet propped, watching episodes of "Millionaire" or some such bullshit.

After the tough guy in the woods – that went down just as I planned - I re-boarded my boat. I had all night, so I didn't mind the miles. Clear my head a little... wash off a little blood. And, it was good to get stealth-like again. I couldn't let myself be seen on the move by anybody - anybody. I am on my game.

So I drive the boat around to Barnhart Cove, slip her at one of the ever-absent homeowner's docks. Again, always pays to be up early. The lone cop walked right into his fate. And that gave me free reign of the Ruins. Talk about a hunter's lair. From deep undercover I let one off, too far out of the age group. It was a risk – I could have come up empty - but I wasn't doing brittle bones. Not for the masterpiece. The extra few hours was worth the wait. Ms. Wisconsin was just the way I like'em. Fit but fleshy. Sad eyes. They always have sad eyes.

I'd never watched one bleed out before. The Ruins afforded me that extra time - I could have disappeared at the snap of a stick. It was surreal watching her blood encircle her. It took me somewhere, back to a time of study. When advancement was important. I'd seen the symbol then. In my readings – the Royal Hellenic Navy. I had to do something. Make her a monument of my work. I knew it would give the cops more to consider. To me it was not about the past, but my intentions for the immediate future. It was perfect, sure. Like Carrie Stowers. I've never anticipated anyone more. Certainly not my wife. I have a plan. I'll change up the M.O. for her. Carrie, or whoever she actually is, isn't one to kill quickly.

CHAPTER 54

"It's time for you to break ranks. End this undercover deal, Detective Stowe."

Mayor Ralph Sneed was on new ground. It was one of his first attempts at being authoritative in his role as leader of Hilton Head Island's Township. It was also his first incursion of a crime scene, and he was obviously distracted. He was stealing glances over Harper Stowe's shoulder at the victim as he spoke.

"All due respect, I can't, Mayor."

"I want you to run the department. Beaumont is out."

Stowe was aware of Sneed's sight line. He wasn't being obvious, but at the same time she sensed he was beginning to pale. His breathing was becoming pronounced. She took him by the shoulders and gently turned him.

"Please Mayor, face this way before your knees buckle. You've had a big day. Now…"

"I must be necrophobic. I didn't know that about myself." Sneed said, first licking, then pursing his lips as though his mouth was dry.

"It's pretty common – a little more traumatic then say, finding your grandfather in his chair. I wouldn't worry about it. Now, why is Lester out?"

"I've heard what went on with Breckenridge. It was a complete breach of city policy and procedure. More than that it was wrong-headed. Idiotic is what it was. A police chief can't make boneheaded decisions like that."

"You don't think he did it because he was looking out for me? That it was the best-possible scenario for keeping me safe?"

Diagram of Death

"That may be true, Harper, but you can't assign a non-employee to a duty like that."

"Mayor. It's not like it was on the books. It was a friend asking a favor of a highly-decorated fellow friend – who was here and involved by choice and under his own recognizance. Putting himself in harm's way."

"That in no way..."

"And - from what I understand, or remember, there's no family to worry about suing us. Maybe we could even use it as a rallying cry for more federal help. But we can't pull me. We think Carrie Stowers might have been a trigger for him. That Carrie might be the final target. That supersedes everything."

Sneed's stare gradually became transfixed, away from Patricia Oldenkamp and the bloody scene, to some random point in the trees.

"Tell me how you think we might use Breckenridge's death as some sort of promotional call-to-arms."

Stowe refrained from body language that would show her anger. *Of course he picked the wrong message to focus on.*

"Come on, Mayor. You've got a professional out there with you. Are you telling me she didn't mention it? A national hero going down for the cause? It's got potential, even if we don't get more help. The main thing is, we don't rock the status quo. Lester needs to keep doing what he's doing, I need to keep being Carrie Stowers. We're close. He's close. I can feel it."

"I don't know, Detective. If we took a poll among law enforcement leaders – Lester's not getting the nod."

"I'm not sure he would either. But there's no time to get nods, Mayor. This is critical – a delicate balance. You can fire us all afterwards if you want to. Are we on the same page?"

Sneed turned a bit more so his back was completely to the scene. He took a deep breath through his nose. His color seemed to be returning.

"Ok, Harper. We are. Suspension lifted. I'll let Lester know."

"Thank you."

"Do you need anything else here?"

"No sir. Just a little more daylight."

Harper shook Sneed's hand. He turned and began to walk away. He stopped and looked back.

"You're very persuasive, Harper. And subtle. I think politics may be in your future."

She smiled. "Doubtful. I'll see you later."

Oh, hell.

In her rush to get to the crime scene, it had again slipped her mind: There was no walking out of The Barnhart Ruins without her police status being revealed. And unlike the Breckenridge crime scene, there was no quick, safe, unobstructed walk to the beach. She looked at the small, visible patch of blue sky the overgrowth of trees provided. The sun hadn't set. It *seemed* later in the Ruins than it actually was because it was shady all day long. As she returned to the group, she pulled out her phone: 8:13.

It'll be dark in an hour. I'll sneak out somehow then.

She stopped at a tree at the edge of the crime scene. She quietly watched as the coroners lifted the yellow body bag that held Patricia Oldenkamp on to a medical stretcher. They faced each other and squatted.

"Ok, on three, Cindy. Two, three," Tom Wilson said.

They lifted the stretcher. Wilson carefully changed his grip and turned around, so he could walk her out facing forward. The whole team stopped and watched silently, as though a casket was leaving a funeral. Stowe waited till they were out of earshot to speak, which really made no sense to her. If they discovered another dead body, it would most likely be Wilson and Lewis immediately returning to the scene.

"Has Pete Waters checked back in?"

"Haven't seen him," said Thorn.

"Let me call him," Stowe said, she paced slowly as she listened to the rings. "There's no answer. Are we all wrapped up here? We're going to have to branch out and look for him."

Paul Clark looked towards the thick underbrush, foliage, and trees of the back two-thirds of The Barnhart Ruins.

"We better pair up," Clark said. "There's no telling what's going on in there."

CHAPTER 55

Since the FBI's arrival on to the island, Harper Stowe had been wise enough to look past Paul Clark's G-man superiority act, and for the most part keep her own territorialism at bay. She knew that both reactions were only human nature, yet if not kept in check, real enough to paralyze an investigation. She realized that most of her irritation about the trio came from the sidekick Jeff Hudson, who seemed to thrust his muscles and mouth into the forefront before his mind. His insistence about nicknaming the murderer - "Nimitz," because of the potential Navy link – had been somewhat irritating. They never used it again after wasting over an hour on it, nor, thankfully, did they share it with the press. "Ocean Oaks Slasher" was gaining ground in the public, and with some news agencies.

Stowe had gained respect for all three agents, mainly through their work ethic and passion for the job. There was little unrelated rhetoric, even from Hudson. Especially in the last few days, as the killing spree multiplied. Now she and Clark were pairing off for a hunt.

"Ok, let's keep the groups about fifty yards apart," Clark said. "But stay in view of your partner. We'll veer left and you all go right until we hit water, right Harper?"

"That's right."

"Should we even separate at all?" Thorn asked.

"Well, if there's a body to find, it could be anywhere," Stowe said. "We'll have to spread out a little. But I agree with Paul. Stay close."

"You think he could still be here?" Thorn asked, pulling her pistol and loading a bullet into the chamber with a quick pull.

Diagram of Death

"I'd say there's a chance, with two officers potentially missing," Hudson said. "We may have trapped him."

"Unless he *wants* to still be there he had three ways out – including a swim," Stowe said. "He could have worked his way out either side. He's gone."

"Why don't we get some backup," Thorn said. "All-available-officers working their way in from the sides. Maybe we really can trap him."

"What if we pull everybody and he hits again in the final zone?" Stowe said. "Like he did here while we were all over at the Breckenridge scene. I hear you, and I'll call in some backup - but we don't want to compromise the other areas. And we've got about forty minutes of daylight."

"She's right. Do it on the move," Hudson said. "Let's go."

They began walking in, separating as they did, the rectangular foundation and the slave shacks behind them.

"Hey Jeff," Stowe said, with a slight smile. "Watch out for snakes and gators."

"You watch out for *the man*. Oh, Nimitz too," he said, winking at Stowe.

After the quick call, a total of nine officers were to go in the front and two sides.

"Make sure they're aware of our presence – two male, two female. It's getting dark. Lots of shadows. Over."

Stowe and Clark were free to explore. Moving through the thickets of brush was arduous. Slowly, the groups' movements from the initial point of attack was creating a letter "V." For a few minutes each pair could hear the others' voices. Then they became whispers. Then nothing but an accordance with the impending darkness.

"I was impressed by your staurogram reference," Stowe said. "On-demand, in-depth facts. Where'd that come from?"

"I was counter-terrorism for my first eight years in the bureau. Religious history - fanaticism – all part of the training. That symbol isn't so far removed from mainstream, believe me."

"Why'd you get out of it?"

"You know that feeling you have, that this'll never end? Counter-terrorism never ends. We're a hated nation."

Clark lifted a branch for Stowe to step under. The brush and bugs were irritating her exposed legs. She ignored it. Daylight was giving way to nightfall, but the heat held firm. The impending darkness she couldn't ignore. Her eyes darted from sky back to root to bush to tree trunk – non-stop.

"I can see that. But…"

"It's that way with all areas of crime though. Maybe I was just burnt out."

"You find this gratifying?"

"When you catch a killer? Damn right. But it's a frustrating road – always. You know. I've checked."

"I've been involved in nine murder investigations – six as lead. Of course none like this. I don't know… I'm sure we could've done better."

"I've been impressed with your work. There're always a few things that could've been done differently - in retrospect. Nobody's perfect. And sometimes you just come up empty."

Stowe angled her head and body to get a better view of something that caught her eye. It was only a downed tree branch.

"Should we spread out a little?"

As she said it, the sound of bushes rustling deeper in the woods halted them in their tracks. They listened. Harper's senses tingled in her neck and shoulders. It stopped, and they proceeded.

"Yes. Not much though."

Diagram of Death

Stowe went to her left as Clark continued moving forward. Their deliberate movements were the only sound they heard. Soon a large live oak separated them.

"Harper, I think I see feet – yeah, and legs."

As he spoke, Wainwright stepped out of the camouflage of greenery and, facing him, deftly slashed Clark's throat. Clark's right hand reacted enough to touch Wainwright's arm, grab on to it, but his strength, his life, was as fleeting as his blood splatter. He let out a gurgling shriek as the blade exited his skin. The damage was done. Eyes wide, Clark sank to his knees, then toppled on to his back.

Wainwright turned, backed up to the tree, sank low and pulled his next weapon – a syringe. Stowe came through the brush with Clark's instant of pain as her compass. Her right hand disappeared in her shirt as she reached for her holstered-sidearm. Just as she touched it, Wainwright's long jab met Stowe at her thigh. The reactionary jerk from the stab left her empty-handed. As he pushed the plunger with the heel of his hand, she hit him with a combination of punches to his face, knocking him off balance and into the tree trunk. She pulled the syringe out of her leg then released a sidekick at a downward angle catching him ineffectively on his hip and waist. Her goal was his groin. She reached for hair and head, either to pull him on to his belly or break his neck, depending on the grip she managed. He swatted the attempt. She came back hard with a backhand to his cheekbone. She followed with another downward kick, scrapping his shinbone, a blow that would have been more painful, debilitating, and advantageous with hard shoes.

As she regained her balance the drug began to find its way through her body and to her brain. She wobbled. Her vision began to blur. She raised her fists, but became more unsteady. Wainwright recognized it and jumped to his feet. Stowe was able to shout "Thorn" but he covered her mouth quickly. It was the first time he attacked without tape on his palm. He knew he wouldn't need it.

Stowe hit him with a weak right to his solar plexus, but then began to tumble. He grabbed her arms, leaned, and pulled her stomach to his shoulder, his hand on the small of her back. He lifted her easily, her arms and legs dangling from his 6-foot-7 frame. He could feel her cell phone on his neck. With his free hand he pulled it out of its holder and tossed it towards Clark's corpse. He turned and disappeared into the brush. He'd hoped in his planning it would be fully dark and it was close. His boat was only five hundred yards away.

CHAPTER 56

Agent Arline Thorn's head snapped like a bear trap. Her finely-trained ears listened to the silence. She knew she had heard something, if ever so faint... and brief.

"Jeff. Did you hear that? Come here. Quick."

From their position to the right side, Agent Jeff Hudson had been working his way to the outside of the Barnhart Ruins' acreage. His quick return to Thorn was as loud as a broad steer forcing its way through the thick underbrush.

"What is it?"

"I heard something. The start of -- it may have been Harper calling out."

Hudson cupped his hands around his mouth. "Harper Stowe. Paul Clark," he shouted. "They stood still and listened briefly. Nothing.

"Let's go."

Hudson took the lead at a quick pace. Trying to run in this jungle was difficult, a moderate jog at best was all he could muster. Thorn trailed closely behind. They were blind to where the pair might have actually stopped. Hudson took a line he believed to be parallel to the road or straight across the expansion.

"They couldn't have gotten much deeper than us – if at all," Hudson said. "You work in a little, I'll go out."

Thorn veered left off of Hudson and slowed, as did he. She could hear the swish of palmettos succumbing to Hudson's chops, as well as the clumping sound of his steps. She wandered aimlessly for another thirty feet.

"God! Over here, Jeff." Thorn sank to her knees at Clark's side. She grabbed his wrist and felt for a heartbeat. His throat was a pulsating, crimson river. She knew. In fact the way Clark had fallen, his shoulders settling on the root of the live oak, his throat lay gaping open. She turned her head to hide her tears and dismay as Hudson slid to the ground by her side.

"Paul! No. Damn it – no!" He looked at Thorn. "Watch our backs."

Thorn, gasping for breath, stood, pulled her sidearm, and scanned the perimeter.

Hudson lifted his colleague's head by placing his hand underneath, then grabbed his shirt and pulled him off of the root. He then let his head rest on the ground.

"I can't believe it," Hudson said. "Paul's dead."

"Where is Harper? We've got to find her. Harper," Thorn shouted. "She's down. Or he must have taken her out that way."

"Let's go."

They negotiated the tree by going right, and within twelve feet they found the bodies of Detective Pete Waters and the patrol officer initially assigned to the Ruins. His nameplate read R.A. Wilkerson. Hudson pulled the voice transmitter from the tiny radio he'd been designated by the group to carry on his belt and sent out a bulletin.

"All law enforcement be advised – Ashanti Alert. This is FBI agent Hudson, we have a female officer missing. Three male officers down - deceased. Our twenty is still Barnhart Ruins, the left or south side. Three down, Harper Stowe - missing. Repeat. Harper Stowe is missing. Fear abduction, possibly out of the southern or southeastern side of Ruins area. Cove side. We are searching, continuing search. Over."

Thorn checked for a pulse in both local officers, hoping one might have survived – that triage was necessary. Nothing.

"We have to keep looking," she said.

The pair continued onward, deeper into the lot.

Diagram of Death

"Be advised also, keep a close eye on zone eight," Hudson said, back on the radio. "Let's not discard zone eight at this point. Or the route between Barnhart and eight. He may be heading there with Stowe – somehow – on foot possibly. Over."

Hudson reattached the device to his belt.

"So where would he be taking Harper if not there? Come on, it hasn't been five minutes."

"If he's had all this planned - bodies are piling up," Hudson said, shaking his head. "And he's rubbing our noses in it."

"Let's get out of this forest. There - there's the cop coming in. That's the edge. The police blanket must be out."

Thorn and Hudson acknowledged the uniformed officer, stepping out of the Ruins lot and on to the manicured lawn of a Barnhart Cove resident.

"Keep looking, Officer. We didn't see her anywhere," Thorn said. "She could be more in the middle. We worked our way out."

The last pink hint of daylight was clinging to the westward treetops, lending nothing but a faint reflection on the shadowy water.

"Well, what do you see?" Hudson said.

"I don't see them - anything. A half dozen boats coming home after enjoying what I'm sure was as beautiful sunset."

"They flat disappeared."

CHAPTER 57

It was a risk, but had I attempted a quick exit out to sea through Barnhart Cove instead of maneuvering inland, up its creek, I would have likely drawn the cops' suspicion. It was an old-man's miracle that I covered the ground I did with Carrie Stowers on my shoulder - one-hundred-twenty pounds of pure gold. I had boarded, untied, turned the engine over, pushed off the dock, and got it moving forward when I saw the surviving pair of cops exit the woods. Had they been able to see the ripples in the water at all, they would have known I had yet to create a wake. It was literally a matter of seconds between being detected and freedom – but five hundred yards is a long way to see after twilight.

Escape became a matter of waiting out their investigation. It would have been easy to cut me off. I would have been forced to abandon ship and flee, which would have hurt me deeply so close to my goal. Eight hours I waited – they had my heart pumping the first couple, I'll admit. But so did she. I shut 'er all down - and waited. Borrowed another dock. No lights on board - blackout. Watched the brilliant stars. Eventually I was able to nap a bit. Then, out to open sea like an early-rising sport fisherman.

Propofol was a risk as well. Straight into a vein would have killed. I partially diluted it with saline and had a second syringe, if necessary. Just enough to get her where I wanted her. I bought it – black market – before I took the preacher boating.

She's a passenger worthy of a French Riviera yacht – like Princess Grace. So seductive. And she's a fighter, my Carrie. I've never been punched so hard – not even in basic training. I'll be more bruised then her. The jaw is throbbing.

Diagram of Death

But that's ok. I'll recover. Now we'll experience a few days of life at sea. Even at the end of this long day she looks incredible. So I'll test her willingness. She can comply or die.

CHAPTER 58

Harper Stowe awoke to the slow rhythm of a calm ocean. She was refreshed, with only soreness at the jab point of her thigh. She was securely blindfolded. Instinctively, she wanted to rub her leg, but she was bound tightly at her wrists. Propped upright by pillows, she believed herself to be lying on a bunk, which was not uncomfortable. The tension on her wrists was, though, and her arms throbbed from being stretched horizontally. She realized that her pain was what woke her. Her throat and mouth felt as though she'd swallowed glue.

She had perfect clarity, though she couldn't tell if it was day or night. The heat was stifling, so she presumed it was the former. At that moment she heard nothing but the hum of the engine through the walls, which made her assume she was alone in a cabin. She twisted gently to try and alleviate her discomfort without drawing attention. She was able to find a little relief. She turned her limp hands to grip the synthetic rope that had her bound. She listened carefully.

Could I hear him breathing if he was in the room? I doubt it, too much engine noise.

She gripped both ropes and slowly began to pull, again hoping she wasn't being watched. She pictured typical boat fixtures, stainless steel but held by no more than a couple of screws. Yet freeing herself was a dreamer's errand. She had no leverage. She pulled until her arms and chest burned.

"It's reinforced," he said. "You won't be pulling yourself free."

She froze. Fear pierced her chest for an instant. She went pale. But after a few seconds regained her composure. She was then in no way afraid. In fact, she was mad, and knew

Diagram of Death

he had made a grave mistake. With her legs untied she could kill him given the opportunity.

"The only way you're getting loose is by my doing."

"Who's driving the boat?"

"I have the wheel tied off. Much like you. Our bearing doesn't have to be precise. We're heading due east – out. No swimming back from here. Move around if you like."

"My arms are numb."

"How's your strength?"

Now is not the time for truth.

"Poor. I'm weak. You're not going to starve me, are you?"

"It depends. It all depends on your behavior. I'm willing to treat you as respectfully as you treat me. I will say, I've got some excellent grub on board, beer, wine, and two lines in the water."

A hundred thoughts went through Stowe's mind. Foremost was whether or not to call him by name, or even admit her knowledge of him and his crimes. Even though they'd met at the church, how would he react to the slap in the face that he was known as the murderer? Would he be flattered or furious? What did it really matter? His murder of Clark would be proof in his eyes that she was a cop and that she knew his involvement. As it stood, he could gut her without reason, pretense, or warning. He could tie her ankles, cut her clothes away, and make her a sex slave.

I'm going to wait, unless he does go to tie my feet. I could engage him about the cluster, find out where that thought came from. But if the cluster is real, why is he taking me out to sea? He's never moved a body... much anyway. Jessica Boyd. Could I get a hint of his plan? No. For now, don't test him. Play the victim. Feign compliance. See where his mind is. Test his level of sympathy.

"How about water?"

"Are you thirsty?"
"Very."
"Sure, give me a minute."
She heard him open a door, take some steps away and then return. He closed the door."
"Open up, tilt your head. Give me a little lip."
She heard the distinct crack of a water bottle lid twisting open. He placed it to her mouth and tipped it slowly, then lowered it. It was ice-cold from a cooler.
She heard his breath stop in his throat – as if by intrigue - then he exhaled. Two drops of cold condensation fell on her shirt.
"More?"
"Please."
He repeated the action. Water never tasted so good to her. It was as if she was waking from the anesthesia of surgery.
"That enough for now?"
"Yes, thank you."
She listened intently to the clump, clump of his footsteps as he walked across the floor and sat back down. Eight lumbering steps straight away from the direction she was facing. She imagined the cabin was not wide. She wiggled her toes. She realized he'd taken off her tennis shoes and socks.
"What about bathroom breaks?"
"I have a plan for that. Do you need to go?"
"Not now. Can I ask a question?"
"You mean another? Kidding."
"Why am I here? What's your plan for me?"
"Well, I don't exactly know. I have to admit I wasn't sure I'd make it this far. And now that I have, losing you seems like an epic waste."
Losing me? You mean slitting my throat?
"I've been admiring you since you moved in."
"You have?"

Diagram of Death

My senses were right.

"Of course. How could I not? But I also figured out your game. I knew you were a cop days ago."

Does that make me a greater conquest?

"Why'd you kill Breckenridge?"

"Is that the man in the woods?"

"Yes."

"I wasn't sure of his intentions. But I was protecting you. Who was he?"

"He was a bounty hunter given a misguided assignment. To protect me."

He laughed coldly.

"So he was after me, not you?"

"That's right."

"Well, more's the pity. The preacher was definitely up to no good. I'm surprised he didn't force his hand on your porch."

"You really *have* been watching. He's gone missing. Know anything about that?"

Wainwright again laughed.

"That Phillies-lovin' bastard? He'll deliver his next sermon to Neptune. He was a disgrace to the Navy. Hell, he was a disgrace to rapists."

There was a pause. Stowe sensed he wanted to continue his thought, but he was becoming agitated. Too much reality? She could hear him fidgeting in his chair, one foot was tapping the floor.

"That's something you law enforcement types need to know about a rapist. They don't change. Or recover. They can fake it enough to get paroled. But you let them out, they'll rape again eventually. They'll just be smarter about it. Bank on it."

"What's that say about you?"

"Just that… like you, I'm in a class by myself."

CHAPTER 59

Reporting the Hilton Head Island murder news concisely was becoming an encumbrance for the media, especially after the Breckenridge homicide and Oldenkamp rape/murder on Thursday. Whittling this news, along with a little background of the six other murders, into even a two-minute report was a burden. The story was gaining worldwide attention, still the major networks and the BBC wanted a 60-second version as well. Secondary and follow-up cuts were as short as thirty seconds.

There was an interesting twist to the Patricia Oldenkamp aftermath, one that burned Rhett Richardson. Worse still, it was making him frantic. It was announced by Mayor Sneed's public relations guru LaDonna Reynolds that Chief Lester Beaumont would make a statement at HHPD headquarters: i.e., vacate the media from Barnhart Ruins ASAP. Richardson knew there was something more going on back in the depths of the Ruins, and assuming the worst meant that it could involve Harper Stowe. He'd watched keenly from the media's designated post across the road as the coroners left with Oldenkamp. There were cops flooding in, but none exiting.

Richardson sent Harper a quick text as he was packing up: *U ok?*

No response.

He sent it again from the parking lot of HHPD.

Nothing.

Little did he know, Harper's cell phone was now in an evidence bag. It was found beside the corpse of Paul Clark, slain along with Pete Waters and R.A. "Ron" Wilkerson.

Diagram of Death

With Mayor Sneed by his side, Beaumont delivered a prepared statement to the media:

"The incidents of senseless violence that our community suffered today was absolutely deplorable. We lost our seventh victim, murdered at Barnhart Ruins, this afternoon. The coroner hasn't ascertained the exact time of death. We also lost a highly-decorated Marine veteran in bail bondsman Chuck Breckenridge in the woods due east of Slack Trimmer Road. The seventh woman's name is being held until her family can be notified. If anybody witnessed any suspicious activity in or around either area throughout the night or all day today please call our office..."

Afterwards, Beaumont answered questions as best he could, the frustration and pressure of the case mounting in every response. Worry lines were deepening around his eyes and forehead. His hair seemed to be graying at an accelerated "presidential" pace. He'd lost weight – not necessarily a bad thing.

Richardson wanted to ask about the activity there at Barnhart Ruins after the fact, but he chose not to. He had enough to work on with a short deadline, and he didn't want to anger Beaumont before he approached him.

When Beaumont exited the interview room for the adjacent hallway, Richardson left his camera, discretely slipped out of the room, and followed.

"Chief Beaumont?"

LaDonna Reynolds was the first to react. She turned and threw up her hand.

"The press conference is over," she said.

"Sir, I have a question unrelated to the case. A private question."

Beaumont studied Richardson with his head cocked to the side, his eyes showing their whites.

"Go ahead with the mayor, LaDonna, and thanks for your assistance. I'll be right there."

She walked down the hallway without him. Beaumont grabbed the lanyard holding Richardson's credentials.

"Are you the boyfriend?"

"I am, sir. Rhett Richardson."

Beaumont shook his hand firmly.

"Harper told me about you."

"I tried to reach her – by text – a couple of times. I know something's going on. Can you tell me about it?"

Beaumont looked at his watch.

"Come with me back here. You need to hear this."

They walked the corridor to Beaumont's office, and rejoined Reynolds and Sneed.

"LaDonna, Mayor Sneed, this is him. Harper's beau... Rhett Richardson. Did you find the number?"

"I did. It's by the phone."

Sneed put his hand on Rhett's shoulder. Their eyes met as they each read the worry in the other's face.

"God, I never wanted to have to do this," Beaumont said.

The chief took a deep breath, exhaled, then rapidly dialed the number on the post-it note.

"Dr. Stowe? This is Chief Lester Beaumont over here at Hilton Head. ... It's good to speak with you, too. ... Sir, there's been a development here involving Harper I have to tell you about. Is your wife with you there? ... Good."

Richardson sat down at a chair in front of Beaumont's desk. Reynolds stood close to Beaumont's supple leather chair, as though she might yank the phone from his hand if he misspoke.

"Sir, I'll be direct. We think Harper's been abducted."

CHAPTER 60

The sea remained calm. From her study of the serial killer, Harper Stowe knew that James Wainwright had broken every rule, every protocol he had by sitting and speaking with her. He had forged new ground. Why? She had to assume that he had some affection, some pull to her that was greater than gravity. More than sexual attraction. What could that be?

She thought back through the volumes of cases she read in hopes of familiarizing herself with similar killers. What did they say about the mother? The killer was typically ignored by both the parents yet sometimes there was that bond that surpassed normal, with disturbing love that dealt with pleasing the mother for acceptance. It would be misguided for her to think he felt that way about her. Yet, what *was* he doing? She thought all this while still blindfolded, and in the confines of his secure ropes.

A few hours had passed since she had awoke. She had twice asked him for water. He complied each time, and she could sense the silent adoration. He hadn't mentioned food again. She was past the groggy, almost-nauseous feeling she had earlier. It was time to test how he would allow her trip to the restroom, before she began to grow weak. He'd come in and out of the cabin a number of times. She knew he was there.

"If it's ok, I think I should go to the bathroom now."

"As you wish. You're not going to try and be some kind of cop now are you?"

How could I not be a cop?

"No, I just want to keep the sheets clean. Thanks again for the water. I think I was close to dehydrated."

"Well, you be good, I'll be good – worth restating."

"You'll get no trouble from me."

"Hold very still. So you know, I'm also armed with your little pistol. Sorry I had to pat you down when I brought you on board."

His plan was a good one. He clasped a handcuff on her right wrist, it sounded like dull wind chimes as it dangled, and another on her left ankle.

"Familiar with these?"

She envisioned his blueprint, and was impressed.

"Pull your left heel to your ass."

He gave the left one another tug after she complied. He untied the knots at her right wrist, lowered and bent her arm, then he attached the two handcuffs together *behind* her back. He gave the joined manacles another safety tug.

"If I untie you, I expect you to keep this civil. Know that it'd mean nothing to me to feed your bloody corpse to the sharks."

I don't believe that.

"I know. I won't."

He untied her left wrist. It was such a relief to have both arms freed she sighed in joy.

He stopped and watched her as she began to move her freed arms and shoulders around as best she could.

"Oh, thank you. Much better."

"You're going to have to hop to the bathroom. Sorry for the inconvenience. You won't be so bound when you sit. Here, let me help you. Swing your legs over the side to me and give me your left hand."

He took her free hand and helped her stand on her right leg.

"The bathroom is close. Just turn left a little. That's good. Hop straight ahead."

Blindly, she began. From behind he first touched, then held her at her biceps.

Diagram of Death

"That's it. Just a few more feet. Almost there. Okay, stop."

He opened the door to the tiny bathroom, and then pulled off her blindfold.

"Help yourself."

She grabbed the door facing with her left hand and took the last hop into the boat's restroom. It was impossible to move her right hand forward enough to help with the process at the sink, washing her face being her first goal. She tugged gently to see just how far she could get her hand. Just a few inches, and as she did her left heel dug into her butt. She did the best she could with her left – not worrying about splashing her shirt. She looked closely at herself in the mirror. Ever the warrior, she was still confident in her prospects.

Ok Harper, be smart. If the sex represents the beginning of the end, you can't let him start. Interpret his motives, his intentions. Woo him. Ask him for dinner on the deck. Tell him you want to be clean, you want him to be clean. Get him talking again.

Despite the long, previous day, their fight, and her night of moderate torture, she still looked vibrant, if not fresh. She knew that if he *was* attracted to her, he still would be. Having him relax into a make-believe relationship would be the easiest way to distract him. She concluded her business, washed and opened the door to find him standing there.

She was seeing him for the first time on the boat. His jaw was bruised on his left side from her punch. His head was nearly touching the ceiling. He seemed to take up the entire living space of the room.

"Can you make it out of there?"

"Yes, thank you."

Facing her now, he again held her arms but looked away from her stare.

"Come this way," he said, as she hopped. He helped her back into her position on the bed by lifting her like a child. She recognized this as a potential attack point.

He'll want to - he'll have to - tie my left hand before he separates the cuffs. When he does, he'll be bent over and awkward. Could I fight him that way? Get him in a chokehold between my knees and thighs? I'd have to grab a handful of hair – pull him off-balance. If he gets away from me, I'm dead most likely. If he did unbind the cuffs first, I could use them like a mid-evil flail for a few blows to the head, then I'd have the killer chokehold.

"That's it… good. Hold still. I'm sorry, but I have to tie you up again."

While she was in the bathroom Wainwright implemented a third rope, at the end of the bed, with an open noose. He secured her right foot first, pulled it tight.

"Give me your left hand, please."

Her previous discomfort returned when he tightened the rope's knot. She wiggled her fingers, then watched as he pulled the handcuff key from his right pocket, placed it in the minute keyhole. The ratchet of the release was a welcomed freedom.

"I have to do some things on deck."

"I hope that includes dinner."

His lifeless eyes became hopeful. She recognized it. He smiled ever-so-slightly.

"It does."

CHAPTER 61

She wants a meal? She's going to get a meal – her last supper. All her condescending thank-yous and pleases. She all but called me Sir - has to go against everything she's about. Her bitch-cop blood must be boiling. I'm sure she wants to cut me down, rip the heart from my chest.

Still, under the right circumstances, I couldn't wish for more than this beautiful woman on my boat. That's fantasy come-to-life – fantasy of a dead man. Doomed by my acts. Carrie Stowers, or whatever her name might actually be, is the prize of all prizes. She's the sweepstakes, the lottery, all rolled into one. With her at my side I would seem legitimate, I would look like somebody. When we docked, people would stop and stare as we walked by arm in arm, laughing and chatting. They would say, "That man must have something on the ball to have such a perfect partner. He must be rich - a venture capitalist, or a market wizard, or maybe he owns a chain of some sort. He has an intriguing look about him."

I'm sure she would be up for anything: skiing, diving, fishing, kayaking, paddle boarding. She looks like a sportsman. She looks like she grew up on a boat. Unlike Victoria. The closest she ever came to a sport in the last ten years was plunging the spiral of a corkscrew into its target. Bull's eye. Victoria was soft. Carrie can kick ass. She'll look incredible in a two-piece – no question.

And, so, a dinner she shall have - my first chance to really impress her. Great food, drinks, conversation. Blue skies, ocean in all directions, a setting sun leading to a near-full moon, stars unimaginably bright away from the lights of man. I wonder if she's seen them before. Breathtaking, like her.

That's what I could talk about. Could I tell her how I feel? That I want to sail her away.

I'm going to put the blindfold back on her and get showered. Then I'll let her do the same. Show a little trust. There's only one way out of that room anyway. I brought some of Victoria's clothes and bathing suits out here – for appearances, I'll look like a lady's man to the Senoritas if I go island hopping.

If she tries to come out of that door before I say it's all right, if she tries to be a super cop, she'll meet my knife blade. That's not what I want though. I want to give this thing a chance. I wish the boys back on the ship could see us having dinner on deck – such a stunner. They always gave me shit about Victoria "the stiff," they'd say. Not that many of them were doing any better. But with Carrie, I would be the envy of all. Even the Admiral would be jealous - probably make a play for her. I would love that. "Back off, get your own. You can't pull rank here, you S.O.B. This is my damned tub."

I'll finish her and complete my cluster – an aerial masterpiece for all the brass that held me back... that put me down. For all the brass that wouldn't let me get there. Then I will sail south.

CHAPTER 62

Initially it seemed that agents Arline Thorn and Jeff Hudson had seen absolutely nothing concerning the Barnhart Ruins murders, or Harper Stowe's abduction. Because of that, Lester Beaumont worried that a search warrant request for James Wainwright's home might be denied. But Beaumont was wrong.

There were pages of Stowe's notes that became typed-documentation and the ongoing Wainwright surveillance lent weight as a timeline, though it was an embarrassment that the larger-than-average suspect had apparently slipped away to launch his most recent murder spree while two LEOs sat outside his house in their car observing. Wainwright was a suspect in the Chuck Breckenridge murder as well, so establishing probable cause was easy and South Carolina Magistrate Court Judge Fredrick L. McBride was quick to comply.

Other mistakes in procedure were becoming evident. Due to the Jessica Boyd murder minutes before Victoria Wainwright's drowning, only the Medical Examiners and Stowe - on the "down low" as Beaumont now learned - were in the Wainwright home that evening.

"Jesus. I feel like this whole thing is getting away from me," Beaumont said to Rhett Richardson. "As if it hadn't already."

"That's not true, Chief," Richardson said, though he was actually in complete agreement with Beaumont. "But we'd better come away from here with something we can use. Harper's life - "

Beaumont interrupted.

"You don't have to finish. I know. Believe me. I can't bear to lose Harper. Keep the obvious rhetoric out of the air when we're in here – please. I'm doing you a favor letting you tag along."

Despite his deep hope of finding Stowe, Beaumont was pragmatic enough to assume that she was likely dead already, but he couldn't say it out loud and certainly not to Richardson. The FBI agents, also present, would agree. With his staff dwindling, Beaumont had asked Richardson to join the investigative group about to enter Wainwright's home. He needed fresh eyes and Richardson had been to more murder scenes as a videographer than anyone left on his staff. Coroners Cindy Lewis and Tom Wilson were ordered on site by Beaumont as well, despite working through the emotionally-charged, colleague-included bloody night, for recognition of any changes to the place. Three newly-promoted, formerly-uniformed officers were also present.

"It seems completely normal," Beaumont told the group upon entering. "Look for anything out of the ordinary. Could be anything."

Some of the group went straight to the bedroom. The coroners went to the back of the house to the doors leading to the pool deck. Beaumont went with them.

"I want to visualize what he must have done to his wife," he said.

"If he drowned her, it could have been a simple thing. No physical trauma, drugs in her system," Wilson said. "She was probably out of it – passed out - never woke up. The scratches to his neck must have been manufactured, and probably a cover up of what Jessica Boyd inflicted on him."

Richardson, visualizing the life of a crazed loner, went straight to the garage, likely the last place the wife would have joined Wainwright.

He stood in one spot, staring at the work area.

Diagram of Death

Yeah, you were here, weren't you Harper? Right here. What did you think? What did you see? Talk to me. Navy recognition – honorable discharge. The spool of rope. Is that a... is that a bilge pump under there? Cheap. Old. Probably been replaced. And, there you go, a cracked rope cleat. Has anyone said it?

Richardson found Beaumont in the living room, where the group had reassembled. The new detectives reported that Wainwright's underwear and shorts drawer seemed low, as if he'd packed a bag. Cindy Lewis informed the group that the knife that was being used at the grill the night his wife died was nowhere to be found.

"So that could have been the murder weapon for all of this," Beaumont said.

"Chief, this man's a boat owner, no question. Harper knew it. She told me. Has that come out?"

The group turned and silently stared at Richardson, waiting for Beaumont's lead on their reaction.

"No. It probably wouldn't come up in the D.M.V. check, but it would've in personal property taxes. That was a big damned whiff by our staffers crunching data. Are you sure?"

"No doubt in my mind."

"Jesus H. Christ. We probably saw him, Arline," Hudson said. "When we came out of the woods last night. Remember, there were a few boats moving."

"Yeah, coming in it looked like. They were all moving inland – up the creek."

"That took balls, if it was him. But that's how he got away with her," Hudson said. "If he'd been busting it out to sea he would have looked suspicious. We would have called the Coast Guard."

"Well we need to call them now," Beaumont said. "We need a records check – if the thing's even registered. We need to go to the marinas, see where he keeps it. You three newbies can get on that. Do either of you remember the type of boats they were?"

"Of course. We're trained for that," Hudson said. "Two were shorter, like these ocean fishing rigs. Tight, little square, upright cabins, lots of poles. But the other was longer – thirty-plus feet - more of a cruiser-type," Hudson said. "Something you could live on."

"Remember, it was barely moving. He must have just pushed it off the dock," Thorn said. "We probably could have chased it down on foot. Now he could be halfway to Miami."

"Or the Bahamas. He'd be tough to find around all those islands," Richardson said.

"He won't leave. Not if Harper's right about his cluster," Beaumont said. "He'll want to finish that. I'll fill you in on it that later, Rhett."

"Wait, no, I know about the cluster – the Navy cluster. I helped her with that – I saw it on her map."

Beaumont stopped to ponder Richardson's statement, as if contemplating whether *his* recognition of the cluster shot holes in the theory, or if he had just recruited a potential true detective. The others again went quiet, as if sensing Beaumont's dilemma. It was Thorn who brought them back on task.

"But the spontaneity of the abduction is gone," Thorn said. "Would he try to take her to the spot to commit the crime? Or would he move her after…"

"Hard to say with this guy. I mean, does a lion want to be fed? What's most important to a serial killer," Hudson said.

"I would think it wouldn't matter to him whether she was dead or alive when he takes her to the area. The body completes the symbol either way," Beaumont said.

"And she'd be easier to move dead – no fight," Hudson said.

"Not true. With a gun to her head or his knife to her throat he could walk her," Richardson said.

"So, we've been assuming he left the creek later in the night for open water," Thorn said. "What if he stayed? He got away with it to begin with. And that would keep him in closer proximity to the final spot if he did plan to walk her. He could have her stashed in an un-rented home."

"We're wasting time," Richardson said. He looked at Beaumont. "Please, you need to call out all the troops. Whatever his plan is, we've got to find that boat fast."

CHAPTER 63

The advantage Harper Stowe seemed to have, James Wainwright's attraction to her, was fragile. She wasn't about to get careless with it, but there was no denying he was at least temporarily abandoning his murderous routine, his immediate lust, his taste for the kill. She also knew his attitude could change like the weather, as she felt the slow rocking of the ocean waves as a prisoner, bound at her wrists and one ankle.

Blindfolded again, the opening and closing of the bedroom door's latch alerted her of his return. On edge, she listened. The jingle of pocket items alerted her that his pants had dropped to the floor. Her uncertainty heightened. She braced to be touched, but instead heard the click of the bathroom door shutting and the flow of water in the shower. Moist heat hit her skin like a sauna when he opened the door, the green and white of Irish Spring and Barbasol emanating as he reemerged. She wondered how he even managed to fit in such a confined space. She pictured a gorilla in a phone booth. As he dried himself, her heart became a drum in her chest. She imagined him naked and just a few feet away, staring at her outstretched and helpless in his bed. He could initiate his intentions. Instead, he quickly began wrestling with his clothes, as though awkward. She heard the snap of his underwear's elastic band on his waist. She'd never been so in tune with her senses, minus sight. She knew then he was going to give her a meal. That he was going to wait, at least until after dinner. She relaxed and began to consider scenarios.

"All right, here's the deal. I'm going to give you some privacy to shower up. There are a few choices of fresh clothes by the bed. Sorry if they don't fit perfectly. When you're ready, knock on the door. I'll open it slightly. You stick your

Diagram of Death

left arm out low to be handcuffed. You will be attached to your dinner chair. It's heavy and awkward. If you think about diving overboard, you'll sink and drown. If you try to attack me with it, you'll lose, I promise. That understood?"

"Yes."

"You don't have to rush. I'm making us a nice meal. But the door will be locked from the outside. There's no other way out of this room. Again, I'll be as nice as you are... no big ideas. Ok?"

"Ok. You'll have no problems with me."

"You've got some fingernails there for knot-loosening, so I'll free your right hand. You can do the rest. Try anything beforehand, the knife is at the ready. Don't move."

For good measure, he touched the cold blade to her throat and softly ran it across her jugular. He let the tip linger a couple of seconds.

"One thrust, one flick of my wrist, and you're done. Got it?"

"I do."

"Oh, one other thing. I think it's time I knew your real name, don't you? It's not Carrie Stowers."

With that said, he removed the blindfold from her eyes. She squinted at the light, though his form was blocking much of it. She was taken aback by his gigantic presence, his broad shoulders. He was dressed in a pale blue, long-sleeved Oxford, plaid shorts of navy and sky blue. His sleeves were rolled to just below his elbows. He wore an impressive, nautical-looking watch. His hair, still wet or possibly gelled, was combed straight back on to his head. His attempt at southern prep, she surmised. The irony of a monster dressing that way was not lost on her.

"Thanks," she said, blinking a few times. She forced her eyes wide, then allowed them to return to normal. "It's Harper, Mr. Wainwright. Harper Kathryn Stowe."

He untied her right wrist. She sighed as her arm dropped to her side.

"That's a poetic name. Powerful. Enjoy your shower... Harper Stowe."

It took less than a minute for her to free herself. Barefoot, she walked to the door and listened. She heard the faint clanging of activity. That was enough. She knew he was busy. She began to scour the room and the bathroom for anything that would give her a shot at opening the handcuff she was about to be locked into. Nothing. Then, she froze. Wainwright had left the shorts he'd changed out of on the floor.

"Oh, I couldn't be that lucky," she whispered.

She picked them up and rifled through the pockets. She felt something, but it turned out to be the spare button sewn on the inside. No key. No buckle on a belt. Nothing else. He'd obviously taken the time to transfer the goods to his new shorts. She ran her fingers through her hair. Before she became a blond pixie to go undercover, she may have had a bobby pin in there. No need now. Her sports bra – synthetic. Holster – a similar blend.

Harper undressed quickly. As she did, she noticed the clothes he'd laid out for her. Nothing too flashy. Everyday wear. One blouse, ivory, had a bit of sophistication to it. The garment would cut low on her chest. She touched the cross on her necklace. A gift from her parents, such a part of her she'd almost forgotten it. Not the tiniest version, but just above. Set on a twenty-inch chain, it hung low on her and was typically hidden, especially with all the running gear she'd been wearing the past few weeks.

Wainwright missed it or deemed it harmless when he took my gun. This could work as a key, if I can bend its end a bit in the cuff. I don't know... longshot. Gold is malleable. A professor taught me that – oddly – in, what, British Literature?

Diagram of Death

Who was the poet that wished peoples' souls were malleable – focus Harper. Get your shower. Keep looking. Keep thinking.

CHAPTER 64

Rhett Richardson's inclusion in Chief Lester Beaumont's hunt for Harper Stowe and her captor was short-lived. In Richardson's mind, the officers at James Wainwright's home were given research assignments – boat ownership queries in state personal property, attempting to find the seller. What the hell good was finding the seller at this point? Maybe a picture to identify the boat, Richardson thought. The FBI agents were sent back out to the tidal creek near Barnhart Ruins Park to make sure the boat they now presumed to be Wainwright's didn't remain there through the morning. At least hands-on, he concluded. The zones of Ocean Oaks were all covered, especially the cluster area yet to be christened by a victim, considered an impossible distance to cover from the boat with Stowe's dead body.

Having been given his walking papers by Beaumont – "Son, I'm going to have to ask that you stay out of the way now" – didn't fly with Richardson. He'd finished his video obligation to the BBC prior to the search of Wainwright's home. The media was in a holding pattern waiting for the next victim, the people of the island - frantic.

There was only one other way to contribute that he could think of – he needed to be on a boat. His parents had one on Fripp Island, but his sense of urgency told him getting there in summer traffic would take too long. And if he was getting on a boat to search, he wanted a gun. Buying one without the waiting period and required background check was easy: two conversations after walking into the door of an island pawn shop. He picked up a 9-mm tactical Glock, with a 33-cartridge magazine. He added two extra clips to be safe.

Diagram of Death

Richardson then sought and found Skull Creek Marina, off Squire Pope Road. The first person he encountered was about his age, a sun-tanned brown, bleached-out version of himself. He had stringy blond hair flaring out at all angles from his worn ball cap, all-encompassing sports sun glasses hid his eyes. No shirt.

"Do y'all rent boats by the hour, day rates, or what?"

"You can go eight hours if you want. Ain't cheap. You familiar with boats?"

"Sure. Grew up on'em. A different version every few years."

"Not pontoons."

"No, we skied on the waterways - and Lake Norman - cruised. 'Course you can ski behind a pontoon. I'm just looking for something small, fast, easy on gas. Sea worthy."

"Oh, you're going out of Port Royal?"

"I'm... doing a grid search. Parallel to the coast."

"The coast ain't straight, you know."

"I'll manage."

"What're you looking for? Maybe I've seen it."

Richardson removed his aviator-style sun glasses, scratched the side of his head, then wiped his wrist across his sweaty brow. He squinted, as he sized up the dock hand. Richardson could tell this guy kept his eyes open.

"What's your name?"

"I'm Dave."

"All right Dave, I'm looking for a local. Real tall, around fifty or so. A Navy retiree, in a cruiser, maybe thirty-plus feet."

"*Last Chance*."

"What do you mean? You just asked me what I - "

"*Last Chance* is his boat. Just bought it. That dude ain't right. Tries to make out like he's one of the guys down here. Stuff shirt, you know? Pompous ass. Strange."

"You don't know the half of it. You seen him lately?"

"His boat's been gone for a couple days. And that was after he took it out for two or three days just before. Quick turnaround."

"Huh. Wonder what he was up to."

"Had a man with him on that first trip, beard, big – not as big as him. The beard wasn't with him when I saw him the next time - I just assumed I'd missed him docking the night before. I'm not here *all* the time."

Reverend Janson, Richardson thought.

"I think I may know who that was," Richardson said. "Ever hear him say where he goes when he's out?"

"No, nothing like that. I avoid that guy. But he fishes so he probably heads out to the Gulf Stream – that's seventy miles out."

Richardson let the irony of that one sink in – a mass-murderer who enjoys the solitude of fishing. Then again, he thought, the rush of sport fishing might be comparable in some way to Wainwright's lustful, violent thrill-seeking.

"So – Dave - can you get me out there or what?"

Dave took his own sun glasses off and began to clean the lenses with a worn bandana pulled from his back pocket. He had the bloodshot eyes of a stoner.

"I'll give you a nineteen-footer, I wouldn't go any smaller with those waves. You'll only get about five and a half hours running wide open. Maybe six."

"Can you give me a few extra gas cans? Just to be safe – get me back in."

"We're not supposed to do that."

Richardson turned and stared at the water, drew out time for a bit as he thought.

"Listen, Dave, you're right about him. This is a bad dude. I've got to track him down."

Dave's eyes grew wide.

Diagram of Death

"He's not the guy that's been raping and killing all these women."

Richardson eyed him solemnly but said nothing.

Dave put his hands to the sides of his head, fingers on his Skull Creek Marina cap.

"Holy shit, man. That's crazy. And yet – somehow - I'm not surprised. I can see it. The man's not right, like I said... So, you some kind of law?"

"No."

"Then why're you doing this?"

"He's got my woman out there. She'll be his next victim if I don't find them. Or the Coast Guard finds him, I guess."

Dave, again wearing his glasses, looked around for any of his superiors. They'd remained alone throughout their conversation. He seemed to have new purpose.

"All right. I'll put you twenty extra gallons in. I'll get you out there quick."

"You're the man, Dave. Thank you."

While Dave readied a boat for launch, Richardson called Beaumont.

"*Last Chance* is the name of his boat, Chief. He definitely has it out."

"Good work, Rhett. Where are you?"

"Skull Creek Marina. You'll tell the Coast Guard won't you? He could be out as far as the Gulf Stream."

A static-laden silence followed as Beaumont digested Richardson's words.

"You're not about to do what I think you are..."

"Just taking a little ride, Chief."

"No, Rhett, now don't get stupid on me son."

"Can't hear you, Chief. I'm just a civilian renting a boat for a leisure ride."

"Rhett, damn it! You leave it to us!"

Andrew Spradling

Richardson hit the end button. Ten minutes later, credit card maxed and void of all cash after heavily tipping Dave, his new best friend, Richardson shoved off into Port Royal Sound: destination the Atlantic Ocean and a rig aptly named *Last Chance*.

CHAPTER 65

Torn. So torn. I admit it. With her I'm laboring towards an outcome I do not want. K.P. was easy. I've tossed a salad, boiled and chilled shrimp to serve with cocktail sauce, I have grits simmering, and fresh tuna steaks rubbed with Cajun spice thrown on my hibachi. Lemons, silver, china, and wine are arranged on a white table cloth, with a breathtaking panoramic backdrop. Dinner will be perfect. She is perfect. While I watched her sleep this morning, I calculated. I've lived nineteen thousand, three hundred and forty-two days – near fifty-three years. And this day, this is the first perfect day. Because of her. Because of her presence on this vessel.

And yet, I know she doesn't want me. I can see motive through those eyes, though she's doing an excellent job of hiding it. She'd cut me down in a heartbeat. Plug me full of holes. Turn my blade on me. Take away the freedom and romance of boat and breeze and cage me like an animal. Make sure my list of crimes preceded my arrival at prison, so I can suffer the rest of my life among the sodomites. She would do all that to me, my Harper, probably more.

But she's not going to act that way now. And it will be just that - an act. The act of a two-faced bitch. Remember that. She wants me dead. She'll try and find a way. It's me against her. She's the enemy. And she must die. After dessert. Eat and drink light. After the key lime pie. She's the one – the exquisite one – the crown jewel. Don't even tape her mouth. Let her plead. Let her scream. Who's going to hear? Take her down, and end this thing.

Perfect day? Perfect day indeed.

CHAPTER 66

Harper Stowe was out of *Last Chance's* cabinet-of-a-shower and finally clean, which felt like Sunday morning to her. Adult Sunday morning, before she would dress for church: robe, bare feet, wet hair, coffee and a light breakfast, back a few years, before she was in high demand, when she wouldn't allow employment to invade the Sabbath unless the shiftwork of being a uniformed patrolman demanded it. Before her caseload was her top obligation, before rushing off to the reality-altering assignments of the day. Or maybe, the assignments were the reality, Sunday mornings and her home life just make-believe.

She knew this moment was fleeting, and the next hour could be the final and most telling test of her life. Wearing a stranger's clothes wasn't comforting, but they would do for the purpose at hand – defeating James Wainwright. Their unfamiliarity could act as a reminder of her mission. Not a shield, but a springboard, because she was certainly exposed.

In what Harper envisioned was about to happen, there was one stroke of luck. The borrowed shorts she was wearing had a hemmed cuff, a perfect veil for holding and hiding her gold cross. She didn't want to attempt concealing it between the fingers of her free hand, nor dig in a pocket for it while she dined with Wainwright facing her. She needed to be cognizant of it when she sat, not letting it fall out and to the floor. On this gold cross hinged her life. She knew well the simplicity of handcuffs. She'd opened hundreds, and was well-schooled in the tricks of would-be escapees. A bobby pin was the common universal substitute. Her cross could do it. It *had* to do it.

Harper approached the door and closed her eyes. *Lord, please give me strength in this task I face. Please help me end*

Diagram of Death

these senseless murders, and return me to my parents and loved ones, to Rhett, and to my department family. I ask in Your name Lord, Amen.

She took a deep, calming breath. She waited as it anesthetized her nerves. She knocked on the door. As promised it opened about six inches. She imagined his abnormally large shoe wedged tight-up against it on the other side, anchored under his weight. She offered her left fist and wrist, and allowed herself to be re-cuffed, this time to her dinner chair, again, as promised by her serial killer. Her metal restraint affixed, he stepped back from the door. He stood before her, politely holding the cumbersome seat low, his arms extended down. She considered an attack now. *I could kick the chair into his abdomen, knock him backward and hopefully to the deck.* She thought better of it. *Best to wait till I'm free of the cuff – stay the course.* Wainwright moved to his right, keeping the chair between them, and sat it on the deck at the table. He raised a palm to it.

"Sit down, please."

She looked at the heavy, wood chair, which seemed out of place on a boat deck, then at the table. Her plan was to be cautiously cold, but cordial. She knew his cynicism meter would be as sensitive as her own, each aware of what Wainwright ultimately wanted, and what the end result could be. He sat the chair where he could assist her like a southern gentleman. She glanced at the table and its arrangement.

"Oh, wow, you've been hard at it. Looks incredible."

As she sat, he pushed her chair in for her. As he did, he leaned and took in her fragrance. His eyes closed in appreciation.

"You, Ms. Stowe, are more elegant than the table."

"Thank you."

"Clothes ok?"

"Yes, fine. What do you think?"

"Excellent choice. They've never looked so... alive. And I love that you're barefoot," he said, letting his own enthusiasm get away from him. He pulled back. "I hope you like tuna."

Wainwright had placed the food on the plates, so Stowe put her right hand in her lap and began on the handcuffs immediately, pulling the short chain tight, resting her left hand on her thigh. *Better to start before I pick up the fork. I knew it would fit in the hole. Now, can I duplicate the angled bend?*

"How could I not love tuna? One of my favorites. You obviously know your way around the kitchen. Your grits look so fluffy. Mine would be clumped up by now."

Don't move your right arm, Harper. Don't tip him off. Thank God, the bend worked. It seems right.

"My wife typically drank her dinner, so I had to learn. I was used to chow lines - wasn't tough rising above that."

Harper thought she should fake laughter but chose not to.

One simple clasp since he didn't double lock it, thank you Mr. Wainwright. I can cover that ratchet click with a cough, or a true laugh, if he says anything actually funny... and if it works.

She pictured the mechanism in her mind. At HHPD they'd been shown videos of clear cuffs, to completely understand the design. She was having trouble catching the latch. Despite a strong ocean breeze from the north, she could feel a traitorous bead of sweat forming on her forehead from her duplicity - concentration and conversation.

"I tried to make everything one-hand friendly," he went on. "Sorry for the inconvenience. Which wine would you prefer?"

"Oh... the white I think. Just a little. I'm famished. It would go straight to my head."

Diagram of Death

"Well, I'm sorry if I neglected you. It wasn't my intention." He finished a moderate pour. "You need your strength. Please. Dig in."

Harper bowed her head, feigning a silent prayer, a perfect opportunity to view her efforts with the cuff. She changed the angle slightly by twisting her right wrist. Just as the ratchet clicked open, she whispered "Amen." She exhaled in relief.

Yes! Thank you Lord. Now get a little sustenance... watch his moves, wait for the right moment. If he goes for seconds, his back would be turned.

She looked around the deck for a blunt tool to possibly hit him with as she returned the cross to her shorts cuff. His hibachi had removable cooking grates with wooden handles. Not a knockout item, but could help her get the jump on him. A rounded fishing gaff stood secured at the front of the boat, many steps away. Then she saw the handle of his knife beside the grill. Problem was it was farther away than the rest of the food. He'd be between it and her. She grabbed the tail of a shrimp, dipped it, and plopped it in her mouth just as he picked up his fork. He smiled.

"It certainly is a beautiful out here. You picked a perfect time for dinner... setting sun."

Not a boat in sight. Anywhere.

"We're not reduced to talking about the weather already, are we?"

"I guess it depends on which way you want to go," Harper said. She picked up her fork and flaked off a bite of tuna. "Mmm... delicious. I mean, I've got questions I could ask. Not necessarily dinner conversation though."

"We're adults and both excellent at what we do. I think we can intellectualize the conversation without getting too graphic, don't you?"

"Sure, Ok," Harper said. She ran her next piece of tuna through the grits and in to her mouth. She stared into his eyes. "Did you drown your wife?"

"Yes."

"Why?"

"The little local, Jessica. Dynamo. She got a shot in on me. Punched and scratched. Lot of spunk, that one... spitfire."

"So you respected Jessica Boyd? More than your wife?"

"There's no comparison, Harper. My wife deserved no respect."

"Can you differentiate between all your victims... rate them in terms of admiration – or distain - or are they just objects?"

"I can rate them, though it's muddled to a degree. I know the woman that got me started on the island thought she was above everyone else. For a while I just went after the stuck-up sort, you know? That, I don't get. We're all on the same trails, have the same means to enjoy them."

"Where does that attitude come from?"

"Is it wrong? Having the common decency to speak to a person you cross paths with? Truth is, they're visiting the island I live on. They're running in *my* neighborhood. ... I've observed you from afar. You're not that way. You're kind."

"So you show them they're elitist by raping and murdering them?

"That's learning the hard way, I'll admit," he chuckled, then dropped a shrimp in his mouth.

"Ok, you were a Navy man, right? Did you ever – I don't know - feel inferior growing up? Or in your work?"

"Not growing up. But in my work, sure. You're all serving, but then there's that wicked-ass chain of command. They either ignore you or have a piece of you – own you - make nasty decisions about you. Randomly check a box on a page or fill out some form and change a man's life... hold up orders."

"Did you get passed over?"

"I got tagged R.O.A.D. by one son-of-a-bitch. He's on the short list, too, if I make it south."

"What's that?"

"R.O.A.D.? It's slang. Hiding – no work – retired on active duty. Pure bullshit though cause I wanted my cluster."

Harper stopped, put her fork down.

"Is that the pattern you're working on? With the bodies?"

He hesitated for the first time, his eyes penetrating hers.

"It is. They'll see it... after. An aerial reminder to not screw a loyal subject." He lingered again. "Unfortunately, you're the final piece Harper. I guess you realize that. Unless... unless I can convince you to sail away with me. I could just do it. Lock you up when I needed to. Enslave you. But it sure would be nicer - fun even - if you'd comply."

Harper picked up her fork, and served herself another bite of fish. As she chewed, she smiled slightly, leaned forward and swallowed.

"I'd rather have you slit my throat right now."

CHAPTER 67

Rhett Richardson knew finding a single, truly-seaworthy boat offshore was the longest of longshots, but he felt he had a good plan of attack. With a lighter, smaller boat, his goal was to cover the outer perimeter, and leave the open water closer to shore to the Coast Guard and any other law enforcement vessels that could be employed. So despite his abruptly-short conversation with Lester Beaumont half an hour prior, he chose to call him back while he had cell service and update him on his thoughts.

"Chief, I'm heading to the Gulf Stream at a 30 degree southeast angle," Richardson said. "I'm going out about 65 miles. When I get there I'll head northeast, try to let the stream ease my gas consumption."

"You said that before. Now why do you think he's out to the Gulf Stream? If he headed south past Tybee he'd have open sea for days."

"Well, can't we get the state of Georgia or the Feds on board to search south of Tybee? He's just hiding, Boss. If he succeeds he's going to want to take her back to Ocean Oaks, right?"

"So why go out that far?"

"Well, he's also a fisherman. That's a good ruse if you're hiding someone. Plus, he's got to eat."

"I don't know, Rhett."

"Listen Chief. You get everyone you can on the inroads. I'll take the outskirts… I'll have, all-told east and west, about a 20 to 24-mile visual if I go up the middle of my zone. Maybe I'll get lucky."

"I just can't abide by this Rhett. Hell, it'll be dark in three hours. You won't know how to get back to the docks."

"But sir – damn it - they're out there. I'm doing it. I just wanted you to know my plan."

"Son, I didn't say this before, and understand that I love her too, but the chances are she's gone already. This guy's not going to wait – "

"I don't want to hear that. I'm not giving up."

"Rhett."

"I'm starting to lose you, sir."

He pressed "end" on his phone.

"That son-of-a bitch!" Rhett yelled to no one but the ocean breeze. He pounded his palm on his boat's side railing, took a deep breath, then refocused.

Understanding well *Last Chance's* body type, he didn't waste time approaching the slimmer, shorter fishing vessels he saw. But three times in route to the Gulf Stream he did change course to take a closer look with binoculars at bigger boats. Each with no luck.

Richardson really had no idea what he was going to do if he had to attempt to overtake Wainwright in open sea. There were a few scenarios he'd come up with. Perhaps he'd dock him playing dumb, a near-out-of-gas idiot begging for a few gallons to get himself back to shore. Maybe he'd play it a little cooler, an unthreatening, lone fisherman, just saying hello. Dave, the dockhand, per his request, had thrown a pole on board for appearances. Or he could pull up gun-a-blazing, though he'd hoped to simply present the firearm to Harper when she boarded. His fear in that choice was that, while he'd shot guns in his life, he was not proficient, and Harper would be in as much danger as Wainwright.

Richardson also had negotiated two of the massive cargo ships coming in and out of Port Savannah. The previous September, he'd fought to cover the wreck of the South Korean ship *Golden Ray*, which had capsized around 70 miles from shore while hauling automobiles, but he failed to find a news agency to foot the bill. Almost 200 meters long, and 25 meters wide – roughly the size of a seven-story building – *Golden Ray* was described to Richardson by a luckier media colleague as a floating shoebox. These ships were a constant, if distant, eyesore, reminding land-bound sun worshipers of the vastness of the oceans.

When the odometer told him he was approaching the Gulf Stream, Richardson slowed his speed. The hairs on his neck raised when he slipped the boat into it, the water just slightly lighter from the diluted phosphorescence of its Caribbean travels. One of nature's greatest forces, his boat seemed to almost turned north on its own. He knew it wasn't the case, but it felt as though a divine intervention had taken place. Or maybe it was. He was on God's magic carpet ride.

After twenty minutes or so, he encountered a third ship in his new northern horizon. He also saw a speck to its right. He proceeded to the port-side wake of this new ship, now his huge blocker. He had a feeling, and he would approach this new boat under cover, popping out to starboard for peeks through the glass until his intuition was confirmed or denied.

CHAPTER 68

The tension at the table between Harper Stowe and James Wainwright was as thick as morning fog, but it lifted quickly. Her suggestion of him slitting her throat brought a brief deliberation, during which he looked deeply into her piercing eyes, but Wainwright defused the situation by simply laughing. It was a deep, throaty laugh, but it was sincere. And it perhaps told as much about Wainwright, faced with staring into the looking-glass of reality concerning Harper's mortality.

"All in due time, my dear. All in due time."

She leaned back in her chair and reassessed, allowing the tension she had created to subside. She watched him take another bite of food. *Well, he's certainly in no hurry. I couldn't prompt him to attack. Still, he's got to be close to launch point. What if I did tell him I'd go south with him. Would he start the engine and go? Abandon his plan... his masterpiece? Would he drop his guard on the trip, or would he keep me bound?*

"Please, Harper, keep eating. You want your strength. Harper... Kathryn Stowe. It's such a strong, southern name. Your parents are no doubt idyllic in their philosophies – full of all that is good in our pathetic little world."

"We'll keep my parents out of this, thank you." To make him more at ease she took another bite of grits.

"Obvious pedigree... professionals. You're certainly not second-generation cop. Big family or lone sib?"

To the south Stowe had noticed a ship coming their way. It was proceeding at a fairly good pace for its size. She hadn't mentioned it and she assumed that Wainwright could hear it, though he'd never turned to check its bearing. It looked as though it would pass them to her right. As she considered allowing the conversation to delve into her family – ill-advised in all phases of law enforcement and the psychology she'd studied – she noticed a small boat coming out from behind the ship. It then disappeared just as quickly behind the cover of the ship.

Oh my God. That could be help. Keep him talking. Control the conversation till you need him distracted.

"All right. I'm an only child. And yes, you're right, I'm not a cop's kid."

"I knew it. What, doctors? Lawyers?"

She laughed.

"One of each."

"You wear it well Harper. Never before have I been privilege to such a blend of... amenities, and yet you're completely oblivious to your own beauty. And, you know, I've been watching you for weeks." He shook his head to the negative. "But – what in the name of Hell's Angels made you want to become a cop?"

"Well, it's never dull." She would only tell him about her great-grandfather if it was necessary for timing. She scooped a bite of tuna up with her fork and put it in her mouth. He was relaxing again as well.

"You've got to give me more than that. I'm sure your momma had a lowland fit at the thought of you putting on a badge."

"You're pretty perceptive." The small boat came into sight a second time. At this point, both vessels were a half mile away.

"True. She was not happy. But she's a prosecutor. I think she felt I'd follow her into that side ultimately. And I guess there's still a chance of it. I know a lot of law. ... but for now they're coping."

"I could see you in a courtroom. You'd wear that well, too."

"Would I wear the islands well?"

Diagram of Death

"Are you kidding?"

He's completely in, no cynicism, no dark distractions.

"You'd be the queen of any and all from Port Saint Lucie south or east. Do you want to test it?"

"I don't want to die."

Wainwright put his own fork down in contemplation.

Damn it. Did I go too far? I just need another minute.

"One of those huge cargo ships is bearing down on us. I guess she'll pass over here," Harper said, raising her hand to her right. "Do you need to turn into her or anything?"

"We can handle her wake, but I don't want to make her change course or widen her berth."

Wainwright stood, walked to the bridge and fired the engine. He pulled the lever down, turned the wheel, and quickly backed her away from the ship's path. He looked over his shoulder at Harper as he did. He smiled. In twenty seconds he had her a couple hundred yards out of the ship's path. He cut the engine, letting *Last Chance* drift backward. He began walking back to the table.

He's taken the bait. And there's the little boat again. Oh my God. Is that Rhett?

"That's the beauty of a boat this size," he said. "Hemingway knew it. We weren't anchored. Just drifting. We could stay for a week or two. As long as you have a good working knowledge of engines. Which I do."

"Of course you do. Hey, since you're on your feet, mind grabbing me a wrap of some kind please? I'm getting chilly."

"Oh, sure."

Wainwright took three long strides to the door and opened it.

That's all I need.

Harper opened the clasp of the handcuff and pushed her chair backwards to rise and run. Whether it was the sounds of her movement or the danger siren in his brain, Wainwright didn't go through the door. He pushed it all the way open in time to see Harper from the other side of the table make a break for the bow of the boat. He stepped quickly and dove towards her flight path and with his massive length was able to catch her right ankle, causing her to fall face down on the deck. He pulled her towards him and then released her to crawl on top, grabbing for the cuff of her shorts at her thigh. She twisted quickly, coiled one leg, and jabbed a downward heel kick to his face, connecting with the bridge of his nose, stunning him briefly, watering his eyes.

      She crawled a few feet away, thinking she again had her opening. She turned to her toes and palms to make a sprinter's release into a swan dive overboard but he recovered enough to again secure an ankle, this time her left. She answered with a heel on his wrist, and another on the top of his hand, which loosened his grip enough for her to again pull away. She jumped to her feet, as did Wainwright.

      She was within an arm's length of him. As much as she'd hoped to avoid it, the fight was on.

CHAPTER 69

When Rhett Richardson realized the boat he was approaching actually was *Last Chance,* he felt that destiny had taken a role in the situation somehow. He hoped with all his being that only Harper would see his quick excursions into plain view, and that she would make a clean getaway to the ladder of his boat, and then into his arms. It was only when he saw the vessel backing away from its spot that Richardson began to worry.

Maybe he saw me pop out from the ship. Maybe I set him into motion to finish his act.

He knew he now had a much greater stretch of ocean to cover – that his element of surprise was gone. As he exposed the boat by going into full view and began closing the distance to *Last Chance*, Richardson saw them both. He saw Wainwright's back and the door opening, Harper stand and begin to move, Wainwright's lunge, and Harper's fall. Now, at sixty yards, he saw nothing. He turned his wheel directly toward the boat, glanced down at the handgun resting there on the console, and prayed Harper would again break free.

"Harper," he yelled as he idled his motor. He was twenty yards out. He would let it drift into the side of *Last Chance*, try to board her. But then he saw Harper stand again and look his way. He was relieved. He turned the wheel away, hoping she could make her break. Then Wainwright also emerged. They were faced off and about to battle. Misjudging his own drift speed, his turn of the wheel caused him to lose his direct line to make contact. He'd have to circle around her. Before he did he picked up the gun, stepped to the boat's side wall and checked his vantage point. While Wainwright was a colorful target with his XXL-blue Oxford, the ocean's bobbing influence made shooting accurately nearly impossible. He tucked the gun into the waist of his pants, went back to the wheel, and slid the lever into forward, his eyes on Harper Stowe the entire time.

CHAPTER 70

James Wainwright wasn't the trained fighter that Harper Stowe was, but he had a foot of height, well over one hundred pounds, and a distinct reach advantage on her. And though he'd killed so many, including the ambushed veteran Chuck Breckenridge, Wainwright was no Cassius Clay on his feet. He didn't have his knife, though it wasn't far. His goal was to subdue her, get her back to the deck. Each faced the other, squared off. Stowe's fighting form was perfect, knees slightly bent, feet shoulder width apart, balanced. She could strike with either foot, or jab and punch in respectable combinations. They began to circle each other.

"I hate to do it, dear, I've never knocked a woman out before. But this new pestilence has to be dealt with."

"You've never knocked a woman out? Least of your sins. I hate to tell you, but bullets will be flying shortly."

"Maybe when you're on the deck. Not before. Then once he's dealt with, I'll take care of my business with you. I promise, you won't suffer."

Harper just wanted to slip free long enough or with enough space to jump overboard. Since Wainwright had twice proved to be an accurate tackler, she felt a few shots to his head or body might make the difference. She wasted no more time going to work, connecting a front kick to his chest. His balance off, she went down to the deck and tried to sweep his feet out from under him. He steadied himself and took the blow without falling.

Damned elephant legs.

Now she was at a disadvantage. She tried to pop up but he knocked her back to the deck with an awkward arm-blow to her back. She dropped, but as he again sluggishly moved to pin her, she quickly gained a little space, and with her free leg scissor-crossed in front of his face and pushed his neck and head farther away and to the deck. She then, like an Olympic wrestler, rolled onto his back, grabbed his hair with both hands, lifted and slammed his face into the deck three times.

"How's that feel Wainwright?"

On her fourth attempt, he raised to his knees and lifted himself up to a woman's pushup position. She locked his neck in her left arm, holding her wrist with her right hand. She wrapped her legs around his abdomen. He could still breathe, but he was shaken. There was blood on the deck from his face. She tightened her grip, pulling backward with all her might. He tried to stand but couldn't. Harper rode him back to the floor, unlocking her legs before he hit.

She jumped to her feet, kicked him twice in the ribs, took five quick strides to free herself and find Rhett's boat. She saw it at starboard. She looked back at Wainwright, who was just rising again. She noticed her cross on the deck between them. Quick as a cat, she returned to him and kicked his face, spinning him on to his back. She picked up her cross and, holding it in her fist, ran to the starboard rail, sprung off both feet and dove over the wall head first into the dark Atlantic.

Harper was submerged in cool water - and freedom – though she knew they were still in danger. She couldn't resist opening her eyes as her momentum slowed and she began her underwater trek. Though blurred, she could make out the boat bottom ahead.

Harper broke through the water's surface. Rhett was in full view. He took her hand and helped her climb into the boat. Once her feet were on deck, she looked back at *Last Chance*. Wainwright had not yet emerged.

She put her cross into Rhett's dry pocket, and flashed a brief and breathless smile.

"Let me see that gun. Do you have more clips?"

Diagram of Death

"Yeah. Three more."

"Good work Rhett - I'm amazed you found me. I can't believe it. Thanks."

She was still catching her breath from her swim and the fight before it.

"I wasn't going to quit, Harper. Are you all right?"

"I am, yes… I'm great… Give me a minute… you better get on the wheel."

She studied the handgun quickly as she spoke, flipped the safety off. Then the sight of Wainwright at the railing of his boat stole her attention. She put him in her unsteady site. The ship that had passed them was in his background.

"I need you to pull forward a little, or go to the other side."

Richardson followed her order, easing forward slightly. He watched as Harper attempted to keep him in-target by moving her arms opposite the waves. Wainwright seemed incoherent. He'd not yet thought of Harper's gun. Rhett's readjusting of the boat put them at thirty yards. She squeezed off three rounds. One hit, spinning him slightly. He dropped out of sight.

"That wasn't a kill shot," Harper said. "Damn it."

The engine of Wainwright's boat coughed twice, then started. They couldn't see him, but he turned south and began moving *Last Chance* forward. He immediately picked up speed.

"We've got to make a choice here, Harper. We probably don't have the gas to get back – maybe just enough. But we can't stick with him. We'll be stranded at open sea."

"We could fill it full of holes – sink him."

He studied her.

"No, I couldn't do that morally - leave him to drown. We'd have to take him back with us. If we didn't, with his luck he'd probably get saved by someone passing by - escape."

"Well, you were going to kill him, weren't you? We could board him. He looked half dead standing there *before* you shot him. There's no doubt he was going to kill you."

"Does Beaumont know you're out here?"

"Yeah. He was pissed."

"Why wasn't *he* out here?"

"He didn't believe Wainwright would bring you all the way out to the Gulf Stream. Plus, rationally, I think he thought you…"

"Were dead already? But you didn't."

"I wasn't giving up. And I thought he'd try to impress you with his fresh catches. Woo you."

There was a pause as Harper thought out the options.

"There should be boats searching closer to shore," Richardson offered. "We'll get picked up if we run dry."

"You say you have a couple of clips?"

He pulled them out of his pocket along with her bent cross and showed her. She took them, forcing them into her wet front pocket.

"You hold on to my cross, please. It – and you – saved my life. Thank you again." She looked into Rhett's eyes, then to *Last Chance*, and back again. "He's got my gun - I'm not letting that son-of-a-bitch go. Let's finish it. We can tow this boat with his. Get this thing up behind him."

Diagram of Death

CHAPTER 71

Maybe superficial wounds are only that if they're someone else's, cause this one hurts like hell. Right through my side flab. Not too much blood loss. Definitely no organ damage, bright red from both holes. I've seen the darker. Should I cauterize with a hot grill spatula? When there's time maybe. Soon. Worse is that Harper shot me. That wound runs deepest. She was lying the whole time. Full of it. She wants me caged... actually dead, I suppose. I should have finished her immediately, not fantasized about some impossible island adventure - where we're holding hands walking the beaches, loving one another. Have I ever known love?

I can't believe the boyfriend found me. In all this damned ocean. Now I've got to shake free - disappear. I can double back later on land to finish my cluster with someone else. Ok, yeah. Heal in the islands. Regroup. I've got a good amount of cash on board. Course I've lost everything I worked for: beach house, ride, pension. So, island bound at last. Free as the wind blows.

What the...? They're following? He can't have the fuel. Ok, I see. She's hell bent on the kill. Bungy-off the wheel – shit - missed me - get your big-ass down. Where's the gun you took off her? Got it. Damn, Harper. You're striking, even in this twilight - even with your intentions. I'll try to shoot the boyfriend. Then she can't shoot straight if she's doing both. Maybe I can get it all back. Her back. She's going to be stranded soon. Stranded at sea. I'll be her hero.... Listen to yourself. Don't be a fool. Too late I suppose.

Ok, rise, aim, fire. Damn it, hit again. Throat – she can shoot – no air – blood, lots of blood. Unload on them. He's all over my wake. Pull it. Wind shield out, but missed them. Don't

Andrew Spradling

get too high. God – one - in the chest. Can't... stand. Give it up. Past pain. Numb. My deck... is cold. Feel the engine rumbling 'neath the floor... what's that from? Vibration tickles my eardrums, like getting a high and tight. A life of buzz cuts. A useless damned life of fades and buzz cuts. Look at the stars. Vast. Endless. Stars guide all sailors. I see Harper in the stars. Beautiful. 0-dark-hundred, man, what a waste...

CHAPTER 72

Harper Stowe's next few steps to Rhett Richardson was a pilgrimage of sorts. She'd become the assassin of a worthless murderer. Rhett was now her mecca. Switching the gun to her left hand, she put her free arm around his side, rested her head on his bobbing shoulder as he awkwardly stood behind his boat's driver's seat, leaning in to grasp the steering wheel. It was not comfortable for either of them. Harper still had the weapon he'd acquired partially raised. He wanted nothing more than to hold her, but there was no time to relax. With only a hint of lingering orange twilight to their right and no sign of land, they were tailing a now-unmanned boat at top speed.

"Great driving Rhett. Were you hit with anything?"

"No, I don't think so. That's plastic anyway," he said, nodding at the windshield. "You're an amazing shot. Think he's dead?"

"Yeah, I do. Or close to it. Throat and chest. We should still be cautious though. He might have a last gasp. I'll have to board her. Think you can get me close enough?"

"I should do the boarding."

"I can give you three or four reasons against it. I don't want you to have to put a bullet in him. I'll live with that. But mainly I'm not sure I can drive this boat well enough. Just don't run me over if I fall off please."

With that she gave him a reassuring smile, a gift he needed. He pulled a life jacket from the side panel and handed it to her.

"Just in case."

She slipped on the blue vest and inserted one plastic latch into the other, which also served as a secure place to wedge the gun. She would need both hands to climb into Wainwright's larger boat.

"Ok, let's just go for the right corner. If all goes well, I'll idle the engine and we can regroup."

"Please, please be careful. Especially with him."

Harper put her hands on both sides of Rhett's face, as much for balance as passion, and pressed her lips firmly to his.

"We'll do better later," she said, letting one hand softly linger on his whiskered-cheek. "Because I'm definitely ready for a few days off. Now get me up there."

Richardson tapped the throttle forward with the heel of his hand, then returned it to the wheel. The elevated wake originating from Wainwright's engine was a like a mountain creek, gushing without knowing why or from where. It, and the crossing wind, were both playing a role in his efforts. But when he surfed off the front of the wake he had more control. As he eased within two feet of the boat wall, he tried, while also holding the wheel with both hands, to shine a flashlight where Harper would attempt to grab.

Wainwright's bloody face appeared at the railing, Harper's Kimber 1911 in the hand he showed, though pointed skyward. Startled briefly, Harper secured her footing, pulled her weapon and squeezed off a round into his forehead at close range. His neck dropped onto the railing, then his chin scraped over it as he disappeared, ending any uncertainty of a surprise attack after boarding. Without speaking she looked back over at Richardson, re-tucked the gun, secured a grip on the railing and leapt. She pulled her chin to the bar and swung a leg over the side with the agility of a gymnast. Seconds later the engine calmed, and the boat coasted to a crawl. Richardson, having moved his boat away from *Last Chance* after Harper boarded safely, pulled beside her and idled his motor as well.

"So how much gas do you really have?" Harper asked.

"Very little."

Diagram of Death

"You would have been stranded?"

"I wasn't quitting," he said. They gazed at each other adorningly through the near-darkness. "We'll have to drive back together. I'm glad of that. See if you can find his deck lights. I'll tie off a couple of lines and throw them to you in the back. Pull me close, I'll get aboard, let her drift a little, and secure it. We'll have to take it slow – it'll take most, if not all, the night."

A few minutes later they were ready to head for land.

"Let's cover him," Harper said. She pointed at the galley door. "Would you grab a sheet out of there please?"

Richardson complied. When he flipped the light on, he froze as he received a surge of Harper's recent reality in the ropes and cuffs that held her captive. He nearly lost it in a flood of emotion as he imagined the scene. He took a deep breath that held awe, relief, and pride, and he pulled the top sheet. He saw a blanket in the corner and grabbed it as well, returning diligently to the deck. He threw the sheet over Wainwright's bloody form without reflection or ceremony. He then picked up the chair to which Harper had been cuffed, the mechanism still attached, and returned it to her as close to the wheel house as he could get it.

"I'll drive home. Should you put on some dry clothes?" he asked, lifting the blanket higher. "You can rest then. This will keep you warm."

With that, Richardson turned the boat towards the last hint of twilight and pushed the throttle forward.

CHAPTER 73

Harper Stowe wanted no recognition or fanfare for what she'd done. Going undercover to take down one of the most horrific serial killers in United States history was her duty, plain and simple. But, due to the second boat they were towing, Rhett Richardson had to bring *Last Chance* back to the docks slowly, an unsubtle prowler of the night. While Harper dozed in the chair he'd provided her, they were boarded first by the Coast Guard, and then by boats carrying state law enforcement. Reports of the case's successful conclusion, James Wainwright's death, the end of the massive manhunt, were radioed to the Hilton Head Police Department - and intercepted by the media. A mad scramble ensued.

Thus, with the backdrop of a brilliant pink and orange South Carolina sunrise, with Chief Lester Beaumont, Mayor Ralph Sneed, P.R. pro LaDonna Reynolds, the FBI, local law enforcement, the coroners, ready to whisk Wainwright's corpse away, an onslaught of national press with their trucks providing live feeds were waiting, hoping to video a true hero, whoever that person might be. The as-yet unknown Harper Stowe could become the focus of the national media. Perhaps.

Richardson committed a hardcore press faux pas by *becoming part of the news*. He was livid with Beaumont and Mayor Sneed at the handling of their return, especially for the sake of Harper, who was mentally and physically exhausted, bruised, battered, and sore from her fight with Wainwright as well as the entire ordeal. When, from a few hundred yards away, Richardson saw a podium set up just off the docks where only a day earlier he'd negotiated with dockhand Dave, he suggested to Harper – and she agreed - to retire to the bedroom. Richardson then went near-ballistic on Beaumont as he came aboard.

"Chief this is bullshit. Harper is in no shape for this. She needs to be checked out - at a hospital. And is this typically how you close a case?"

"Don't tell me my business… And let's not jump to conclusions, here Rhett. Let me talk to Harper."

"You should be ashamed. Twice over."

Beaumont stepped back towards him.

"Watch it now. You're a hero, too. Or, you could be charged with interfering in a government investigation. Don't fall out of favor with me, son. Besides, this is your chance to go big-time. What do you call yourself now, a stringer? A freelancer? Or, no, it's rent-a-lens, right?"

Richardson was about to react to Beaumont's impertinence, but he swallowed his words and looked away. He pointed at the door.

Harper was in the tiny bathroom washing her face when Beaumont knocked. She backed out of it, opened the bedroom door and allowed her boss in. They hugged. She cut it off.

"You don't know how relieved I am that you're safe, Harper."

She looked at him and shook her head.

"I know," she said, refraining from letting an eyebrow rise in skepticism.

"Let me offer both a congratulations and thank you on behalf of everybody. Just give me a quick synopsis – I'll do all the talking - and we'll get you to a hospital. That'll be our excuse for a quick exit. We'll fill out a report, close the case, and you can take a few weeks off. You've certainly earned it."

"I don't *need* to go to a hospital, but I *can't* do this. My cover will be blown. I'll be no good to the force. What will I do after this?"

"It couldn't be helped, Harper. We didn't call them."

"I'm your detective, Chief. I don't need – or want – the exposure. And look at me. I'm three days removed from fresh eyeliner, and I'm wearing someone else's clothes."

"I'm not surprised that I'm saying this, but you look great. Especially for what you've been through. Please, you and Rhett just stand beside me. I'll make it quick. This could help him even more than you."

"Don't try to rationalize this. I'm not doing it. I just… there's not been any time to digest any of this. I mean, I feel like it was fifteen minutes ago I was in the woods with Paul Clark – before he went down. Did Wainwright kill Pete Waters too?"

Beaumont looked at the floor.

"He did. And another… Ron Wilkerson. It was four that night, along with Patricia Oldenkamp. I was afraid you were the fifth. Thank God you weren't."

"And thank Rhett. He gave me another option – a better option - in case I couldn't beat him outright."

"Did you?"

"Just enough. I suppose I would have even without the option of diving overboard. Wainwright had a good plan…"

Harper picked up one of the ropes on the bed, contemplating the past day and a half. Then she dropped it.

"He had me in a vulnerable position at first. But I enjoyed smashing his face into the deck at the end. I had him."

"So what happened?"

"I'll tell you the story, Lester, but I'm not giving up my career for a little fanfare. I need to be in the field."

"I understand, Harper, I do. But this is more than a little fanfare. You could be the toast of the entire country, hell, the world. A celebrity – a bona fide hero. They'd probably let you play yourself in the movie."

She laughed, but refused to entertain the temptation.

"Get Rhett in here. We can give him all the credit, or you can kill off a fictitious detective. If the press saw me from a distance I can be an un-named, near-next-victim who prefers to remain anonymous. I'll leave after it's over - or they can haul me out in a body bag. But the media hasn't seen me. Let's keep it that way."

"One thing. Your parents are out there."

Harper looked at Beaumont, still annoyed that he allowed the impending circus to gather.

"Along with two hundred other people," she said. She opened the door and motioned Rhett into the room.

"Lester, can I borrow your phone please? I'll text my mom. You two can work out the details of the lie."

CHAPTER 74

FBI agent Arline Thorn was brought on board *Last Chance*, along with Mayor Ralph Sneed and LaDonna Reynolds, joining Harper Stowe, Rhett Richardson and Lester Beaumont. Thorn and Harper hugged with both professional respect and sisterly affection.

"I'm so proud of you, Harper," Thorn said. "You will inspire a generation of young women into law enforcement."

Harper, continuing to hold her colleague by the shoulders, smiled softly. She pulled back slightly, and through her own tired eyes she looked knowingly into Thorn's. There was a connection, as though through osmosis they'd experienced each other's unspoken battle scars.

"No, for now, I can't," Harper said. "If I walk out there my career is over. Wouldn't you agree?"

"Oh, with the gravity of the crimes, your looks, your charisma, if you walk out there *your life* will never be the same. You'd go viral in seconds. Your career – as an undercover detective – will definitely be over."

"Wait a minute, what are you saying?" Reynolds asked. "You can't deny the media this story. You can't! What lie do you think you can perpetuate... here, from the confines of this boat?"

"That's why you're aboard," Richardson said. "You have to help make it happen."

"What in the hell do you think you can say?" Reynolds said.

Beaumont stepped forward.

"What if, Harper, you own up to it, and become chief? This is great publicity for the department. You – our

Diagram of Death

department – solved the case," Beaumont said, "I could step down. I'm ready to step down."

"I don't want your job – an administrative job - yet. I'm not ready for that."

The room went silent as everyone pondered the problem.

"This is ridiculous," Richardson said. "Harper shouldn't have to decide the next chapter of her life here on this boat – at this time – after what she's been through. You all should be helping her defer."

"He's the answer," Harper said, lifting a hand towards Richardson. "Just give it all to Rhett. He had a hunch based on the events at Barnhart Ruins, or maybe he knew the victim or witnessed the abduction, he was hungry for the story, so he rented a boat, went out and got lucky - ran into Wainwright's boat - the victim gave him a sign, he won the gun fight. It's simple."

"There's only one hole in that story when the questions start flying," Richardson said, turning and facing Harper. "No footage. No video. I was so focused on finding you, I didn't even think to take my camera."

The room again quiet, the affection in the journalist's statement was lost on no one. Thorn drew a quick breath that bordered on a gasp. Harper took the few impassioned steps necessary to reach Richardson and planted a fiery kiss on his lips. When they broke, they gripped each other as though their love was insatiable.

CHAPTER 75

Ten minutes later Rhett Richardson and Chief Lester Beaumont stepped on to the dock and up to the podium with Agent Thorn, Mayor Sneed, and a tight-lipped LaDonna Reynolds in formation behind them. Muriel and Carter Stowe had discreetly vacated the area after receiving Harper's text. They departed to await their daughter at her condo. Harper remained hidden on the boat.

Beaumont took the lead and, still craving credit for Hilton Head PD, explained how Richardson had been all but "deputized" after he'd recognized the reporter's experience in crime scene investigation. They'd gone so far as to take Richardson and his fresh eyes to James Wainwright's abandoned home.

"From limited clues, it was Rhett Richardson who realized that Wainwright was a boat owner, and he took it upon himself, like the bulldog journalist that he is, not only to find where *Last Chance* was docked, but to go out and search for her when he found her slip empty," Beaumont said, raising a hand toward the boat's painted moniker. With a wink he added, "No offense, but I imagine most of you lay low on what looks to be a slow news day. Not this young man."

The media horde lapped it all up with a spoon, accepting the privacy wishes of the near-victim as well. Richardson appeared humble in his lies.

"I was going for footage initially. His first shot hit my camera – knocked it off my shoulder – and, well, shaken, I'd never been shot at before, I couldn't catch it. It dropped it in the water," Richardson said. "That, of course, eliminated any doubt that he was the man I was searching for, even though I knew it was his boat. I hit the deck and then came up shooting.

Diagram of Death

As you can see, he took out my windshield as well. I guess I just got lucky."

Over twenty-four hours had passed since Richardson had slept, but the media – both those operating the cameras and those in front of them - found him freshly sincere, heroic, and handsome. Some knew him already, others – network talent - dispatched to Hilton Head at the story's conclusion, were impressed by his courage. It was a great situation for a young man in search of a gig as a correspondent. And he knew it. With the cameras still rolling at the end of his interview he put Beaumont on the spot for HHPD to help with any damages – and perhaps the original rental fee – of the small boat. The joyous Beaumont complied as the crowd laughed.

Reynolds had put together a short bio of James Wainwright's life, along with a Navy photograph, taken from his home. As to his motives, Beaumont explained the unfinished cluster and had to assume his motivation, from his briefing by Harper, was perhaps related to his lack of Navy promotion. He turned and looked at the table where Harper had dined with the murderer. He was flooded with a sense of ineffable pride for Harper.

As to the trigger of his exacerbated killing spree – Rev. William Jansen, Chuck Breckenridge and other male law enforcement officers - especially after Wainwright's every-other-Friday routine had been set and followed for over two months, Beaumont lied when he said, "I have absolutely no earthly idea."

CHAPTER 76

The following day, Harper Stowe arose well-rested but sore for an 11 a.m. meeting in Mayor Ralph Sneed's office. She dressed casually but tastefully in sandals, white capris, and a sleeveless, floral blouse, sending the message that she was definitely on vacation. She, in fact, was meeting her parents for lunch at noon.

Sneed presented Harper with a gift card basket in which most all the businesses on Hilton Head Island were represented. Rhett Richardson and LaDonna Reynolds were absent, tending to his national interview requests, conducted from local affiliates' stations. Reynolds, always hoping to be close to the center of attention, was more than happy to escort Richardson and keep close to what was trending.

"Share these with Rhett if you like," Sneed said, "but enjoying meals with him now may put you in the spotlight as much as if you'd just accepted your rightful praise. Until he gets a job and ends up in North Korea or Iraq or Russia, or somewhere really dangerous."

Harper thanked him mindlessly, instead deeply contemplating each part of his statement and their ramifications. *If Rhett reaches his goal, he'll be a national correspondent somewhere overseas.*

Bennett Boyd, husband of victim Jessica, joined the group, along with Chief Lester Beaumont. Boyd had spent a good deal of time with Sneed in the past few days, thus Boyd now knew the truth about Harper, not just the "new neighbor" persona she'd used at Jessica's wake. He pledged an oath of secrecy. Boyd hugged Harper. He whispered into her ear, "Thank you for vindicating Jessica, Harper. For vindicating them all. I only wish this could be more."

Diagram of Death

He again hugged Harper, then he presented her with a $100,000 reward check. "Use it to move into the neighborhood. For real this time."

He smiled, holding back tears.

"I can't take this money, Mr. Boyd," Harper said.

"You can, and you will. Don't offend me," Boyd said. "Had you actually been living in Ocean Oaks prior to her death, I believe you and Jessica would have eventually become good friends."

She kissed Boyd's cheek as she took the check. "Thank you, sir. I believe you're right about that."

"There's more, Harper. A lot more," Mayor Sneed said. "We've been checking in to it. Federal and state rewards, some attached to the cold cases. You deserve it all."

"I don't deserve any of it. If I'd done my job well, I would have saved a half dozen lives at least."

"Don't say that, Harper," Beaumont said. "You did an incredible job. You were born for that case. You can't blame yourself for the work – the allusiveness - of a mad man. Anyway, think of the money as hazard pay. Just like our troops. You certainly risked everything."

"This isn't me. It's not what I'm about. The risk *is* the reward. I just want to work, be in the field, solve crimes, see that criminals are put away."

"Folks will respect you even more for that. You'll be beloved," Sneed said. "One day. When the actual truth comes out."

Harper smiled in appreciation, nodding upward once at Mayor Sneed. She slid the gift basket closer to her, casually glancing at the offerings, all in elevated plastic card holders, like those in flower arrangements. She imagined Rhett sitting under hot lights and in front of a television camera in some cheap-looking studio, getting flirted with by the female on-air talent while waiting for the start of yet another interview.

She laughed to herself. Then she remembered the wings of her soaring spirit when she realized it was Rhett manning the rescue boat in the open ocean the night before. She pulled her phone from her purse and texted, "*Picking up Fishcamp for 8:30 dinner behind canary-yellow door. Walking beach after. Interested?*"

The reading bubbles appeared immediately. Harper's heart fluttered with anticipation.

Rhett texted back a thumb's up with a red heart. "*I can't wait.*"

Diagram of Death

THE END

Andrew Spradling

ACKNOWLEDGEMENTS

Completing a project like this one brings an array of emotions: mostly relief, followed by joy and satisfaction, equaled by a large helping of pressure-induced nerves. As I think back to the people I've asked for advice and instruction, it also brings a great deal of gratitude.

First and foremost, I must thank the boys from our Shelton College Writers Group, Larry Ellis and Joe Bird, who painstakingly read my rough copy and helped it along. Their patience, guidance, and encouragement is much appreciated.

From the law enforcement world I must thank Lt. Philip Bass, and Chief Joe Crawford, both of the St. Albans, West Virginia, Police Department, and especially Robyn Lewis, a forensics specialist for the West Virginia State Police, for both reading and legitimizing my forensic foul balls.

Thank you to Dr. Rebecca Goodwin, resident grammar guru, for her beta read and advice.

Thanks also to Michele Carroll, WOWK-TV, Charleston, WV, for advice in the world of television journalism.

Special thanks to lifelong friend Barry Thaxton for laptop, technical, guns and ammo advice and support.

To my SAHS Hall of Fame Committee brothers Mike Eakle, Dr. Randy Robinson, Pat Quinlin, J.D. Adkins, Coach Tex Williams and especially "Hall" inductee Doak Turner, thank you for your continued support and "good-word" sharing.

To literary agent Diane Nine, of Nine Speakers, Washington D.C., special thanks for believing my efforts have earned me a place in the world literary scene.

Dr. Alan Morris, thank you sincerely for sharing with us a window into the lowland world that we love so much.

Having dipped my toe in educational waters the last couple of years I developed a newfound appreciation and respect for the teachers that devote so much time and effort in advancing the minds of our youth for so little reward. Also in that vein, I must share that FBI Agent Arline Thorn was named in honor of one of my inspiring professors of English, Dr. Arline Thorn, West Virginia State University, remembered fondly, and taken well before her time.

To my nearly all full-grown children, Evan, Audrey, and Claire I wish for you love and happiness, and that all your dreams come true. Thanks for your assistance, be it discussing ranks, kicking around character names, or posing as book cover models. To my wife, best friend, and soulmate, Mylissa, thank you sincerely for your great ideas, your support, inspiration, and love.

And to you, the reader, thank you sincerely for your time and continued support. If you are so moved, please consider writing a short review on Amazon.com.

For news about my next book, follow me at: andrewspradling.wordpress.com

ALSO BY ANDREW SPRADLING

The Long Shadow of Hope

The Lost Lantern

Available on Amazon.com/author/andrewspradling

Andrew Spradling

Diagram of Death

Andrew Spradling

Diagram of Death

Made in the USA
Columbia, SC
01 October 2024